The Cairo Vendetta
Ernest Dempsey

Get the four-book Ernest Dempsey starter library absolutely FREE.

Become a VIP reader and get all the great stuff by visiting ernestdempsey.net or
check out more details at the end of the book.

Prologue
Tanzania, Western Border

In the blink of an eye, the peaceful surroundings of the forest turned into hell on earth.

Darkness had come early for the five men in SEAL Team Four. They'd been lurking in the shadows for almost three hours, waiting for the opportune moment to strike. Just a hundred meters from their hiding place, their target—a compound run by a ruthless warlord—began settling down for the night.

Most of the men running patrols had since disappeared behind the feeble-looking gate. Only a few guards remained. They appeared to be young, fifteen at most. Every member of the strike team had been apprised of the situation. Their target—a warlord by the name of Baku Toli—had been abducting children to serve in his rebel army.

That wasn't even the worst of it. Intelligence reported Toli had also obtained biological weapons. There was no word as to where he planned on using the weapons or what his motives might be, but one thing was obvious: his intentions weren't good.

"Two guards at main gate, sir. Two in the tower to the north. Same with the tower to the south." Petty Officer Alberto Garza was quick to assess the situation. Not terrible odds. Six on five was better than what they usually faced. But as soon as the first shot was fired, the rest of the warlord's small army would hit back—hard. The SEALs would have to move fast.

Lt. j.g. Fletcher Collins was the commander of the mission. Affectionately known as Fletch to the others, he made quick decisions and was a natural leader. He'd glanced over at the others to give the signal to move up when the first shot was fired from behind their position.

And that's when everything came unraveled.

First the dirt exploded around them again and again as bullets flew at their position. Other rounds thudded into the trees and clipped branches nearby. Next, Petty Officer Max Wilson took a bullet to the leg. He grimaced and dropped to his knees before another round zipped through the base of his neck. He fell over prostrate, grasping at his throat for five seconds before slowing to intermittent twitches. Then he stopped moving altogether.

The remaining four SEALs returned fire immediately. In the dark it was difficult to see the enemy, but the muzzle flashes illuminated the gunmen in bright bursts and effectively gave away their positions. The ambush was coming from a wide arch, surrounding the Americans in such a way that would make escape nearly impossible.

Fletch dove for cover behind a huge tree stump and continued firing on the right flank. The other three took up positions behind the biggest tree trunks they could find.

Petty Officer Tevin Simmons, a young man of twenty-seven, squeezed the trigger on his assault rifle. A second later a yelp merged into the rat-a-tat-tat of the gunfire. "One down," he said. The voice had sounded like a child's. The men all knew they would be facing some of the child soldiers Toli had abducted and brainwashed. Now it was eerily real.

Senior Chief Mark Mueller was in the center with Garza. Their weapons swiveled to the left and right with every muzzle flash. Even though they were firing into darkness, the reckless shooting by the enemy exposed them every time they pulled the trigger. For a unit as elite as Team Four, that was all the light they needed. One after the other, the SEALs dropped the shooters until only a few were left. Whoever the enemy was, they were wildly inaccurate—better at hitting stumps and rocks than their targets.

Fletch gave the signal for the other three to fan out and press the attack. He started to leave the protection of the stump when suddenly he felt the cold metal of a rifle muzzle against the back of his neck. A chill shot through his body, and he froze stiff.

"Don't move, American."

The voice was young. The kid couldn't have been more than twelve. Fletch didn't turn around to look. For a second, the idea of dropping to the ground and sweeping the kid's legs rushed through his brain. That notion was lost to fantasy the second he saw three other child soldiers with guns appear to his right. Their barrels were leveled at their hips, pointing straight at him.

Fletch dropped his weapon and raised his hands. Garza looked back from his advanced position and noticed his commander in trouble. Before he could react, though, a line of young soldiers appeared. They charged out of the gate toward the battle, covering the span in fifteen seconds in spite of the heavy weapons they bore. Garza and the others spun around, ready to fire at the new threat.

"Stand down, boys," Fletch ordered. He knew a no-win situation when he saw one. There was zero chance he and the others would get out alive if they tried to fight their way out. "There's too many of them."

Fletch glanced over at the lifeless body of Wilson lying face down in the dirt. The sight caused Fletch to clench his jaw. Based on the poor aim of the so-called soldiers, Wilson had been unlucky. He was only twenty-five years old—a good kid. Now he was gone. Just like that. Fletch had lost a member of his team once before, and he never stopped blaming himself for it. The old demons started to flame up before his eyes as he imagined how heartbroken Wilson's family would be. He was engaged to be married in a few months. Now his parents and his fiancée would have a hole in their lives until the end of time.

All because of Baku Toli.

The American commander's thoughts were interrupted by a man's voice from amid the cluster of soldiers swarming the area.

"What have we here?" the man asked. "Americans?"

Fletch kept facing away from the sound of the voice. He wasn't about to make a sudden move, not without being told. As it turned out, he didn't have to move at all. The dark face of the man they'd come to kill appeared as Toli stepped around in front of him.

He wore a red beret, dark camouflage fatigues, and had two bandoliers of bullets stretching from his shoulders across his chest.

Fletch had seen the face a dozen times while he studied the mission. He'd learned all he could about Toli, but information was scarce. It was as if he'd appeared from nowhere, a creation of Fletch's imagination. Fletch wished he was a figment. Toli was real enough, though, and now he was standing face to face with the American.

"What are you doing here?" Toli asked in his thick East African accent. "It was not wise for you to come to my fortress. Now I will have to kill you."

Fletch looked out of the corner of his eye. He saw the remainder of his team reluctantly surrendering their weapons.

"Well we all do dumb things every now and then." He flashed his eyes at one of the children hovering close by. "What kind of sick coward abducts kids and uses them to fight for him? You always stand behind someone else's gun? Too afraid to use one yourself?"

Toli pulled a pistol from the holster on his hip and smacked it across Fletch's face. When the American recovered, he found himself staring down the wrong end of the barrel.

"These boys must learn what it means to become men," Toli said. He waved a finger around. "And they must learn what it means to serve the Almighty."

Perfect. Another religious fanatic who thinks he's the savior. "There have been men like you before, Baku. In fact, there was one not too far north of here in Uganda. Things didn't work out too well for him, if you catch my drift."

Toli was unimpressed. His reply was a derisive snort followed by a wave of the hand. "Take them to the basement in the main building," he ordered one of the few men he had serving. "Make sure they are watched at all times." Toli stared hard into Fletch's eyes. "I have plans for these Americans. Soon the *world* will know who we are."

1

Atlanta, Georgia

Sean didn't think. He didn't worry about the consequences. He simply saw the threat and reacted.

He'd seen the suspicious guy lurk into the stadium midway through the fourth inning. The man looked like any other middle-aged guy attending a baseball game. He wore a cap, the team jacket bulging out around his belly, and jeans that had seen their fair share of washings—the blue almost faded completely.

He wasn't, however, an ordinary man attending a baseball game.

From the moment he sat down at the end of the aisle — two rows ahead of Sean and in the adjacent section — he'd acted oddly. No one else had noticed; at least it didn't seem that way. Everyone's attention was focused on either the game or their concessions: beer, nachos, and that old American staple—hot dogs.

The primary reason Sean even noted the man was that the game was half over and the guy was just showing up. *Who comes to a baseball game halfway through it?*

To be fair, he hadn't missed much. The Braves were losing by two, and the home crowd was already growing restless.

Sean had watched as the guy looked around, checking to his left and then his right as he eased into his seat. It was almost as if he was looking for someone. Maybe he wasn't sure if he was in the right row. Whatever the reason, Sean's instincts had kicked in immediately.

He'd spent the last few innings half watching the game while he kept an eye on the guy. When the seventh-inning stretch began, he realized what the man had planned.

The guy in the jacket looked around nervously. Sean watched as the man reached into his jacket and pulled out a pistol, keeping it close to his chest as he stepped toward the railing only two rows away.

Sean had only taken a few karate classes in his youth, though he'd been in his fair share of brawls in high school and college. Trouble had a way of finding him, much like it was now. Fortunately, for the last six months he'd been through one of the most rigorous training programs the U.S. government had to offer—a program that only graduated 5 percent of the people who went in. His senses felt heightened. His muscles tensed.

None of the other fans seemed to see what was happening. The security guards that lined the edge of the field were looking up into the stands, but they were spaced in such a way that the gunman approaching the front row blended in with the rest of the crowd.

Sean charged down the steps, giving no thought to his personal safety. The man pulled out his weapon and took aim at the first baseman, whose back was turned as the team warmed up for the bottom of the inning. There wasn't any time to think. Sean leaped from two rows away and sailed through the air. As the man's finger tensed on the trigger, Sean's shoulder plowed into his lower back. The jarring blow caused his hand to flail in the air as the weapon fired, sending the round off into space to land somewhere—hopefully harmlessly—outside the stadium.

The momentum from Sean's flying tackle sent both of them toward the brick wall separating the fans from the field. The gunman's body protected Sean. The gunman, however, had no protection—and being caught off guard, was unable to react fast enough to brace himself. His face smacked against the top corner of the wall, shattering the cheekbone below his eye. Dazed and suddenly in agonizing pain, he dropped the weapon and grabbed his face. A gash had opened up in the skin and oozed crimson through his fingers. Sean worked hard to stay on top of him, holding on to the writhing gunman like he was roping a calf in a rodeo.

"Freeze!" a voice commanded from nearby.

Sean released the man and kicked the weapon away while still straddling him. He slowly put his hands up.

Two police officers were pointing guns at the man on the ground, each with menacing expressions on their faces.

The closest security guard hopped over the wall and grabbed Sean under the armpits. He pulled him up a few steps and held on.

"That guy had a gun," Sean explained.

"Just let the cops do their thing."

Another police officer descended the steps with a radio in hand. The crowd of fans in the closest two areas were in a panic and flooding out to the aisles as far away from the gunman as they could get. The players were being ushered to the opposing team's dugout for safety.

Sean bit his tongue and watched as the police cuffed the gunman and dragged him up the stairs and out onto the concourse.

One of the cops stopped and questioned the security guard. "What's this guy's deal?"

Sean knew better than to chime in. If he'd learned anything about cops, it was to speak only when spoken to. Sean could have been arrogant, especially given the fact that he'd just saved the first baseman's life. Or he could have played the *I have security clearance you've never even heard of* card. Instead he let the guard answer for him.

"This guy took down the man with the gun. I'm just holding him here to make sure you all didn't think he was part of the problem."

The cop, a guy probably in his midforties, narrowed his brown eyes as he assessed whether or not the guard was right.

"That true, son?"

Sean nodded. "Yes, sir. I noticed the gunman walking toward the field during the seventh-inning stretch. When he reached in his pocket, I rushed him."

It wasn't like Sean to sound so submissive. But in this case, he'd prefer to give the cop whatever info he wanted and get the heck out of Dodge. Too many people had seen him as it was. No question he'd get grief about it when he got back to the office in the morning. If it took that long.

"So you're just a good Samaritan, doing his part to help the world?"

Something in the cop's tone carried a barb of sarcasm.

Sean ignored it and remained respectful. "Yes, sir." He grabbed his shoulder and winced, faking an injury. "If you don't mind, I think I'm going to go take some ibuprofen. I hit my shoulder pretty hard when I tackled that guy, and it's getting sore. Am I free to go?"

The way the cop was deliberating caused Sean a degree of concern. Of course he hadn't done anything wrong, but he also knew how cops were when it came to protocol, statements, reports, and all that nonsense. Sean was getting the overwhelming feeling that not only would he be missing the rest of the game, he'd also be heading downtown to give some kind of testimony.

"I'll take care of this one," a female voice interrupted the tense moment.

Sean cautiously twisted his head around. Most of the fans had already cleared out and were stampeding their way down the concourse. Alone on the steps a few rows back was a woman with light brown, shoulder-length hair. She wore a gray business suit and looked the spitting image of a corporate CEO. Her fingers clutched a foldout with a government-issue identification card inside. The cop couldn't see all the card's details from his vantage point, but apparently he saw enough to know when to back off. At least from questioning her ID's validity.

"What are the feds doing here?" he asked. He put both hands on his hips. "We already got the gunman in custody. What do you want with this one?"

The woman took a few steps down the stairs toward the three men and slid her foldout back into a jacket pocket. Sean let a sly grin escape and crease across his face.

"This one," she said, "is one of ours. He's been tracking that gunman for over a month now. He knew the guy's plan and waited for the right moment to take him down."

The cop was perplexed by the tale but couldn't find an argument for it. "You mean this guy is one of yours?"

Sean couldn't hold back his instincts any longer. "That's what the lady said. Now if you don't mind," he looked down at the cop's badge, "Officer Wilkins, I'm going to go see if I can get our suspect out of police hands and into federal custody. So thanks for screwing up and costing me at least a half a day."

Suddenly the cop got apologetic. "I didn't realize you all were working on a case. I'll put in a call downtown..."

"Don't bother," the woman said. "We know who to call."

She grabbed Sean by the arm and led him away from the cop and the guard, who were both staring wide mouthed at the two as they disappeared into the thinning flow of people.

Once they were out of sight, the woman picked up her pace and turned right, heading for one of the elevators in the recesses of the stadium.

"Nice job, Emily," Sean said.

"Less than a week with the agency, and I'm already bailing you out? Not a good way to start, Agent Wyatt. I certainly hope this isn't going to be a recurring theme."

Sean had graduated from the University of Tennessee with a degree in psychology and not a clue how he was going to use it. He had an affinity for history, but there wasn't much of a future in that, unless of course he went to work for his friend Tommy Schultz. That would be a last resort. Tommy, being the friend that he was, had offered Sean a good-paying job as a security specialist for his fledgling artifact recovery agency, but Sean had always wanted to forge his own path.

An interview with the Justice Department had led to some unexpected opportunities. Eventually, he was corralled into a special branch of the government called Axis, a small agency that carried only a handful of field agents at any given time. Sean had never imagined in a million years that he would become a spy. But after passing the series of strenuous tests, he'd been left with few reasons to say no. The only thing that held him back was how heartbreaking it would be to his parents if he were to be killed in the line of duty. The money was good, though, and the job played to Sean's strengths.

He was the kind of person who excelled under pressure, and he almost never cracked. When others panicked, Sean made calm decisions. Those qualities were something the government prized for its field agents. Apparently, Axis was even more stringent with *their* requirements.

"Don't worry, Em. I won't get in too much trouble. I doubt you'll have to bail me out more than two or three times." He twisted his head to the side and passed her a wry grin.

The elevator doors opened, and they stepped in. When the doors closed, she spoke, keeping her eyes forward as she did so. "Please don't call me that, Agent Wyatt. You and I are not friends. We work for the same agency and therefore are teammates, but do not mistake that for some kind of platonic relationship."

He pursed his lips and nodded. "Fair enough, Agent Starks. Although it would be a lot simpler if we just used first names. Just saying."

"I disagree."

He gave a nod and stared ahead at the doors. A moment later they opened again, and the two found themselves on the ground floor. They exited, and Emily led the way out and to the right toward one of the private parking lots where the players kept their vehicles.

"I'm sorry," Sean said. "Where are we going? My car is on the other side of the stadium. And that reminds me: What in the world are you doing here anyway? You don't look like you're dressed for a baseball game."

"I'm not," she said. Her shoes clicked loudly on the brickwork underfoot. "And your car will be fine here. We received a call. The director asked me to bring you in."

Sean's somewhat jovial mood immediately darkened. His eyes narrowed, and he glanced at her as they stalked down the sidewalk into the lot. It was never good news when the director called.

"What's going on?"

She stopped at a red Volvo sedan and got in the driver's side. He hopped in next to her and stared, waiting for an answer.

Emily revved the engine to life and backed out of her parking spot, spun the wheel around, and steered the vehicle out onto the packed city street.

"I don't know, exactly," she answered after coming to a stop at a red light. "The director didn't tell me. He just said to bring you in and told me where you were sitting at the Braves game."

Sean frowned. "He knew where I was sitting? I scalped that ticket."

She turned slightly to the right and shot him a devious glance. "They know everything, Sean. Sooner you understand that, the better."

He shook off the thought. "I guess it's a good thing I'm on the team then, huh?"

"We'll see."

The light turned green, and before he could question her sinister comment she stepped on the gas and whipped the car onto the street to the left. She sped ahead and then jerked the wheel right to merge onto the ramp that took them onto Interstate 75 heading north.

"We really need lights on our cars, you know?" He made the comment as Emily swerved around slower cars in the right two lanes.

"That would draw too much attention. Sort of like your little stunt at the game earlier today."

Sean was incredulous. "Wait a minute. That guy was going to kill someone. I did what I was supposed to do."

"Maybe," she said. "Or maybe that is a police matter."

He could feel the blood pulsing into his head, pounding hard with every heartbeat. "What, you're saying I should have just let that guy kill the first baseman?"

"Not necessarily. But you're essentially a spy now, Agent Wyatt. If you draw attention to yourself, your identity could be compromised."

Emily Starks hadn't been with Axis much longer than Sean. From time to time, however, she used that sliver of experience to give him guidance—guidance he felt wasn't needed.

He decided to use his go-to move that usually worked in situations like this. "You're right. I'm sorry. I'll be more careful in the future." Sean knew an unwinnable argument when he heard one.

She bought his fake surrender. "Good. You know I tell you these things for your own good, right? I just don't want you to get compromised. That leads to trouble."

"That's very sweet of you."

She yanked the wheel to the right, and his head smacked against the window. He winced from the sudden pain and grabbed his scalp.

"It's not just for your own good. It's for the good of the agency and all of us who work for Axis. You screw up; we all pay the price. If one of us gets tagged, the rest of us can, too. I'd prefer not to be dodging bullets when I'm not on a mission."

He went on the offensive. "Seems to me that part of the job is we're always on a mission, even when we aren't necessarily taking orders."

She went silent, which he took to mean she agreed.

Emily exited the freeway and navigated the traffic across the main part of downtown until they reached the area close to the Georgia Dome.

"I thought we were going to the main office," Sean said. "The airport is the other direction."

"One, you probably should have mentioned that before we headed north. And two, I know. We're taking a helicopter to the airport. I'm dropping off this vehicle for another agent."

"Oh." He felt silly for asking.

"Sooner or later, Agent Wyatt, you're going to need to learn to trust me."

He responded by muttering under his breath, "And sooner or later, we are going to need to start using first names."

Her head snapped in his direction, but he was staring out the window as the Peach Tree Westin passed by in the window. "What was that?"

"Hmm?" Sean looked over at her and shook his head. "Oh, nothing."

2

Washington, DC

"Thank you for coming in on such short notice, Sean."

The Axis director gave a curt nod from the other side of his massive desk.

Sean cast a sideways smirk at Emily in the seat next to him. He considered saying, "See? First name," but thought better of it.

Director Forrest Stone had been with the agency for nearly thirty years. More and more, he talked about retirement. But something was holding him back.

Sean had a feeling it was being uncertain of who his successor might be. Being low man on the totem pole, Sean doubted it would be him. He'd not been there long enough to learn everything. But Emily would make a great director. She, too, however, had only been there a short while in comparison to Director Stone's extensive experience.

"No problem, sir. What's happening?"

Stone picked up a remote from his desk, stepped to the left, and pressed a button. The flatscreen on the wall behind him lit up and immediately displayed the southeastern quadrant of Africa. Tanzania was highlighted and a moment later zoomed in on a small city on the nation's southwestern border with Zambia—a city called Mbeya.

"A warlord by the name of Baku Toli is causing trouble," the director started. "At first he was just a minor irritation, hitting small villages here and there. But the problem has gotten worse."

The screen zoomed to a satellite image of a compound on the outskirts of the city. "What we didn't know is that he's been abducting children to build his Tanzanian Liberation Army, if you can call it that. The kids are taken to this compound and brainwashed until they will do his bidding."

Emily cut in. "With all due respect, Director, what has the Tanzanian government done about all this?"

"Right now they are in political flux. Their current leader is weak. And there's a power struggle going on that could turn into a full-blown civil war."

Sean frowned. "I thought they were one of the more stable countries in that region."

The director nodded. "They are. Right now, this warlord's activities are fairly localized. But the more he continues doing what he's doing, the worse it will get." He paused for a moment to take a drink of water from the bottle on his desk. When he began again, his tone lowered. "There's something else you need to know." His eyes went from Emily, to Sean, and back. "We have reason to believe this warlord, Toli, has been amassing a stockpile of biological weapons."

Sean cast a concerned glance over at Emily and then back at the director. "Are you sure?"

Director Stone smirked and snorted a short laugh. "Son, ever since the debacle in Iraq, we always make sure. But we aren't calling the United Nations on this one. They work too slow, always trying to do everything by the book. The president has asked that we go in and take down Toli before his momentum reaches a fever pitch."

Emily still had questions. "I'm sorry, sir, but this sounds like a mission better suited for one of the special ops units."

"Funny you should say that, Starks. A team was sent in four days ago. They failed to check back in, which means they're either dead, captured, or lost. Since you could drop those guys off in the middle of the North Pole with nothing but a toothbrush and they'd still make it home, I think we can rule out the latter."

Sean shifted in his seat. The thought of American soldiers being killed or captured was unsettling. "If they're alive, sir, we'll find them. Where would we start?"

"I like the enthusiasm, son." Director Stone turned to the screen and pointed at one of the buildings. It didn't look like much: tin roof, two stories, probably built out of cinderblocks. Based on the structures around it, Sean guessed maybe three thousand square feet. "This building is where we've seen the most activity. Our satellites have been monitoring it for the last few weeks. It's where we sent the SEAL team. Our last contact with them was just before they went in."

"So why not use another team to go in after them?" Emily asked.

"We thought about that," Stone replied. "Unfortunately, doing so risks letting the Tanzanians know we're running ops in their backyard. As far as we know, they are unaware of what has gone on so far. But the more people we send in, the bigger our footprint. If you get my drift."

"Clearly."

"So," Sean said, "you need a smaller footprint."

Stone nodded. "The Tanzanians have good relations with the United States. They're an up and comer in that part of the world, and we want to continue to foster that growth. If we go in and start throwing our weight around like a bunch of bullies, however, that could change things. But we need to get our boys back, if possible. And moreover, we need to find out if they really do have bioweaponry, how much, and where it's coming from."

Emily raised an eyebrow. "You think someone's bankrolling them? Middle East?"

"Starks, you've been in this game long enough to know that someone is always footing the bill. It's clear there's money going to Toli. So far, we have no idea where it's coming from. Obviously, we look to the Middle East first since, historically, that's where most of the money comes from. Right now, however, the few leads we had are coming up cold."

Sean crossed one leg over his knee and folded his hands. "Go in, save a bunch of Navy SEALs, liberate a child army, and take out some weapons of mass destruction. Sounds like a good weekend to me."

Stone set the remote down on his desk and eased into his chair. "Don't be fooled, Sean. They may be kids, but many of them have been brainwashed to the point of no return. If you're spotted, they *will* try to kill you. And you're going to have to fight back."

Sean's eyebrows knit together. "The second someone starts shooting at me, the gloves come off."

Stone cocked his head to the side for a second and then straightened up. "You say that now, son, but nothing in your training has prepared you for taking down a ten-year-old who's shooting at you with a Kalashnikov."

"Who will be running the show on this one?" Emily asked.

"Agent Fitzsimmons is coordinating your mission. He'll accompany you to the drop point, fall back, and monitor your progress. He will also be your eyes and ears. We will keep surveillance as much as possible, but that has its limitations. I'm hoping that this drone program they keep talking about has some legs. Those satellite-controlled planes will give us a much better view of everything and for a sustained period of time. Until then, we'll have to do it the old-fashioned way." He tossed a file across the desk. It slid to a stop just before going over the edge. "Look through that, both of you. It has all the intel you need. You rendezvous with Fitz in twenty-four hours. So I suggest you get moving."

Sean and Emily moved toward the door. They were about to open it when the director stopped them one last time. "By the way, your cover will be with a group of archaeologists. They're in the region recovering some kind of ancient artifacts for the Tanzanians. The group is based out of Atlanta."

"IAA?" Sean said. "What are the odds?"

"In all the tea joints in all the world. Yeah, I know you and the guy in charge of that little agency go way back. Just see to it he doesn't meddle with your mission. We're using them for a cover. Nothing else. Understood?"

Sean nodded. "Of course." He opened the door and stepped out.

When the door closed, Emily shot Sean a look that needed no explanation. It was followed immediately by the question, "What was that last bit about?"

Sean ignored her for a second and started walking. She grabbed him by the shoulder and raised an eyebrow.

"The group of archaeologists he mentioned?"

She gave a nod that said hurry up with the explanation.

"My best friend runs that organization. And it's a good bet he'll be there."

Emily frowned. "That's not going to be a problem, is it?"

Sean shook his head and turned away. "Nope. In fact, he might be able to help us."

"This mission is highly classified, Agent Wyatt. No one else can know what we're doing."

Sean waved a dismissive hand. "Yeah, yeah. I know. I won't say a word."

As the two agents walked down the hall away from Director Stone's office, Sean flipped through the files. He stopped on a page with an image of Toli. He was staring off to the side, but his face was instantly imprinted on Sean's mind. Ever since he was a child, Sean had possessed an uncanny ability to remember names and faces. He'd seen enough and passed the file over to Emily as they rounded a corner toward their adjacent offices.

"That guy is messed up," Sean said, glancing at the file as she opened it. "Using children to fight his stupid war? I'd like to get my hands on him."

She didn't look up as she answered. "Pretty sure that's exactly what the director expects you to do. Let's just hope we can get in and out quickly. The last thing you want is to end up getting captured by a guy like this. I've heard some pretty bad stories from guys who were prisoners of war. And the more rogue the enemy leader, the worse it gets."

3

Mbeya, Tanzania

The guards shoved Alberto through the door and watched him stumble then fall onto the moist concrete. They'd taken him up the stairs nearly an hour ago. It was difficult to see much in the room. The only light came from a single naked bulb hanging in the center of the ceiling. The power running to it was weak and produced only a faint yellow hue.

Fletch was sitting in a corner against the wall when Alberto crashed to the floor. The commander stood up and hurried over to his comrade. He put an arm under Alberto's shoulder and tried to help him up.

Alberto shook his head and waved a dismissive hand. "I'm all right, Cap. Just give me a minute."

"You sure?"

Alberto gave a weak nod. "Yeah. I mean, considering they just used me as a human punching bag." He raised his head, and then Fletch and the other two saw what Alberto meant.

One eye—discolored a purplish blue—was swollen shut, like he'd just lost a boxing match to a heavyweight champ. A long cut oozed blood from his right cheek. He tried to sit back but immediately grabbed the ribs on his left and winced.

"I think they may have broken a rib or two." He let out an agonizing sigh.

Simmons and Mueller huddled around, both putting a consoling hand on Alberto's back.

They'd all received similar treatment. Alberto had simply been the last one to go. Fletch had been first. They beat him up on the first night and left him bleeding on the basement floor. Simmons had been next, then Mueller. Fletch had a bad feeling they were spacing it out to let the Americans recuperate for a few days just so they could put them through the torture all over again.

Toli's lieutenants—mostly men over twenty-five—had overseen the measures taken against the American soldiers. They demonstrated to some of the boy soldiers and then forced the children to take part—just one more layer to the already deeply-rooted brainwashing.

"They didn't even ask me any questions," Alberto muttered.

"Just take it easy, buddy. Don't try to move." It was all the advice Fletch could muster. He'd experienced the same thing. Their tormentors never said anything to the Americans. They just wailed away at them.

The door to the stairs opened again, and the light from without poured down onto the basement floor, creating a bright rectangle. A long silhouette appeared in the doorway. Toli had come to pay a visit.

Fletch stood up, defiant, with fists clenched. It took all the energy he could muster to fight off the urge to charge the warlord.

"What do you want with us, Toli? Are you just torturing us for your own personal amusement?"

Toli clicked his tongue and wagged a finger left to right. "Typical Americans," he said. "Always so shortsighted. Your people never think about the long term." He laughed. "Of course, torturing is one of the side benefits of your being here. But the main point of putting you and all your men through that was to send footage of it to your leaders. And to the American people."

"Didn't think that one through, did you, moron?" Simmons snarled in the background. "You just pissed in a hornet's nest."

Toli drew his head back, staring at Simmons with curious eyes. "Oh, you mean the American public that no longer has the stomach to do anything? Sure, your faces will be plastered all over your news outlets for a few days. And then everyone will forget about you. You'll be yesterday's news."

Fletch took over the conversation again. "So why keep us here? Why not just kill us or let us go? Honestly, I don't care which. Listening to you talk makes me want the latter."

Toli held up his finger again to emphasize his point. "Ah, because dead Americans aren't worth as much as live ones. I have friends who will pay a pretty penny for the likes of you four."

"Money?" Alberto spat. A little glop of blood shot out of his mouth and splattered on the floor. "That's all?"

"Of course it's for money. How do you think I'll be able to finance my war, with bananas? Revolutions cost money. While mine is already well funded, a little more never hurts."

So someone is backing this lunatic, Fletch thought. His mind raced with possible financiers, but with no way to narrow it down the endeavor was pointless.

"If you think you are going to make us beg, you're mistaken."

Toli squinted one eye. "Oh, I don't intend to make you beg. I know you won't do that. You and your little group are probably American special forces of some kind. I know well enough that you are trained to resist any form of torture I could put you through.

"Your public, however, will cry for you to be freed. They will demand that your government pay the ransom to get you back. Your families and friends will make sure it happens."

Fletch gritted his teeth.

Mueller had been silent, but now he spoke up. "Our government doesn't negotiate with terrorists."

"I beg to differ." Toli wagged his finger around. It was an annoying little habit that had already worn thin on the American leader. "Just recently, your government arranged the exchange of prisoners you'd been keeping since the September 11 attacks. They will pay. After all, it's only money. And if Americans are good at anything, it's spending money." He ended the sentence with another laugh. It sounded like a blend between someone who was jovial and insane all at once.

"You think no one is going to try to come find us?" Fletch asked. "They're coming. And if you kill us, they'll make sure you pay. If you have half a mind, you'll let us go. But I'm warning you, this is your last chance."

Toli laughed, and two of the men nearest him joined in. "You are in no position to threaten me. I can see you have forgotten how much pain you were in just a few days ago." He turned to one of his lieutenants. "Sachu, take him upstairs and remind him."

Fletch grimaced as the men grabbed him under his armpits and dragged him up the stairs. The other three Americans protested but were kept at bay by the weapons pointed at them by Toli's guards.

"You would be wise to keep your mouths shut, Americans. But don't worry. This will all be over soon. I'll have money to fund my war. And you will be free." He took a step forward and his eyes took on an icy stare. "Or you will all die."

He turned and disappeared into the stairwell. The door closed after the two guards followed. A second later the three remaining American soldiers heard two locks sliding into place.

They exchanged uncertain glances.

Tevin broke the silence. "You think Cap was right?" he asked. "You think someone is coming for us?"

"I wouldn't get your hopes up," Mueller answered. "I'm sure the military is going to do all they can, but when we dropped in on this one, we went dark. They don't have a lot to go on. Even if they can pinpoint our location, as soon as Toli smells an attack, he'll have us killed."

Alberto spit out another glop of blood onto the floor. He stared at the floor with his one good eye. When he spoke, his voice was full of resolve. "They'll send someone. And when they get here, it's best that we all be ready."

4
Washington, DC

"Senator, this is Omar Khalif."

The senator's assistant made the introduction and then stepped aside so the two could shake hands.

Sen. Harold Thorpe put his hand out and took the other, grasping it firmly. No cameras flashed. No press begged to ask a question. The meeting was held in secret—an arrangement between one of Pakistan's wealthiest men and a powerful United States senator.

"I know who the man is, Gary." Thorpe blew off his assistant's introduction.

Khalif was an imposing figure, well over six feet tall with dark hair, matching eyebrows, and a goatee that capped his shallow chin. He wore an expensive suit that likely cost more than a week's wages for the young legislative aide.

The American leader dressed slightly more conservative for the meeting, wearing his standard red tie on top of a white shirt and black jacket/pants combination.

"It's a pleasure to meet you, Mr. Khalif."

The Pakistani returned the greeting with a pleasant smile and bowed his head. "And it is a great pleasure to meet you, in person."

The two eased into a couple of club chairs tilted in at an angle toward each other. A butler stepped into the room and set a cup of coffee down next to each man.

Khalif picked up his cup and let the aroma spiral upward into his nostrils. He cast a curious glance at the senator. "No cream or sugar?"

The senator snorted. "I make it a habit to know people, Mr. Khalif. I am well aware you don't use sugar or creamer in your coffee. You prefer it black."

Khalif nodded, impressed. "I can see your CIA does its job well."

"The CIA didn't tell me that. Let's just say I pay attention."

Khalif took a sip of the coffee and savored it for a moment before setting the cup down on the end table. "Well, good coffee doesn't need to be tainted. And this, my friend, is definitely good."

The senator grinned, satisfied his guest approved. "Thank you. I had it brought in from a small farm in Guatemala. They only produce two hundred pounds of this variety every year. Very difficult to come by."

"I'm impressed. But you didn't bring me here to talk about coffee, Senator. You brought me here to talk about something else."

Senator Thorpe motioned for his assistant to leave. The younger man nodded and disappeared through a side door. When the door closed, Thorpe turned back to his guest.

"Omar, you and I go back a long way, before either of us were leaders in our countries."

"That's how I know you want something from me, Harold. A United States senator doesn't call on someone like me just to chat about coffee. How can I help you?"

The senator took a cautious look around before speaking again. "We have word that the number two terrorist on our hit list is hiding out somewhere in Pakistan. His name is Abdullah Qafar. The problem is that we can't go after him without it making everything look messy for our tenuous friendship with your fellow countrymen."

Khalif claimed residence in Pakistan but had homes all over the world.

"So you need my permission to come find this man and kill him? I have to say, Harold, it wouldn't look good if a bunch of your soldiers were traipsing through my streets." The American politician noted the way Khalif used the possessive form with his words, as if he owned the country. It wasn't far from the truth.

The senator waved a dismissive hand and shook his head. "No, nothing like that. The last thing we need is for the media to know we're conducting military missions in your backyard. The rest of the world wouldn't stand for it, and obviously you would need deniability for something like that."

Khalif raised a puzzled eyebrow. "If not that, then what?"

"We need you to take him out. Think of it as a way of solidifying our alliance."

Khalif's mouth opened wide, and he whispered, "Ah. I see."

He stood up and put his hands behind his back, then paced over to the far wall. "What you ask is very difficult, my old friend. Many of my people treat some of these terrorists like heroes. They love them and stand behind them. You say this man is in my country; how do you know? Are you certain?"

"You're right to ask that question. Let's just say we used a lot of resources to track him down. Yes, we are sure of Qafar's whereabouts. We just need you to take him out. I know you have the resources to pull off an operation like that. And your relationship with the Pakistani leaders is good enough that they'll let you do whatever you want." The senator leaned forward and picked up a red folder that was lying on a coffee table. He extended it to his guest.

"Everything your special ops units might need is in that folder. You take him down, and let the world see you do it."

Khalif took the folder and stared at the sticker on the cover. The word *Classified* stared back at him. "Now I see why you had your assistant leave. It would not do to have too many people know what you just asked me to do, and that you gave me this." He motioned with the file.

"Omar, the American people have questions. They want to know why we haven't stepped in with the growing tension between Pakistan and India. They're afraid that you are the enemy because you're a Muslim nation. I know better, but the people need proof. You take this guy down; it will go a long way with the American public. You'll be a hero instantly, and so will your leaders."

Khalif liked the idea. The senator could see it in his eyes. Everyone liked to have their ego stroked every now and then, and the American leader was using that to his advantage.

"It is a good plan," Khalif said after a moment of thought. "But I will need additional compensation."

The senator shrugged. "Of course. I wouldn't do this sort of deal otherwise. Just tell me what you need, and I'll take care of it."

Khalif pivoted around and took four steps in the other direction, as if contemplating what he would ask. He spun again and faced the senator, now with his hands folded in front of his chest.

"Double."

The senator was taken aback by the request. He crossed one leg over a knee and leaned back in his chair. "Done. But I have to ask. You're not planning on starting a war, are you?"

Khalif shook his head. "No, my old friend. You know as well as I do that the Indians have a nuclear arsenal while we are left with nothing. We must be able to defend ourselves with equal force."

"I'm not giving you nuclear weapons, Omar. You know I can't do that."

"And I wouldn't ask you to. I don't need nuclear weapons, Harold. In addition to the shipment, I will also need your word that if it comes to war, America will not interfere."

"So long as you don't do anything stupid, like try to invade India, we prefer to remain neutral."

Khalif unfolded his hands and splayed them out wide. "It is only for self-defense. If they should attack, we would like to be able to defend ourselves or respond in kind."

The senator thought about it for nearly a minute. He scratched his chin as he tried to figure out the most prudent course of action.

Thorpe and Khalif had been friends a long time. They'd studied together at Oxford, both men of extraordinarily high intelligence. It was a friendship that had lasted through difficult times and one that had been beneficial for both. More weapons to Pakistan would leave a bigger footprint and a much larger paper trail.

The mess surrounding the Iran-Contra affair had been a major blight on one senator's career. If not for having several fall guys in place, it could have been catastrophic. The latter gave Thorpe an idea. He could do the same thing, put names in place that would be there just in case information came to light.

He'd be careful. He always was. And with his term ending in the coming years, having his legacy untarnished was of increasingly great importance.

"I'll figure it out, Omar. You'll get your weapons. I have connections that can make it happen, as always."

Khalif bowed low. "Thank you, my friend. I know it is a great risk for you to do something like this. But it is appreciated."

"It's no problem. Just remember, take out Qafar. And let the world know you did it."

Thorpe turned around and left the room. Khalif lingered for a moment, considering what the senator had asked.

Eliminating Qafar would be problematic, especially since Khalif had been the one to give him safe haven while the United States and the rest of the Western world's militaries were scouring the globe for him.

If Thorpe was correct and the U.S. military knew Qafar's location, it was possible they could have connected the dots back to Khalif.

He shook off the thought. Were that the case, the Americans would have arrested him the moment he set foot off the plane. The fact that they'd found Qafar, however, meant that they could also find out about Khalif's connection with him. If that happened, everything he'd worked for would come crashing down. That was something he could not abide.

Khalif called in his assistant and whispered into his ear. "I have an assignment for you. It would appear that our special guest has overstayed his welcome."

5
Dar es Salaam, Tanzania

Sean knew the dust-covered Range Rover was their ride before Agent Fitzsimmons ever got out of the driver's seat.

The flight into Julius Nyerere International Airport had been comfortable enough. From the first sight of the antique SUV, Sean doubted their ground journey would be the same.

The door flung open with a loud creak, and a ginger-headed, freckled young man stepped out. He wore an eager, toothy grin as he greeted Sean and Emily. *God, he looks like a Boy Scout*, thought Sean.

"Welcome to Tanzania," he said. "I'm Patrick Fitzsimmons. You can call me Fitz. How was the flight?"

"Patrick Fitzsimmons? Went a little heavy on the Irish there, don't you think?"

"Yeah, I have my parents to thank for that. My grandparents were from Ireland, so there you go. I'll take that," he pointed at Emily's baggage, and before she could protest had scooped it up and was heading toward the vehicle's rear.

Sean started after him and glanced back at Emily. "Seems like a nice guy."

After the luggage was loaded, the three jumped into the SUV and took off amid a throng of glowing red lights.

"Sorry about the traffic," Fitz said. "It's crazy this time of night around here."

Emily looked over at him from the front passenger seat. "How long have you been here?" she asked.

"Just a few weeks now. The director had me come over here to monitor the strike team that went in last week. But that wasn't the only reason."

"He sent you here as a backup plan, didn't he?" Sean chimed in from the back seat.

"You know the director. Always have a Plan B. His idea was that if something should go wrong with the strike team, we would already have a cover in place to disguise our movements."

"Smart," Emily commented.

"That's why he's the director."

Fitz steered the car around a slow-moving truck loaded down with people in the back. "Our compound is fairly close to Mbeya. There were a few locations that were closer, but we figured setting up nearby would draw too much attention on top of posing an obvious safety risk."

"Safety risk?" Sean asked.

Fitz gave a nod and glanced back in the rearview mirror. "Yeah, Toli's soldiers have been branching out. Four days ago they hit a village about ten miles from our compound. In a few more weeks they'll be brazen enough to go even farther."

"I can't believe the government isn't doing more to stop this," Emily piped in.

"This little quarter of the country isn't a high priority. They're a growing nation and are too focused on the big cities. A military presence has been sent out to patrol certain areas, but they never see anything. That means when they report back, the government hears nothing but good news. It's almost like Toli knows when to venture out and when to stay hidden."

"Sounds like he has someone working on the inside," Sean said.

"Probably. But he won't know you two are coming."

The drive to the compound took nearly ninety minutes. After traveling on paved highways for half the drive, the remaining forty-five minutes were spent on bumpy dirt roads leading out into the savannah.

Eventually the outline of the Axis compound rose up from against the starry backdrop. Out so far away from civilization, billions of stars twinkled in the night sky. The Milky Way was in full view like a cosmic soup of dust, gas, and celestial bodies. *So much beauty above a country so drenched in blood*, Sean thought with a grimace.

Fitz pulled up next to a wooden building with a tin roof and stopped the SUV. Sean stepped out and gazed up into the sky.

"You don't get a view like this in Atlanta. That's for sure."

The others exited the vehicle and shared the moment, staring up into the heavens.

Fitz cut the silence. "I have rooms for you two in this building here," he pointed at the closest structure. "It isn't much. No air conditioning, but right now the temperatures at night are bearable."

"So long as there aren't any mosquitoes, I'm good," Emily said.

"Yeah, what she said," Sean agreed. "There aren't *going* to be, are there?"

Fitz chuckled. "We have nets set up to keep them out, but now and then one slips through. Have some extra bug spray just in case, but for the most part, those guys are not easily deterred by that stuff."

"Great!" Sean smirked.

"Come on," Fitz said, laughing again. "I'll show you to your quarters."

He led the way up a simple set of steps and through the front door. Inside he pointed to two doors on opposing sides of the hall. "Take your pick. They're both the same. Bathroom is down the hall on the right. We have a shower here from rainwater, and electricity all comes from solar and batteries. We'll go over everything in the morning. You should plan on leaving here at one in the afternoon local time. That should put you close to Toli's compound near dusk.

"For now, get some sleep. You're going to need it. Let me know if you need anything. I'm in the building across the way."

"Thanks, Fitz," Sean said.

"Yes, thank you," Emily echoed.

"No problem. See you guys in the morning."

He spun around to leave, but Sean stopped him. "Hey, any chance Tommy Schultz is around here? I heard his archaeology group was in the area. We're kind of using them for cover if I'm not mistaken. Correct?"

Fitz nodded. "Yeah. They were here, but most of them headed out yesterday to investigate something in the hills. What they were looking for, I have no idea."

Sean felt a pang of disappointment. It was instantly replaced by a sense of relief. Probably better that his friend wasn't around.

Fitz turned and disappeared out the door, leaving Sean and Emily alone in the hallway.

"I guess I'll take this one," Sean said. He jerked his thumb at the closest door.

"Fine by me. Sleep tight."

After spending a few minutes getting ready, Sean climbed into the modest bed and pulled the sheets over him. In spite of no air conditioning, the room's temperature was in the upper 60s.

Butterflies crept up in his stomach. He'd only been with Axis a short time. And this was his first real field mission. There'd been one other that involved doing some recon work, but it had been a fairly safe scenario.

This one was different. He'd be shot at. And he would have to use lethal force.

Surprisingly, neither of those things bothered him. His nerves were more from excitement.

The possibility of dying wasn't something that Sean spent a lot of time worrying about. Ever since the death of his girlfriend in a tragic motorcycle accident, he'd almost tempted the grim reaper on a regular basis. The guilt inside him may have had something to do with that. He'd survived the crash. She hadn't. And Sean would have to live with that for the rest of his life.

While the accident hadn't been his fault, he was still riddled with guilt. The car that struck them ran a red light. Both Sean and his passenger were thrown across the intersection. Miraculously, he was nearly unharmed. But she struck a pole and was killed almost instantly.

The visions of that fateful evening clouded his mind most nights before he fell asleep. *It should have been me.* That same thought ran through his head over and over again before eventually exhaustion took over. Even out in the middle of Nowhere, Tanzania, he couldn't avoid it.

Fortunately, he had a job to do. And what he did for Axis was something that required total focus. Lose that at any second, and he would be dead. Sean didn't want to die. He didn't have some sick vision of going out in a blaze of glory. His guilt, however, pushed him to his limits. In a way, it made him a better agent.

He closed his eyes and redirected his thoughts to the mission and what he had to do. The layout of Toli's compound appeared in his mind: the buildings, the fence, the gate, the guard towers. It was a veritable fortress—built to keep out a substantial attack. The warlord's anticipation of large-scale assault would be to Sean and Emily's advantage. Although if the strike team was indeed captured or killed, Toli would likely be on full alert and ready for anything. Sean and Emily would have to be careful. Otherwise, they could end up in the same boat as the special ops unit. Or worse.

6
Mbeya

Cold, dirty water splashed across Fletch's face, rousing him from his sleep. If one could call it that.

He and his men had been given little more than thin, flimsy blankets to sleep on. The basement was cold, damp, and more than a few times in the night he'd heard things crawling on the concrete. Rats? Insects? He didn't know. Part of him didn't want to.

Between the awful conditions and the gripping hunger in his belly, slumber was hard to come by. Every time he'd dozed off, something would wake him up only minutes later.

It was a barrage on the senses.

Any normal human would have broken after the first twenty-four hours. Fletch and his men, however, were anything but normal. The SEAL training was the most rigorous in the world for a reason.

As he lay on his side on the hard floor, Fletch remembered back to that training. He recalled wondering what kind of hellish situation would call for them to be able to tolerate such conditions. Now he understood.

Of course it had always been a possibility.

With every mission, their risk was always the greatest. The SEALs often operated behind the curtain, so to speak. The operations they carried out put them in tremendous danger—and usually with no reinforcements to come to their aid should the need arise. Every man on the team knew that. And they didn't just accept it; they embraced it.

Now that resolve was being tested.

They'd been beaten severely. Tevin had been electrocuted. Fletch knew that was coming for him soon, too. As savage as Toli and his soldiers were, they had a firm grasp on just how far they could push the limits of the human body.

He looked up at the face of the young soldier who'd thrown the water on him.

The soldier was just a boy. Couldn't have been more than fourteen years of age. The kid was holding a rusty tin bucket and staring blankly at Fletch with vapid, zombie-like eyes—as if his soul had been sucked from his body leaving nothing but a hollow skin-robot.

The noise of the water splashing roused the other three from their tenuous slumber. They sat up but didn't dare stand. Four guards plus the kid with the bucket were in the room, all of them armed with Kalashnikovs leveled at the Americans' heads.

Toli stepped into the room from the glowing yellow light of the staircase.

Fletch wondered if he was going to say something clichéd. Most guys like Toli were still watching 1980s American television.

"Good morning, gentlemen," Toli said.

Yep, Fletch thought.

The warlord went on. "You don't look as if you slept well last night. Are the accommodations not to your liking?" He looked around the room and held his hands up high as if showing off a palace.

"We slept fine. Which one of us are you going to torture today, Toli?"

"Always straight to the point. I have heard Americans are this way. Always in a hurry. But I will answer your question." He pivoted to the left and took one step. He wiped his nose with his index finger and continued. "I was going to conduct a test tonight. Unfortunately, I didn't have anyone to use as a test subject."

"Sounds like a personal problem," Fletch spat.

Toli raised a finger in the air. "Ah, it was. Until you showed up on my doorstep. You see, my test was going to be done on animals since we are a bit shorthanded on volunteers."

Mueller jumped into the conversation. "What? You don't force your child soldiers to be guinea pigs, you sick freak?"

Toli's head twitched to the side, but he remained calm. "Sadly, I need them for something else. I'd considered going into one of the villages and taking a few people to serve as my test subjects. That was my plan until you arrived. Then a solution to my problem presented itself." He spun and faced the four Americans again. "You're all in peak physical condition, in the prime of your lives. If my weapons work on you four, they will work on everyone."

"You're a madman," Tevin chimed in.

Fletch shook his head. "You'll never get away with this."

"And why is that?" Toli pried his prisoner with his eyes, searching for the answer. "Is there another group of you coming? Perhaps we should test our weapons on them as well."

Fletch chuckled. "Now I know you're bluffing. You'll kill us all, yourself included, if you use those things within a five-mile radius. Maybe ten if the wind is blowing right."

It was Toli's turn to laugh. He looked up at the cracked ceiling as he bellowed. When he finally stopped, his face took on a sinister appearance. "You misunderstand me, American. If there are, in fact, reinforcements on their way, we will be long gone by the time they arrive."

Fletch searched him for the truth. He couldn't find a lie anywhere on the man's face. Then it hit him. "You have this place rigged."

"Very good. Of course, I will leave a few of my men here to give the appearance that the place is still occupied. I'll use the youngest ones.

They're not extremely adept at fighting yet anyway. Better to sacrifice them, as you suggested."

Fletch stood up off the ground, but one of the nearest guards—one probably in his early twenties—smacked the American in the face with the stock of his assault rifle. The blow sent Fletch sprawling. His men tried to react and keep him from hitting the floor, but their reflexes had slowed over the past days.

Toli turned to the guard and put his hand on the man's shoulder. "Be sure to keep an eye on them today. Now that they know what we are going to do to them, they'll be desperate. If they do anything stupid, shoot them in the legs. I don't want my test subjects dying before I get a chance to try out my new toys."

He turned and ascended the steps, followed closely by the guards who kept their weapons aimed at the prisoners until the door was closed.

Garza and Mueller helped Fletch sit up. He wiped his lip with his forearm. A streak of crimson smeared across the skin.

"You all right, boss?"

Fletch grunted. "I've taken worse. I'll be fine."

"You think he was lying about the place being rigged to blow?" Tevin sounded dubious.

"No idea. But Toli is definitely crazy enough to do something like that. If there's one thing I've learned through the years, it's to never underestimate the lengths an insane person is willing to go to."

Alberto spoke next. "Someone will come get us out of here. They're probably on their way as we speak."

Fletch took a long, painful breath and sighed. A sharp, stabbing pain radiated from the left side of his ribcage. He was pretty sure one of the ribs was broken but didn't mention it to the rest of his team. They all had injuries. He could suck it up, though it made breathing an exercise in agony.

"Well, if they are on their way," Fletch said, "they'll need to get here soon. And if they don't, we'll have to make our move."

Mueller never said much. He preferred to speak with action. He'd been sitting farthest from the other three, listening. Now he spoke up. "We'll have to rush them. As soon as they open the door, we charge."

"Exactly," Fletch agreed. "Each time they open the door, one of them looks through the slit before unlocking it. They probably do that to make sure we aren't close. Even so, when it opens, their guns are ready. Next time they come in, we sit around here in the middle of the room. As soon as that slit closes, I'll get next to the doorway, and when the first gun barrel comes through, I'll grab it."

Alberto liked the plan. "That should take care of both guards because the other one will instinctively turn toward the trouble."

"Right. And that's when you guys go after him."

The other three nodded.

Fletch winced again at the pain in his side.

Tevin put his hand on Fletch's shoulder. "You sure you're up for this, boss? Maybe I should go after the guard. You're hurt."

Fletch's head twitched back and forth. "No. We're all hurt. I'll be fine. Just a bruise. You know how those things are. Feels worse than it is. That's the plan. And we *are* going to stick to it. Once we have the two guards' guns, we shoot our way out. Everyone remember the layout of this place?"

The other three nodded. They'd studied Toli's compound for weeks, making sure they knew it like their own homes.

"Good. I figure we have about four hours. We'll take one of their Jeeps once we're outside. Grab as many weapons and ammo as you can along the way. Could be a tough fight to get out."

It was a desperate plan. But the time for sitting and waiting around for the cavalry had passed. Better to make a move than sit around and wait to die.

"Rise and shine, campers! Time to get to it!" Agent Fitzsimmons stood in the middle of the hallway as he called out to the other two.

Sean groaned and stumbled to the door. Their concierge was a little too chipper considering Sean and Emily were about to jump into the proverbial lion's den. He opened his door at almost the same time Emily cracked hers and stared at their host.

Fitz was holding a steaming cup of black coffee, wearing a pair of black tortoiseshell glasses and a white button-up linen shirt.

"Good morning," he said cheerfully. "Sleep well?"

Sean nodded and scratched his head. "Well enough."

"How about you?" Fitz turned to Emily.

"Same. Got any more of that coffee?"

"Definitely. It's set up in the main building where we'll go over your plan. Go ahead and have a shower. I'll be waiting. Just follow all the wires. You won't get lost."

He spun around and disappeared out the door again without waiting for them to say anything else.

Sean raised an eyebrow. "You go ahead and hit the shower first. I'll wait. Need to wrap my head around this time change anyway."

Emily nodded and returned to her room.

Sean closed the door behind him and fell face down into his pillow. A few more minutes of sleep wouldn't kill him. But he needed to stay awake. Today was going to be long. Hopefully everything would go according to plan. Most likely, it wouldn't. Things never went as planned, which was why Axis agents had to be exceptional at thinking on their feet.

He heard the shower turn on through the thin walls, and the water was splashing around inconsistently. Sean looked over at the modest wooden nightstand next to the bed and grabbed the file he'd set on top. He pulled himself up to a sitting position with his back against the headboard and began flipping through the mission briefing he'd already read at least four times.

Sean's mind was like glue. Everything he'd studied before only took one pass to stick, but there was always something, some tiny detail, that could have been missed. And he didn't want to miss a thing.

He stared at the image of Toli in a beret and full fatigues. The warlord considered himself a general of sorts, a leader of the people. Beyond that, he believed God was on his side and that with divine help, Toli's army would overthrow the government and lead the people to freedom.

It was an odd goal considering Tanzania was one of the more stable governments on the continent. The people seemed to be happy, and the economy was beginning to thrive, unlike most of their neighbors. Someone like Toli could ruin all that. The bigger issue was the crimes against humanity. Stopping men who did horrible things to innocent people was one of the reasons Sean joined Axis.

Sean had seen atrocities from afar but never up close. He wasn't sure how he was going to handle it. He reminded himself that that was what made him human. Some viewed assets like him and Emily as some kinds of robots in a skin suit, incapable of feeling empathy or having fears.

It couldn't be further from the truth.

Stable but fragile governments could be toppled if the right crazy person was given some guns, a little money, and an ego the size of Texas. It seemed to happen too often in Central America and Central African nations. And the countries usually took decades to recover from the carnage.

After Emily finished in the shower, Sean got cleaned up, and the two headed over to where Fitz said to meet. They found him in a room surrounded by gadgets, computers, monitors, and wires. Seeing all the technology in what was essentially a glorified shack was almost humorous.

"Nice setup," Sean commented. His head swiveled around, taking in the array Fitz had put together.

Fitz looked up from a computer screen. "Thanks. Gotta say, it doesn't suck to have an almost unlimited budget."

"Almost?"

"Well," Fitz shrugged, "there are a few things the director wouldn't approve. But you can't have it all, right?"

Emily cut through the boys' conversation and got down to business. "I don't mean to break up this little bromance you two have going on, but could we take a look at the plan?"

Fitz scratched his head. Something about his expression didn't fill his two guests with a ton of reassurance. "Yeah. That's something we need to discuss. We're going to have to move up our timetable."

Sean stole a glance at Emily. "What do you mean, move it up? We're still going after dark, right?"

Fitz squinted and lifted his shoulders. "Not exactly."

"Not exactly?" Emily crossed her arms.

"Yeah, I'm with Em...Agent Starks on this one. Our best play is to go in after dark. If we don't, that kinda throws out the element of surprise."

"True," Fitz nodded. "But there's another possibility. You could go in through the front gate." He held up his hand before the other two could protest. "Hear me out. You take one of our Jeeps that just so happens to look just like most of Toli's. Put some scarves around your faces, and drive up."

He walked around to a screen that displayed the rebels' compound and pointed at a section where the roofs of two towers were located. "There will be a couple of guards here. You'll have to take them out and then crash the gates. Inside, you'll need to move fast."

Sean cut him off before he could finish. "No offense, Fitz, but that isn't going to work. Once we're inside, this whole thing is one big kill box." Sean ran his finger along the outline of the big courtyard. "The guards in these towers won't have to be good to take us out. We'll be dead before we can even get out of the Jeep."

"Why are we having to move up the operation, Fitz?" Emily asked the question that had been bugging her for the last few minutes.

"Because," he replied with a sigh, "we have word there's been a bunch activity around Toli's compound. Several transport trucks going in and out all morning. We think he's moving the weapons. And if we don't act fast, we could lose them."

"Track them," Sean said. "If we can keep an eye on the compound, we can keep an eye on where those trucks are headed."

Fitz shook his head. "They're going in different directions. We can't watch them all. It's like a shell game."

Emily took a step closer to the big screen and leaned in. "Sean, you said that if we stormed the gate we would be dead before we could get out of the vehicle."

"Yeah. Ever heard the expression 'shooting fish in a barrel?' Well, that's the closest thing to it."

"Right, but what you said about getting out of the Jeep gives me an idea." She looked over at a pile of linens and mosquito nets in the corner. "You using those for anything, Fitz?"

Their host glanced over at the stuff in the corner and then back at Emily. "No. It's extra. What do you have in mind?"

8
Mbeya

The SEALs heard footsteps coming down the stairs beyond the metal door. Toli's men served them rations every day at the same time for lunch—if you could call them rations. Bowls of lukewarm dirty water and a few scraps of stale bread were hardly enough to survive on.

The fact that he was feeding them at all showed the four Americans that the warlord wanted to keep them alive, if for no other reason than to torture them, or perhaps to get information. His men had asked relatively few questions, so Fletch ruled out the latter.

"Get ready," he hissed in the darkness.

The four clustered together in the center of the room. Fletch lay on his back while the other three propped themselves on their sides. The door's little window slid open. Two dead eyes peered through, making sure the prisoners were in view. A second later it slid shut.

Before the first lock bolt started sliding, Fletch was on his feet and rushing over to the corner of the door. The second lock clicked inside the door as he readied himself. Garza positioned himself on the opposite side. Tevin and Mueller waited on the floor, their muscles tensed and ready to spring.

The door inched open, creaking on its hinges. The first muzzle appeared—same as it had the last several days—at waist level, ready to take aim at the prisoners. As soon as the gap between the door and the frame opened wide enough, Fletch made his move.

He reached out and wrapped his hand around the weapon's barrel. He yanked it toward him, pulling the guard through the door in the process. As he pulled, he twisted his body to the right in case the guard fired, but the younger man's grip on the Kalashnikov was loose, and in an instant the American spun the assault rifle around and took aim, pointing it straight at the guard's chest.

The second guard stepped in immediately. He pointed his weapon at Fletch, but before he could take a shot, Alberto tackled him from behind and drove him to the floor at the feet of the other two.

He wrestled the gun from the guard and thumped him on the back of the head with the stock. The blow knocked the second guard out, leaving him lying on the floor, limp. Once he was unconscious, Alberto knocked out Fletch's prisoner with a blow to the base of the man's skull.

Tevin and Mueller stood up and stepped toward the door. A third person was standing on the threshold. It was a boy who couldn't have been more than ten, maybe eleven. He was holding a tray of food, staring with wide eyes into the unfolding scene before him.

Alberto looked over at Fletch for instructions. The leader moved over to the boy and crouched down. "What's your name?"

The boy appeared uncertain if he should answer. "Charles."

Fletch put his hand on the boy's shoulder. "Okay, Charles. We need your help. Can you stay here and guard the door? We're going to go upstairs for a few minutes, and when we come back we'll take you back to your family. You want to see your family?"

The boy nodded, his eyes still vacant.

"Okay," Fletch patted him on the back. "Leave that food on the floor, and stand guard here. We'll be back in a bit."

Charles set the tray down just inside the basement and then took up a position at the bottom of the stairs.

With the door locked, the four Americans hurried up the stairs and found themselves in a short hallway. There were two doors, one on either side before the passage turned left. They could hear a television in one of the rooms. It sounded like they were watching a soccer game.

Fletch took point to the left, Alberto to the right. They stepped through open doors simultaneously. Fletch found a soldier sitting in the little room with his elbows on his knees, watching the game. As soon as the man turned his head to see the American, Fletch smacked him in the face with the stock. The guard toppled out of his chair and onto the floor with a thud.

Mueller stepped around Fletch and picked up an assault rifle that was leaning against the wall. He checked the magazine and made sure a round was in the pipe. Satisfied, he gave a curt nod to Fletch, who led the way back out into the hall.

Alberto was already there—crouched on one knee with his weapon aimed down the corridor in case anyone else appeared. Tevin was behind him holding a sidearm he'd found in the room. It was a cheap 9mm, but it would do. And he'd found an extra magazine, which would definitely come in handy.

Tevin looked at Fletch. "You sure we should leave that kid there? How do we know he isn't going to unlock the door and let those two out?"

"We don't. But I'm not going to put him in the basement either. Just gotta hope he does what we asked."

"You really going back for him?"

Fletch nodded. "Yeah, if there are more kids like him here, we need to get them out. First things first, though."

He pushed down the hall and stopped at the corner. There was a closed door. From the sounds coming from just beyond, it led outside. The night they'd been captured had been a blur. In the darkness, Fletch had tried to memorize where Toli's men had taken them, but it had been difficult. Once they were in the light, he would figure out their next move. He'd have to do it fast. As soon as that door opened, they'd be sitting ducks.

Fletch pointed at the door and motioned for Mueller to open it. Then he motioned to Tevin to clear the guards he felt sure were standing right outside. As soon as the first shot was fired, chaos would ensue.

Tevin moved forward and waited for Mueller to twist the latch. The two gave each other a nod. Mueller yanked the handle and pushed the door open. Tevin rushed through and twisted to the right. He fired the pistol, putting a bullet through a guard's temple. He spun back left and squeezed the trigger again, zipping a round through another guard's forehead before the man could raise his weapon.

The other three filed through the door. They stayed low and assessed the situation in an instant.

Fletch's assumption that the doorway led outside was incorrect. They found themselves in what had the appearance of a sort of guard station. There were two windows in the front wall and one in both side walls. Beyond the glass the Americans could see the flurry of activity going on in the courtyard. Transport trucks were being loaded with long wooden crates. The markings on the sides were difficult to read from the SEALs' vantage point, but they already knew what the crates contained.

"Toli's moving his weapons. We need to move, too." Fletch said.

Alberto pointed out the obvious problem. "Yeah but this place is swarming with his soldiers. There must be hundreds of them."

"We can't sit here all day and wait. If we're going to get out of here, now is the time."

He looked into the eyes of each of his men. Their resolve was as strong as his. And they knew he was right. If they waited around, they'd never get out alive.

9
Mbeya

"You know this is never gonna work, right?" Sean asked. He finished propping up linens to make the shape look as much like a human figure as possible.

"Maybe," Emily said. "But we need a diversion."

She looked out at the plains leading up to the walls of Toli's compound. "The land here is flat. So even if the Jeep veers off the road, it's going to hit something. Might be the gate. Might be the wall."

"Or it might just steer itself off course and into the jungle."

"Either way, it will draw some attention from the guards. If Toli is half the paranoid control freak we believe he is, I'm sure those guards in the towers have been told to shoot on sight."

"True. This Jeep will be Swiss cheese before it gets close."

"Probably. And while they're destroying that one, we'll flank them with this one."

They'd taken two of the old SUVs from the camp after Emily laid out the plan to the men. Her idea was to sacrifice one Jeep, sending it crashing into the compound walls. It would draw out some of Toli's men and the attention of pretty much everyone inside. Then they would be able to circle around and enter from the smaller gate in the back. It would be a tight window, but Sean agreed it could be done, even though he was giving her a hard time about the plan not working.

He finished making the dummy prop and checked everything one last time. "Good to go. You ready?"

Emily nodded.

They were tucked safely behind a short ridge, just beyond the guard towers' lines of sight. Once the Jeep was over the knoll, it was another seven hundred yards to the compound. Sean's timing would have to be perfect. If he waited too long to bail out of the Jeep, the guards atop the towers might see him. If that happened, the plan wouldn't work.

He propped a tree limb in the passenger side and started up the hill.

She followed close behind and sped up to walk next to him. Once they reached the crest, the two cut off the dirt road to a lone tree perched nearby. They kept low until they reached the broad trunk and then tucked in behind it. Each of them had binoculars and spied on the facility, careful to make sure they stayed close to the shadow of the tree.

From their vantage point they couldn't see what was going on inside the compound. A cloud of dust rose up from inside, but other than that there was no movement.

Sean moved the binoculars up a little and saw the guards in one of the towers. "Looks like we've got two in each tower," he said. Moving his view to the right confirmed there were two more in the opposite lookout station.

He spoke into his radio. "You know, Fitz, for moving up the timetable on this operation, I gotta say there isn't a lot going on down there. You sure Toli's making a move?"

Fitz's voice crackled in the earpiece. "Just going with the intel I received, Sean."

"Someone else is coming to the party," Emily said. "Two o'clock."

Sean took his eyes away from the binoculars for a second and then redirected them to where a new dust cloud was billowing into the sky. A transport truck was rumbling toward the fortress via the north road. Sean adjusted the focus of the binoculars.

"Got a transport truck heading into the compound," he said.

"See?" Fitz answered. "Word is those things have been coming and going all day."

Sean nodded. "Okay. Okay. I get it. Trust the intel. Point taken."

Emily spoke up. "Sorry to cut in on this again, boys, but as soon as that transport goes in, we should take advantage."

"Agreed," Sean said. "They'll be occupied with loading the truck. The diversion will add an additional element of panic to the situation."

"Exactly."

Sean looked over at her. "Ready then?"

She gave a nod. "Now or never."

They crept back through the weeds to the road and then hurried down the short descent to the Jeeps.

Emily hopped into hers and turned the key. The motor grumbled for a moment and then evened out to a smooth hum.

Sean started the sacrificial Jeep and shifted it into gear. He eased it up the hill until he could barely see the top of the gate over the ridge. The transport truck was just going through the opening. The guards quickly closed the massive doors as soon as the truck was clear.

The road down to the main gate was a straight shot. As hopeful as he was that the Jeep would stay on the road and break down the gate, he knew better than to expect that. He shifted it into neutral and attached the two rubber cables he'd found in the back to the steering wheel. Then he connected them to the door handles. When he jumped out he'd have to go over the door. Fortunately, the Jeeps' tops were long gone. The only thing that would make the maneuver difficult was jumping from a higher point. That, and the ground was rocky.

Satisfied the steering wheel was stabilized, he gave Emily the thumbs-up. She flicked her head up, giving him the go-ahead. "I'll be right behind you."

Hopefully not right behind me, he thought. *I'd rather not be run over.* He took the stick out of the passenger seat and wedged it between his seat and the steering wheel.

Again, Sean shifted the Jeep into gear and stepped on the gas. At the same time, he jammed the fork of the branch into the gas pedal. The Jeep groaned and lurched forward. He'd started it in second gear to make sure the vehicle had a little more speed as it rolled toward the compound.

Sean crossed the crest of the hill and began the descent. He let go of the wheel, climbed up on the seat and over the door. Holding onto the edge with his fingertips, he lowered himself down as the Jeep picked up speed. With no time to hesitate, Sean let go and tucked his head between his arms.

He hit the hard dirt and rolled fifteen feet before coming to a stop. The second his momentum halted, he pushed himself off the ground and sprinted back toward the ridge where Emily was waiting just out of view. Behind him, the Jeep bounced along the road, kicking up a dusty fog.

Sean didn't look back. He had to get out of sight or the entire plan would fail. His legs churned harder, and as he reached the top of the hill he dove forward and rolled into the weeds.

Emily was waiting a few yards away with her engine running. She motioned for him to hurry. Again, he got up off the ground and rushed over to the Jeep. He flung himself inside the open door, and Emily stepped on the gas.

The prairie outside the compound was mostly flat but extremely bumpy. Fortunately for the two agents, it was also grassy, which meant they wouldn't leave a trail of dust to let Toli's soldiers know where they were.

Their heads bobbed forward and back with every bump, like they were at a heavy metal concert. Emily kept her hands on the wheel, deftly guiding the vehicle around rocks and over a few humps that nearly sent them airborne.

In the distance, they heard the first sounds of the guards firing their weapons at the other Jeep. Emily eased the wheel to the right, keeping them on a course parallel with the compound's southern wall.

"You gonna make the turn?" Sean asked. He looked at her with anxious eyes.

"Wait for it."

"Wait for it? They're shooting at the other Jeep."

"Ten more seconds."

"Okay, but you wanted a distraction. They're distracted."

The ridgeline leveled out, and the compound came into view five hundred yards away.

Sean looked back at the gate just in time to see the other Jeep smash into it. From their point of view, he couldn't tell where the vehicle struck. Not that it mattered. The fact that it hit the target at all was pretty incredible.

Before he could say anything, Emily jerked the wheel to the right and put the Jeep on course for a smaller gate close to the rear. It had barbed wire attached at the top, but the weak chain-link fencing wouldn't stop them. Especially not at top speed.

Sean grabbed his assault rifle and pressed the stock against his shoulder. He checked the wall with his sights to make sure there were no other guards looking their way.

He noticed one, but the man was running in the other direction. The diversion had worked.

Emily's knuckles were white as she gripped the wheel. The secondary gate was only a few hundred feet away.

"Once we're inside, you turn this thing around and leave the engine running!" Sean shouted over the combination of motor and wind. "I'll take out the first guards, then we press to where they're holding the SEALs."

She didn't acknowledge his order. They'd already gone over the plan. Now it was time to execute it. The gate loomed a hundred feet away as Emily kept the pedal pressed firmly against the floor.

10

Mbeya

Fletch was crouching next to the door, about to burst through when the thunderous gunfire started. He looked over at Mueller and then the other two with the same questions in his eyes that they had.

He moved back to the nearest window and peeked around the edge. The soldiers outside were shouting and running toward the front gate.

"What's going on?" Tevin asked. "Backup arrived?"

"No idea. But whatever it is, it's got Toli's men distracted. They're all heading to the main gate. This might be a good time for us to..."

A huge bang erupted outside, cutting his comment short. The men looked around at each other and then back at Fletch. "I say we go out the back."

He sidled back over to the door and flung it open. A group of four soldiers were running by. They didn't notice the four Americans inside. All their attention was on the main gate where a column of black smoke roiled into the air.

Fletch stepped out and turned left, right into a group of three more of Toli's men. His weapon was already trained on them, and before they could react he cut them down in a barrage of metal. The other three poured out of the building, Alberto joining Fletch, and the other two covering the back.

The gunfire at the front had ceased, which caused the shots Fletch fired to receive more attention than the Americans would have preferred. Two guys came around from behind a transport truck and were cut down by Alberto. The group who'd been running by as the SEALs left the building turned around to see what was going on behind them. Tevin and Mueller took care of them, firing one shot at a time in quick succession to maximize the number of rounds they had on hand.

Fletch kept the group pushing forward to the rear gate. He scooped up one of the dead men's rifles in his hand and slung the strap over his shoulder. The others rearmed themselves as well.

They stayed together in a tight formation and cut left behind the corner of the building where they'd been held. Immediately, Fletch and the others realized their position was not advantageous.

"We need a way out of here," he stated the obvious.

"May as well take one of Toli's trucks," Mueller said.

Fletch nodded.

It was a forty-yard sprint across the courtyard to reach the nearest transport truck. And it would put them out in the open—easy targets for anyone on the wall with a weapon.

The leader didn't wait for one of the others to volunteer to go first. He took off at a dead run, pumping his legs as fast as he could. Halfway to the truck, the dirt around him exploded in little bursts. He slid to one knee and spun around. The shooter was on the wall around thirty yards away.

"Move!" Fletch yelled at the other three. They ran toward him as he took aim. He felt the trigger tense under his finger and then squeezed. The muzzle erupted six times. The barrel tried to ride up, but Fletch kept it tightly locked on the target, peppering the gunman with four of the six rounds.

More shots were fired behind him as his companions ran headlong into a rally by Toli's men.

The rebels were terrible soldiers and gave no thought to strategy or planning. Dozens of them were cut down in a wave of heavy fire from the SEALs. But the victory was only temporary.

Tevin was the first to signal he was out of ammunition. Mueller came next. More gunmen were running down the causeway above the wall. Fletch emptied his magazine, clipping one of them in the leg. But four others took up positions and started firing.

Pinned against the back of the transport truck, they were trapped, out of ammo, and out of options.

Toli's troops flooded the courtyard from the different buildings and charged the Americans.

Suddenly, a crashing and screeching blasted through the courtyard from the rear gate. An ancient tan Jeep burst into the area with a brunette woman driving and a blond man with an M16 in the passenger seat.

In an instant, the muzzle blazed hot metal at the enemy, slicing through their ranks and sending them scattering for cover.

The woman jerked the wheel to the left, pushed the Jeep into a power slide that finished with it aiming toward the gate they'd just plowed through.

"Come on!" the blond man yelled as he hopped to the ground and crouched next to the Jeep.

He took aim at the men atop the wall and fired. One. Two. Three. Four shots, three dead. The fourth gunman dropped below the wall's concrete railing and stayed hidden.

Toli had gone to the front gate to see what had happened. At first he'd believed it was some kind of brash attack or perhaps someone who'd strayed away from the main road, killed by his men in the towers.

It didn't take long for him to realize what was really going on. Someone had planned a diversion to help the Americans escape. He ordered the men who had been tending to the wreckage to move to the rear of the compound.

Furious, he took an RPG from one of his men and strode down the north wall toward the battle.

He saw the tan Jeep crash through the back gate. And he saw the blond man shooting at his soldiers, easily taking out three on the far wall. His four prisoners were running toward the Jeep.

"Time to finish this," he said.

Taking up a position with his elbows propped on the wall, he pressed his eye to the scope and aimed at the Jeep.

The woman glanced in the rearview mirror and saw Toli on the wall. She yelled something at the others and jumped out of the vehicle as he pulled the trigger.

A moment later, the Jeep exploded in a searing hot orange flame. In seconds it was ablaze, sending plumes of black smoke into the sky.

Toli stood up and handed the weapon to a young soldier standing beside him. He tightened his beret and stalked toward the stairs leading down into the courtyard.

The ground crunched under his boots as he walked past the dead. He'd lost at least thirty men in the battle. Some of them had fallen on top of each other as they ran recklessly into the storm of bullets pounding their ranks.

Now the courtyard had fallen into an eerie peace. The blazing Jeep crackled, the only disruption in the otherwise quiet space.

The remainder of Toli's forces gathered around him as he approached the burning vehicle. The woman was on the ground, face down, clawing at the dirt in an effort to stand up. The blond man who'd accompanied her was prostrate on the ground. A thin stream of blood oozed from a cut in his neck, likely a wound from the explosion.

Toli's four prisoners had been charging to the Jeep when it blew. Three of them were rolling around, grasping at various wounds. One lay still on his back, staring up at the sky with blank, lifeless eyes.

The warlord shook his head and put his hands on his hips. He stared at the carnage for long moment as if not believing they'd tried something so stupid. He shouted at Fletch.

"You see what happens? Huh? Now another of your men is dead! And I have two more prisoners!"

Fletch didn't respond. He was clutching his ears in an effort to stop the ringing. He looked over and saw Alberto wincing in pain. Mueller was squeezing his shoulder to slow the blood from a fresh wound. But Tevin didn't move.

Before Fletch could bring a word to his lips, Toli barked at his troops. "Round them up over there!" He pointed at an area near the wall, thirty feet from the newly destroyed rear gate. "Line them up."

His soldiers gathered the Americans and dragged them over to the spot Toli had indicated. Two of them picked up Tevin's body under the armpits and pulled him to the wall before dumping him in a heap.

"Put them on their knees," Toli commanded. He turned to the boy next to him and told him to retrieve the camera. The kid ran off to one of the buildings near the north wall and disappeared through a doorway.

By the time he returned, the five American prisoners were on their knees, facing the courtyard. The blond man winced and looked up at the warlord. The woman said nothing but was equally as defiant.

"We won't kill her," Toli said, pointing at the woman. He looked at his second in command, a tall, muscular man with a matching set of fatigues. "We could use her, huh?"

The man bellowed a deep laugh. His head rocked back and forth.

She sniffled air through her nose but said nothing, showing no fear.

The boy finished setting up the camera and stepped away. Toli moved over to it and hit the red button on the back.

"As you can see, America, this is what happens when you meddle with affairs that are not your own. We have your soldiers. We have your women. You dare to challenge my strength? I am here on a divine mission!"

Toli stepped in front of the camera and raised his arms to the sky. About forty of his soldiers had gathered around the scene. When their leader put his hands up, they all started shouting in celebration. Then he lowered them and signaled for silence.

He stared into the camera. "You can see one of your soldiers is already dead. But I can assure you, the fate that awaits the others is far worse than death. I have an arsenal of bioweapons that will kill millions unless my demands are met. I was going to use one of those warheads on these men here." He put his hand back, displaying the four male prisoners. "But I think I will just kill them instead and choose one of your cities to be my proving ground."

Toli pulled the pistol out of his holster and walked over to Fletch. The American leader was still grimacing from the ringing in his ears and the pain in his ribs. The warlord pressed the pistol to the side of his head and tensed his finger on the trigger.

"This man is an American soldier. Witness my power."

A truck horn honked at the front gate.

Toli's head snapped to the side, his face furious with indignation.

"Another delivery, sir," his second in command offered.

The anger left Toli's face, and he motioned for the gate to be opened. He stepped away from Fletch and back toward the camera. "I'll be right back." He glanced at the camera. "We can always edit it later, right?" He laughed at his own joke. Some of his men joined in the laughter albeit slightly uneasy as to whether they should or not.

The gate swung open, and the transport truck rumbled through. Toli's men parted to let him through as he strode into the open courtyard. He waved at the truck and grinned.

The truck's driver shifted into a higher gear, and the engine groaned as he stepped on the accelerator. Toli's eyes narrowed, trying to see through the windshield.

Suddenly, the driver's door opened and the driver fell out, tumbling and rolling to a stop on the ground. The truck was bearing down on Toli at a dangerous speed, but the leader was frozen at the sight. He wasn't sure whether to run left or right. Black exhaust poured from the smokestack behind the driver's door as the truck barreled toward Toli.

At the last second, the rebel leader tried to jolt to his left, but the truck lurched that way and smacked into him. Toli fell under the front tire and was finished off by the rear a split second later, his body crushed under the heavy truck.

His soldiers stood motionless, paralyzed by what they'd just seen. In the next instant, their paralysis was broken. The truck's new driver—a stout man slightly under six feet tall with short brown hair—jumped out with a pistol in each hand. He opened fire on the crowd of soldiers who suddenly scattered like cockroaches in lamplight.

Some of them were struck by bullets and fell to the ground. Another man joined the fray from the back of the truck and opened fire with an assault rifle.

The American prisoners seized the moment and sprang into action.

Calling on every ounce of strength he had left, Fletch launched at Toli's second in command and tackled him. The rebel reached for his sidearm, but Fletch got to it first. He pressed the muzzle into the man's ribcage and fired three times. The rebel's massive hands reached up to choke Fletch, but as the bullets ripped through his torso and into his vital organs, his fingers weakened and he fell limp to the ground.

Sean charged at the nearest rebel soldier—a guy who looked like he was probably fifteen. Sean's fists were raised, but before he could strike, the boy dropped his weapon and ran. Sean stopped and watched as the kid disappeared through the destroyed rear gate. Emily stood up and joined him as more and more of Toli's soldiers dropped their weapons and ran through any exit they could find, fleeing the compound.

The two men from the truck ceased fire and lowered their weapons. The brown-haired one sauntered over to the others.

He spoke in a dry tone. "You know, one of these days I'm guessing you're going to have to bail me out of something."

Sean laughed and met the other guy with a big hug. He slapped him on the back and put his hand on the man's shoulders. "Tommy, am I glad to see you."

Mbeya

Tommy sat on a stool next to Fitz, across from Sean and Emily. The SEALs had loaded up their fallen comrade in one of Toli's trucks and left for the exfiltration point.

Their leader, Fletch, had hesitated. "They could come back, you know. You sure you don't want us to stick around and help clean up?"

Sean had insisted they get medical treatment and take care of their own. He and his friends would be fine. "Besides, most of those kids are probably miles from here by now."

Fletch had asked who Sean was, but all he could get out of him was a first name. "Don't worry about the rest," Sean had said.

"Good enough."

They'd driven off toward the east. Sean figured a helicopter would be on its way to get them out of the area.

He looked over at his childhood friend and took a swig of water from a bottle. "I gotta say, I didn't expect to see you here."

Tommy shrugged. "When I got back from the dig site, Fitz told me what was going on."

Fitz put his hands out. "I figured he was a friend of yours so it was okay."

Sean's head twisted back and forth. "Not very classified of you, Fitz."

"You should be glad he did," Tommy said, raising a finger. "That was a crazy idea you two had."

"To be fair, it was Emily's idea."

She backhanded his shoulder and jolted him. "Hey."

Sean guffawed and put up a defensive hand. "Sorry. Agent Starks's idea."

She raised her hand again but didn't strike.

Tommy interrupted their little play fight. "Either way, it wasn't a good call. I mean, the diversion thing was pretty good. But always have two moves planned. Not just one."

Sean raised an eyebrow at his friend. "What are you, the chess master now? We had a good plan. And a second one." He struggled with the last sentence, giving away his bluff.

"What was it? Get shot by a Tanzanian warlord?"

Fitz cut in. "The point is that you guys are okay and Toli is dead. We won! Mission accomplished."

Sean shook his head and stood up. "We won the battle, Fitz." He walked over to the closer of the two trucks in the compound and opened the back tailgate. The cargo area was empty. A stack of crates sat against the wall on the other side of the courtyard.

He wandered over and pried open a lid. The others joined him around the wooden boxes and looked inside. The crates had been packed with shipping popcorn to keep the contents stable during transport. Sean brushed aside some of the foam to reveal a six-foot-long missile. It was only about five inches in diameter.

"We need to get these somewhere safe," Sean said.

"Yeah. And we need to confirm whether or not these things can do what Toli said," Emily added.

Fitz appeared confused. "I don't understand. These are short-range missiles. Relatively speaking, of course."

Tommy's area of expertise was in history and archaeology. So he was lost. "What do you mean, relatively speaking?"

"These can only travel two, maybe three hundred miles at most."

"That's a pretty long distance."

Fitz nodded. "Hence why I said relatively speaking. They aren't like long-range nuclear missiles. Those things can travel thousands of miles."

Something troubling had been on Sean's mind since the SEALs left. "Fitz, before we stormed this place, you said trucks had been coming and going all day."

"Yep." He realized what Sean was getting at before he spoke.

"So where did the other missiles go?" Emily asked, voicing the question they all had in their heads.

Sean pointed at the first truck. "I'll check the cab and see if there's anything inside. You guys check this one."

Before they could ask what to look for, he ran over to the other truck and jumped in the cab. He sifted through the glove compartment, checked under and behind the seat, and even under the floor mats. *Nothing.*

He hopped out, ran around to the back, and climbed into the cargo bed. The truck was loaded with crates, but there was nothing that suggested where the load might be headed.

Sean walked back to the others, disappointed but undeterred. "Find anything?"

The others shook their heads.

"Nothing," Fitz said. "I doubt Toli was dumb enough to leave manifests lying around for this sort of thing."

"Maybe. But we have to try. If we don't find those other missiles, there could be a lot of people in danger."

Tommy interjected, somewhat uncertain. "I don't mean to interrupt your special ops thing here, but isn't the bad guy dead?" He jerked his thumb at Toli's body on the ground. "I mean, threat eliminated. Right? You guys won!"

"He's got a good point," Emily agreed. "With Toli gone, his little army will fall apart."

"And then what?" Sean asked. "Whoever has those weapons will sell them on the black market. Or there could be something else going on."

"Something else?"

"Yeah."

He walked back over to the open crate and flipped the lid off completely. Again he brushed away the foam popcorn and ran his fingers along the missile body. "We need to find some paint thinner."

Fitz frowned. "Paint thinner? Why?"

"These have been painted recently. Who paints a missile unless they want to cover their tracks? I'm willing to bet there might be some markings that could indicate this thing's origin."

"There's a shed over there that might have something like that," Emily said, pointing at a small building with a tin roof in the far corner.

"Worth a look," Sean sighed.

Emily stopped them in their tracks. "Wait." She took a slow step to the crate and inspected the missile's body. "This is American made."

The other three exchanged questioning looks and then stared at her, awaiting explanation.

"You don't need any paint thinner. I've seen these before."

"You have?" Sean asked. "You're sure?"

Emily nodded. "These were designed to be surface-to-air defense missiles. They were part of a new defense program for Israel called *Reaper*."

"*Project Reaper*," Fitz added.

"Right." Emily went on. "No other missiles this small can travel two hundred miles. These can."

"And because of their size, they can slip by defenses much more easily than larger payload weapons."

"Much."

Tommy still couldn't put the pieces together. "I don't understand. What would someone like Toli want with these?"

"Apparently he figured out a way to arm the warheads with a bioweapon. What that is, isn't clear at this point. We'll need the labs to confirm it."

"By the time that happens," Sean said, "it could be too late. We need to know where those other rockets went. And I want to know how in the world someone like Toli got his hands on so much American tech."

Emily took a step back and looked around the courtyard. "First things first. We need to search this place high and low for anything remotely close to a manifest or shipping order."

A groan came from the other side of the truck, like someone was in excruciating pain.

The four Americans stepped around the vehicle and looked out into the courtyard. There on the ground, grabbing his head with both hands, was the driver Tommy had tossed out of the cab.

Tommy pointed at him. "Or we could just make *him* tell us everything."

The driver shook violently to try to escape the chair. The four Americans watched, somewhat amused, as his muscles tensed against the ropes.

"You know, it will just be way easier if you tell us everything we want to know," Sean said.

He stood a few feet away from the prisoner, facing him with arms crossed and a stern look in his eyes.

The man shook his head and wiggled again, as if this time would be the lucky try that freed him.

"Not sure where you think you're going to go if you get out of that," Tommy chimed in. "We'll just shoot you in the knees and drag you back over here. Then you'll be in the chair *and* in agonizing pain."

Sean looked over his shoulder at his friend standing next to him and smirked. "Yeah, you know he's right?" he asked the driver. "That's what we'll do. Of course, we don't have to wait for you to try to get away." Sean pulled out his pistol and pressed it to the prisoner's right knee.

The man screamed in anticipation of the shot.

Emily was standing behind the other two with Fitz and started to move forward, but Fitz put out his hand to stop her. "Hold on," he whispered.

"Is that what you want?" Sean's voice escalated. "I got no problem blowing off your kneecap right now!"

The driver shook his head and yelled. "No! Okay! What do you want to know?"

They'd already asked him several times about where he was headed with the delivery. Maybe he was stalling, or perhaps he just needed a reminder.

Emily stepped in. "Where were you taking the missiles?"

The man looked genuinely puzzled. "Missiles? What missiles?"

Sean jammed the muzzle of his weapon deeper into the man's leg.

He yelled in pain and fear. "I swear! I don't know anything about any missiles! I was told we were running guns to the coast. I only know where to pick them up and where to drop them off. But I swear, I don't know anything about missiles."

Sean looked over at his friend, then at Emily. "He's telling the truth."

Emily wasn't so sure. "How do you know?"

"I always know a bluff when I see one." He turned back to the driver. "I don't suppose you know who Toli was delivering these crates to?"

The man's head snapped back and forth rapidly. "I already told you. I don't know anything about it except the pick-up and drop-off points."

Fitz took a step forward. "Show us."

They propped the prisoner in front of a map they'd spread out on a bare table. Sean kept a wary eye through one of the windows in the room to make sure no one was entering the courtyard. As far as he could tell, everyone had abandoned the place with no intention of returning.

"There's a port, in Dar es Salaam. Heavily guarded. The men there are not Tanzanian." He virtually vomited the words.

"Wait," Emily stopped him. "What men? The guards?"

The driver nodded eagerly. "Yes. The guards and the ones loading the ships. They are not from this country."

"Where are they from?"

"I don't know for sure. They were speaking another language. All I know is they are of Arab descent."

Tommy looked at Sean. "The plot thickens."

"You said they were loading ships. What kinds of ships?" Sean asked.

The prisoner raised his shoulders as far as he could. "I don't know. Different kinds. Some were big. Others were smaller."

Sean took in a deep breath and sighed. "Whoever is moving the missiles is trying to hide their tracks. By using different kinds of vessels, it will make it harder to identify any kind of pattern or similarity. Smart."

"Hard to police every boat in the ocean," Tommy added.

"What I still don't get," Fitz spoke up, "is why this charade with Toli? A guy like him wouldn't have the connections with American manufacturers to get this kind of haul. So what was his part of the deal?"

"It's a shell game," Emily said. "Just like with the trucks and the boats. The big picture is one giant shell game. Toli was a cover. They brought the missiles to this part of the world and delivered them to a crazy warlord desperate to get his hands on some powerful new weaponry. Whoever is behind all this probably promised Toli a few of the missiles in exchange for the risk he was taking holding them until they were moved."

"He was certainly crazy enough to take on that risk," Sean commented.

13

Cairo, Egypt

The sounds of the *Maghrib*, or sunset prayer, echoed through the streets of the city. When the chanting ended, Omar Khalif stood from his usual place near the window and dusted off his knees.

He looked out over the Garden District with satisfaction. Growing up in utter poverty, no one would have believed that he would have achieved such stratospheric success. Yet here he was, on top of the world.

Khalif had been born to poor parents in the slums of Cairo. He'd spent many years away from the ancient city—moving to Pakistan for the better part of the last two decades. There he established himself as a global financial player.

But Khalif's heart beckoned to remember the lessons Cairo taught him. From an early age he learned how to survive on the street and quickly developed the necessary skills to make money. It began when he conned other kids out of *their* money. Later, he turned to outright thievery.

His destiny had long been on a troubled path.

When his mother died, Khalif's father didn't want anything to do with him. He pushed the boy away, shunning him almost entirely. Young Omar grieved the loss of his mother. And at the same time he loathed his father.

Realizing there was nothing for him in Cairo but pain and hatred, Khalif planned to leave. Running away wasn't a cowardly thing to do; at least not in his mind. But why should he stay?

He gathered his things and took off, running down the city's sidewalks and alleys. Khalif had no idea where he was going. He'd not thought that far ahead. He just had to leave his home and go wherever his feet would take him.

Now Khalif smiled as he remembered that day. He'd turned a corner and run into the man who changed his life forever. That man became his spiritual father and taught him everything about God and the universe.

Young Omar had bumped into the man in white robes at nearly full speed. Yet the older man had simply smiled. He'd asked, "Running away, are we?"

The wise, beady eyes narrowed with a sun-wrinkled smile.

How did he know?

Khalif had been mesmerized by that simple question.

He'd cried to the older man, told him everything about his life. The man in robes listened and let young Omar spill his guts. And when he was finished, he uttered words that Khalif had remembered, and would remember, for the rest of his life.

"Come with me, and I will show you the purpose God has for you."

Some might have considered it weird or dangerous to go off with a stranger like that. But Khalif had never sensed anything sinister or evil about the man he eventually called "Teacher."

His real name was Asar al-Farrat. Khalif never called him that, out of respect.

Al-Farrat had been in Cairo on a visit. He'd been recruiting young men to come to his spiritual academy in Tripoli, Libya.

Khalif had never even left his neighborhood, much less the city or country. Traveling so far away seemed like a major undertaking. But he was ready for the adventure. And he was anxious to learn what this teacher had to tell him about God.

Al-Farrat taught Omar and the others about the different paths God had planned for them. He started them off about how God forgave them for their past sins and that they could each have eternal life if they pledged allegiance to Him.

It was an easy thing for Omar to do, though he had trouble believing he could so easily be forgiven for all the wrongs he'd done in the past. Al-Farrat reassured him, and promised that there were also things he could do to make the past right.

Years went by, and the little academy became a small community of more than sixty people. They prayed five times each day, and dedicated their lives to studying the scriptures.

Someone interrupted Khalif's thoughts from the doorway with a clearing of the throat. "Excuse me, sir. Your coffee is ready."

The rippling orange sun was setting behind the deserts to the west. Khalif turned away from the window and saw his assistant standing in the doorway holding a silver tray with a matching coffee pot and two porcelain cups. There were also two cigars on the platter.

"Please," he motioned with his hand. "Come in, my friend. I was just enjoying this spectacular sunset."

"It must be an incredible feeling for you, sir, to be able to look out on the city where you were born, especially after coming from such a lowly state."

"Mmm," Khalif nodded and looked over his shoulder again at the setting sun. A few miles away were the slums where he'd grown up.

Indeed, he had come far. From a poor boy on the streets of Cairo to one of the wealthiest businessmen in Pakistan. Pulling off that last trick had taken an incredible amount of work. And he had every disadvantage the world could have thrown at him. Fortunately, what the street-savvy Khalif had learned as a boy served him well as a businessman. Now he was worth billions. And when it came election time, no one could come close to whomever he chose to support.

Still, there were a few who'd crossed him in the past. Those people had disappeared from the face of the earth.

Winning a political office had little meaning to Khalif. He didn't care about politics, and he certainly didn't care about Pakistan. He preferred to stay in the background, a marionette pulling his puppets' strings.

His assistant, Ahmed, brought the tray in and set it on a glass table in front of a plush sofa. He poured two cups and set one down on an end table next to a club chair. Then he picked up a cigar, clipped the end with a golden cigar cutter, and set to lighting it. He deftly spun the cigar in his fingers while barely touching the tip with the blue flame from a butane jet lighter. The white smoke circled into the air and formed a thin fog over the living room. When the tip was engulfed in bright orange, he blew gently on it and then passed it to Khalif, who graciously took it with a bow.

Ahmed repeated the process with his own cigar as his friend eased into the seat and took a long draw. He puffed the smoke out in little rings and then looked at the cigar with satisfaction on his face.

"So tell me, Ahmed, how are we progressing with the issue at home?"

Khalif's assistant finished lighting his cigar and sat back on the couch, pinching it between his fingers. "The problem should be eliminated this evening. Our forces are moving in on Qafar as we speak."

"Good." Khalif took a sip of the dark coffee and licked his lips before putting the cigar back in his mouth for another draw. He released the smoke into the air. "And our team knows what to do?"

Ahmed gave a slow nod. "Yes, sir. They have cameras with them to document Qafar's death." He hesitated to say anything else.

Khalif saw through the facade and pulled the doubts out of his friend. "What is it, Ahmed? You look worried."

The assistant leaned his head to the left and then rolled his shoulders. "We have been allies with Abdullah Qafar for many years. He has helped us in times when others would not. It seems we are biting a hand that has fed us."

Khalif's head bobbed up and down. "A valid point, my friend. Qafar *has* been a useful ally. And we rewarded him with asylum in our country where he has lived without worry for a good amount of time."

"I don't mean to question your leadership or your decisions, sir. But why are we killing him?"

Khalif's mind veered off course for a moment. It drifted back to a night long ago, when he was still at the teacher's academy. He'd gone out for a walk to look at the stars when the Israeli bomb hit the compound, killing everyone inside. The Israelis had called it a terrorist camp. They'd been misinformed. Or had they? Rumors abounded about Israel's "accidental" attacks on such religious facilities. The precision of the attacks combined with modern warfare technology caused Khalif to believe it was less a mistake and more a direct, purposeful strike.

Khalif grieved for days at the loss of his mentor and the other students. When the time for grieving passed, he'd sworn to avenge their deaths and make those responsible pay for what they'd done.

"Because," Khalif said, returning to the conversation, "sometimes the best way to attack an enemy is to go through a friend."

Ahmed was still puzzled and cocked his head to the side.

"The Americans have supplied us with weapons. They want Qafar dead. I'm willing to trade his life to get what we need."

Khalif's assistant was the only person on the planet who knew the motive behind the elaborate plan. It was years in the making. And now things were being set in motion.

"I see," Ahmed said. "We eliminate Qafar and look like heroes to the Americans. And while it looks like we are doing our part to rid the world of terrorists, we hit Israel while nobody is looking."

"And when the attack happens, we will be the last ones they suspect. The world will look everywhere for the culprits. Of course, we will happily give them information that suggests some of Qafar's generals carried out the attack."

"Brilliant. But one part of it still doesn't make sense to me. Why involve the Tanzanian?"

"Ah," Khalif raised a finger in the air. "Because we can't have those weapons coming directly to our front door. We needed an intermediary. Toli provided the perfect cover. In exchange, we give him a few dummy missiles, which he believes will make him powerful. He delivers the other weapons to our ships, which take them to Arish, just a few miles from the Israeli border."

"Won't their defenses shoot down the missiles?"

"Some, perhaps. But not all. Those missiles were designed to fly at low altitude. The Israeli defenses won't have enough time to adjust and take them all down. And the warheads are equipped with enough nerve gas to kill hundreds of thousands. Possibly millions."

"And all the while, the Americans will be chasing ghosts to figure out who is to blame."

Khalif took another puff on the cigar. "Exactly. Of course, we will offer any assistance we can provide to bring those responsible to justice. They will eventually find a scapegoat and eliminate them." He waved a dismissive hand. "But it won't save Israel. The West Bank will be overrun, and Islam will once more rule the land that belonged to our ancestors."

14
Sibi, Pakistan

A hard knock came from the front door of Abdullah Qafar's hideout. He'd been stuck there for nearly ten months, lying low to keep the Americans and all their toadies off his trail. The noise interrupted his evening tea as he sat with some of his guards in the bonus room upstairs.

He'd been the brains behind a major attack on three different European cities almost a year before. The attacks were so spread out, and looked so random, it was difficult to track down the mastermind behind it all.

Of course his men took the fall. The ones with the guns were always the first ones to get taken. Two of the shooters killed more than fifty people in a playhouse in Frankfurt. The city's police were on the scene before the men could escape. They were shot and killed just inside the theater.

Several others were arrested over the ensuing weeks. Four of his men who'd set off bombs near a church in Amsterdam lasted nearly a month before they were apprehended in Geneva.

One by one, they'd all fallen. Had Qafar underestimated the resolve or ability of the Western dogs to track them down? Maybe. But the mission was an absolute success. All told, more than 140 infidels had been killed.

His eternal reward would be assured.

The knocking on the door resumed, longer and more fervent this time. Qafar looked over at one of his men. The underling, a skinny Iranian named Afi, returned the questioning expression.

"Go answer it," Qafar said.

The guy nodded and started for the stairs.

"Wait," Qafar stopped him. He pointed at a pistol on the end table. "Take that with you just in case."

Afi gave another curt bob of the head and picked up the weapon. There was another man standing guard at the door but didn't dare open it without permission. He had an AK-47 slung over his shoulder and was leaning against the wall. Afi stopped halfway down the stairs and extended his weapon, aiming it at the doorway. He nodded to the other guard.

"Open it."

The man did as told, unlocking the two deadbolts and the doorknob lock. He glanced back up the stairs to make sure. Afi confirmed with a flick of his head.

The guard swallowed and pulled the door open.

A man with a dark tan, black eyebrows and hair, and an olive green military uniform stepped into the foyer.

"What is the meaning of this?" He looked at the door guard with disdain. "What took you so long?"

Then he saw Afi on the stairs with the pistol.

The man in the uniform shot him an irritated glare. "Put that thing down, Afi. You might accidentally fire it. Wouldn't do you any good to kill the hand that's kept you and your friend safe."

Afi lowered the weapon. "Sorry, sir. I didn't know it was you."

"Who else knows you're here? You haven't been talking to the delivery boy who brings your supplies, have you?"

Afi shook his head. "No. Of course not. He leaves them just inside the gate, and we don't go out to get them until he's gone."

The uniformed man was named Nasir. He'd risen through the ranks of the Pakistani army and become a powerful officer. What the general public didn't know about was his sympathy for Qafar and his mission. Nasir had worked hard to keep the terrorist's location secret. Qafar and his men often wondered if Nasir was really committed to what they were doing or if he was just taking orders from someone higher up.

"Is he still awake? We need to talk." Nasir had a sense of urgency in his tone.

Afi nodded.

"Good. Tell him I'm coming up."

Nasir was halfway up the stairs when Qafar appeared on the landing. He put his hands on the rail and smiled at the military man as he reached the top. Qafar opened his arms and embraced Nasir, who accepted the gesture reluctantly. He'd never cared much for hugging but went along with it.

Qafar smiled. "Please, come in, my friend. What brings you here at such a late hour? Would you like some tea?"

Nasir followed him into the makeshift living room. A flatscreen television hung in the corner. It was connected to a video game system and a Blu-ray player. The room smelled of tea and flavored tobacco. The latter came from a hookah sitting in the corner nearest the door.

"Some tea would be appreciated." Nasir did his best to sound gracious.

Being sociable wasn't one of his best attributes. He was a guy who specialized in getting things done. It was why he'd risen so quickly in the Pakistani military. There were, however, occasions such as this that required him to put on a friendly face and pretend to enjoy customary social interaction.

Qafar walked over to the teapot he'd left on a tray atop a coffee table in the middle of the room. He picked it up and poured a steaming cup for his guest. Then he looked up, still leaning over the table. "You like yours without sugar, yes?"

Nasir nodded.

Qafar acknowledged the response and picked up the cup. "Good. That's how I like mine as well, though occasionally I will sweeten it a little just to change things up."

Nasir accepted the cup and took a sip. He sighed with satisfaction and raised the porcelain. "Thank you. Delicious as always." As hard as he tried to sound honest, his voice smacked of insincerity.

Qafar either didn't recognize his guest's tone or he simply ignored it. "I'm glad you like it." He eased back in the deep leather couch and put his arms out across the back. "So to what do I owe the pleasure?"

Nasir took another sip and then set the cup down on the glossy wooden end table close to his chair. "We have a problem."

Qafar's smile disappeared. "What do you mean, a problem?"

"We have word from our sources that you may have been compromised. From what we know, it sounds like the Americans are putting together an operation to come after you."

"What? How could this be?" Qafar didn't believe it. He leaned forward and put his hands on his knees, staring hard at Nasir.

"You've been in this place almost a year. You have a dozen men here. Over that amount of time, with that many people, you start to leave a footprint. Not sure if you've noticed. But there are a lot of people looking for your footprints right now."

Qafar's eyes narrowed. "My men haven't spoken to anyone. We keep to ourselves here. Honestly, it's like a prison. The only place we get out is in the backyard."

Nasir looked around the room with mocking eyes. He put his hands out wide. "If this palace is a prison, I'd hate to see what you think of a real one." Before Qafar could react, he went on. "I know it is difficult staying in hiding, especially when you're trapped in one place for so long. But we have worked out a solution for you that will help alleviate both problems."

"We?" It wasn't the first time Nasir had referred to multiple people being involved with his safe asylum.

"Yes. We. And *we* are going to get you safely out of this country and into a place where you'll be able to resume your normal life, whatever that is."

Qafar bit his lower lip, still wary about whatever plan his guest was going to relay. At this point, what options did he have other than to listen? "Fine, let's hear your plan."

"We have someone on the inside with the American military." It was a powerful opening line and immediately got Qafar's attention. "They told us that there has been a lot of attention on Pakistan lately in regards to harboring known terrorists. Specifically, they are zeroing in on this city.

We might have a few days, possibly a week or two. But it's always best to err on the side of caution. If we wait too long, the enemy could be on your doorstep and you'd be trapped."

"So you want me to run? Like a coward?"

"You've run before. And you survived."

"That was different."

"And look at all you've accomplished. Think of all you will accomplish if you escape again."

Nasir was saying all the right things. Whether he was full of lies or not was yet to be proven. Qafar had no reason to discount the man. Nasir had kept him safe from the infidels for almost a year. Now he was offering further assistance.

"Where will I go?" Qafar asked. "How will I get there? If the Americans are watching this place, getting out could be difficult."

Nasir acknowledged the statement with a nod. "You will leave in an escorted convoy to the outskirts of the city. There you and your men will be transferred to different vehicles. Some of the cars won't be pretty. They'll be old, rusted, beat up. Some will be new. We want to make it look natural. Getting you across the border in similar vehicles might draw attention."

"Okay," Qafar said. He was following the plan so far, but Nasir still hadn't answered his first question. "But where are we going?"

"Tajikistan. You will cross the border in the mountains. You'll be safe there. We've already made the arrangements with our contacts there."

Qafar's mouth opened wide. "Tajikistan? That's a long journey."

"It isn't that far. And you'll adapt easily. You'll need to cut your hair. Maybe grow a beard. A change of appearance will help. We would go through Afghanistan, but that would be running right into the lion's mouth with the American presence there."

He was right about that. The place was overrun with American troops. While they were preoccupied with hunting the Taliban, that didn't mean they should tempt fate.

"And if I agree to this plan of yours...when will we be leaving?"

"Tonight."

Qafar was taken aback. "Tonight? That's a little sudden, isn't it?"

"You can either accept our help and do what we say, or you can stay here and be killed by the Americans."

Qafar stood up and paced back and forth. He ran his fingers through his hair and let out a long sigh. He stopped and faced Nasir. "I don't understand. How is it that your government is going to allow the Americans to conduct operations here? They can't do that."

"My friend, it is important to always know with whom you pick your battles. Do you really think anyone in our government is going to tell the

United States no? If they find out we are harboring one of the top ten sought-after men in the world, what do you think they will do?"

"Then stand up to them."

Nasir chuckled. "And do what? Fight them? They will annihilate us. And the Indians will help them."

"So you let them come into your home and do as they please?" Qafar spat the words out. He was disgusted by what he was hearing. Politics enraged him. He was a man of action, not committees or back alley dealings.

"If that is what keeps the people safe." Nasir rolled his shoulders. "I suggest you take our offer, Abdullah. It is your only chance for survival. The convoy will be here in two hours. Take only what you need. You can always buy new things. You can't buy a new life."

Nasir turned and walked out of the room, leaving Qafar alone. Afi stood just outside the doorway as Nasir passed by. The military man stopped and put his hand on Afi's shoulder. "Talk some sense into him, Afi. If you don't, the cause he has worked so hard for will be lost."

The front door closed behind Nasir as he left. Qafar had been standing silently in the bonus room, running through his limited set of options. He was tired of running, tried of hiding. It was cowardly. He knew it. But it was also necessary. Combine that with the fact that he didn't want to die, and there was only one clear choice.

Afi hesitated in the doorway and then entered. He was reluctant to speak but eventually forced the words out. "It sounds like we need to get ready to leave."

Qafar was staring at the floor with his chin in hand. He scratched his scruffy beard with his index finger a few times. He looked over at his friend and nodded. "So it would seem. Tell the rest of the men we will be leaving in two hours. Our friend Nasir has provided us with a means of escaping death once more. Take only what you need. Leave the rest."

15
Sibi

Qafar watched the street from the window in the upstairs sitting area. He glanced down at his watch and checked the time. It was almost time, but there was no sign of Nasir.

Qafar and his men had spent the last hour and fifty-plus minutes getting ready to leave. He had all he needed in a book bag sitting at his feet. The rest of the men were packed equally as light.

One minute before the hour, Qafar saw headlight beams approaching from just down the hill. In seconds, one pair of lights appeared, then another, and another. Six black SUVs pulled up to the curb in front of the compound's wall. The door flew open, and Pakistani soldiers dressed in black got out and waited next to the vehicles.

"Looks like our ride is here," Qafar said to Afi. "Get the others loaded up. Let's not keep our friend waiting."

Afi rushed down the stairs and started barking out orders.

Nasir exited the lead SUV, opened the front gate, and walked to the door. Before he could knock, one of the guards opened it and motioned for him to enter.

Inside, Nasir found a flurry of activity. Qafar's dozen men were rushing around to make sure they'd collected everything they needed for the relocation.

Qafar appeared at the top of the stairs with his backpack slung over his shoulder. "I was beginning to wonder if you were going to be late, or if you were going to show at all."

Nasir checked his watch. "I'm never late."

"That's what I've heard about you."

Qafar descended the steps and joined Nasir on the main floor.

"We have weapons for your men," Nasir said as they walked out onto the front porch. "I don't trust the guns they have. Unreliable Chinese guns. Jam too much. If we get in a firefight on the way to the rendezvous, they'll need weapons that work."

"These guns work fine," he said and pointed to one of the Kalashnikovs hanging on a nearby soldier's shoulder.

Nasir's head jerked back and forth. "I'm afraid I must insist. You haven't seen what I've seen in battle. Trust me; we have you covered."

"I hope you're not expecting some kind of attack." Qafar probed Nasir for the truth.

"No. That's why we're making this move tonight. No one knows what is happening other than my drivers and me. But I like to be cautious. Always."

The lips on the right half of Qafar's face creased slightly. "Safe is good, my friend. I trust you."

"Good. The weapons are in the back of the trucks. Tell your men to exchange them before they get in. They are much smaller, submachine guns. But they'll fire with just as much accuracy and are much more compact for travel."

Qafar considered what Nasir was saying. Then he told Afi to make sure the men all exchanged weapons with Nasir's men. Afi didn't ask why. He simply relayed the message to the rest of Qafar's men.

One of Nasir's soldiers approached the house and ascended the front steps carrying a black box. He stopped in front of Qafar and turned to his commander.

"Thank you. See to it that the rest are loaded up and ready to go in the next five minutes." The soldier stomped his foot on the ground, confirming the order. He double-timed it back out the door to assist with the evacuation.

Nasir turned to Qafar with the black box and pried the lid open. "In honor of our friendship, I took the liberty of having these made for you. I hope you like them."

Qafar looked as if he'd been smacked in the face. "You bought me a gift?"

Nasir raised his shoulders. "I can be sentimental from time to time."

Qafar stepped close and looked in the box. Twin 9mm pistols lay in a bed of crushed velvet. They were cerakoted with the images of golden dragons rising up from the grip and down along the sides. Their mouths breathed fire close to the muzzle.

"They're beautiful," Qafar said. He took the weapons out and waved them around, then took aim at a mirror on the other side of the room.

"They're loaded and chambered," Nasir warned. "So don't pull the trigger just yet. We don't want to rouse the neighbors."

Qafar was clearly pleased. He stared with admiration at the two guns before placing them back in the box. "Thank you for everything, my friend. I appreciate all you have done. Allah will bless you for it. I promise."

Nasir closed his eyes slowly as he nodded. "I certainly hope so. Now, we must be going. We don't want to be late for our rendezvous."

The drive through the small city didn't take more than fifteen minutes before the convoy was on the outskirts where the neighborhoods turned into farms and occasional factories.

Qafar held the black box in his lap as his SUV—the second in line—followed the lead vehicle through the winding streets and down onto the flats of the plains below. The moon was high in the cloudless night sky, obscuring the view of some of the nearby stars with its bright light.

A dark silhouette rose on the horizon on the right side of the road. As the convoy drew closer, the passengers could see it was an old warehouse. Qafar looked down at his watch again. *Nearly half past the hour.* A nervous tension filled his veins. He didn't know why. Maybe the sooner he got out of Pakistan, the better he'd feel. Nasir's words about the Americans being on his trail had filled him with a new sense of dread.

The convoy turned off the main road and into the gravel drive leading into the warehouse property. The lead vehicle—with Nasir in it—drove around to the back and then through an opening where two huge doors hung on either side.

All six vehicles pulled into hangar-like building and came to a stop in the center. Qafar looked out at the dark, vacuous room. Rusted beams supported a skeletal metal frame underneath a tin roof. It looked like the place had been abandoned for decades, maybe more.

"This is where we're changing vehicles?" Qafar asked.

The driver nodded. "The other cars should be here shortly. Stay here. I'm going to go check."

Qafar accepted the explanation with a nod and looked out the window once more. His driver walked up to the lead SUV and got in the back.

Afi was in the rear seat of Qafar's ride and leaned forward. He put his hand on Qafar's headrest. "Soon, my friend, this will all be over, and we won't have to worry about looking over our shoulders anymore."

"I hope so, my friend. It will be nice to be able to come and go as we please. If what Nasir says is true, we will be free men once more."

The words barely escaped his mouth when Nasir's SUV lurched forward and came to a stop at the other end of the warehouse—a good eighty feet away.

"What's he doing?" Afi asked.

Qafar noticed movement on a catwalk high up over the floor to the right. In the darkness, it was difficult to see what it was. A second later, he had his answer. A muzzle flashed over and over.

More bright explosions of gunfire immediately accompanied it. The weapons were quiet—silenced by suppressors—but still popped loud enough to hear in the SUVs.

"It's a trap!" Qafar shouted.

Bullets thumped into the roof of the SUV, shattered the windows and windshield, and pierced the tires.

Afi reacted quickly, kicking open his door and taking aim at the shooter closest to their vehicle. He opened fire, emptying his magazine at the gunman but missed with every shot. The second after his weapon clicked, the shooters fired at him again, showering the back seat of the SUV with hail of deadly metal. Afi's body shook violently with every round that tore through him until he fell into the seat and stopped moving.

Qafar instinctively grabbed the pistols out of the black box and flung open his door. The two closest shooters were reloading. His eyes shot over to the far side of the warehouse. There was a door in the back corner—the darkest part of the building. He could make it. He had to make it.

Qafar clutched his new pistols in both hands and took off as fast as he could go. The men on the catwalk saw their target running and quickly adjusted their aim as he passed underneath. They opened fire, but Qafar jumped to the left and right, avoiding the bullets pinging off the concrete around him.

When he reached the darker part of the room, he virtually disappeared, making hitting him even more difficult.

The men called down to someone on the floor for assistance.

The door was only thirty feet away. He didn't dare look back. Not now. Not when he was so close.

He slid to a stop and stuffed one of the pistols in his belt to grab the door handle. When he tried to push it down, though, a sickening feeling coursed through him in an instant. The door was locked. He took the pistol in his hand to fire at where he thought the lock might be, but a familiar voice stopped him cold.

"What exactly were you planning on doing once you got outside, Abdullah?"

Qafar spun around to see Nasir's face, barely visible in the shadows.

"You betrayed me. You betrayed all of us. Our blood is on your hands."

"Oh, I know." Nasir stepped forward to a point where a ray of pale moonlight shone through an opening in the roof. "I can't tell you how many nights it will keep me up. But sometimes we have to do these kinds of things."

The sarcasm wasn't lost on Qafar.

He panted for breath but noticed Nasir was holding his pistol at his side. Qafar reacted quickly and raised his weapon, aiming it at Nasir's head. He took the second gun out of his belt and held it next to the other.

"It seems you forgot about these, old friend. Now here is what is going to happen. You're going to walk me back over there. You will tell your men to stand down, to put their weapons in your truck, and then you and I are going to take a long ride."

Nasir almost looked amused. His right eyebrow rose. "Oh? And where are we going?"

"Like you said. We're going to Tajikistan. When we cross the border, I'll let you go. If you do anything stupid before that, I will kill you with the very guns you gave me."

His fingers felt the cold of the triggers. Qafar almost wanted Nasir to try something. But the Pakistani officer was his ultimate bargaining chip, a virtual guarantee of safe passage.

"There was never any plan to take you to Tajikistan, Abdullah. There will be no safety for you there. We will hunt you down no matter where you go. It's over."

Qafar's face tensed, and one of his eyes twitched. "No!" he yelled. "It's not over yet! It will be over when I say it is!"

Nasir's expression softened to an almost devilish smile. "All your men are dead. Afi along with them. There's nowhere for you to run. Now you can put down your guns and die like a man. Or you can die like a dog. Doesn't matter to me which one you choose."

Afi's lifeless face passed before Qafar's eyes. He looked beyond Nasir at the bodies of his men being dragged out of the SUVs. All the shooting had stopped. Four soldiers in black were standing twenty feet behind Nasir. Qafar couldn't believe it was ending this way. But if he was going to die, he would take Nasir with him—and as many of the others as he could.

"If I die, you die, too, old friend." He let out a yell as he squeezed the triggers. "Ahhhhhhhhhh!"

His fingers alternated, firing one shot and then another at Nasir who stood motionless, watching the muzzles blaze until both weapons clicked. Qafar's fingers kept pulling even after he realized his magazines were empty.

He stared in disbelief at Nasir, who was untouched by the bullets. "How? That's impossible!"

Nasir took a casual step forward so that only his face was illuminated by the moonlight. He pouted and shook his head once. "You should always check to make sure you're using live rounds when someone hands you a gun, Abdullah. You remember the guns we gave you? They all had blanks."

Qafar was incensed. Rage boiled up inside him, and he started to charge. Nasir merely raised his weapon and unloaded ten rounds into Qafar's chest.

The terrorist stumbled, struggling to keep his balance and stay on his feet. He swallowed, then coughed. His mind fought the mortal wounds as long as he could before he dropped to his knees. Qafar desperately fought to keep conscious. Across the room, on the other side of the warehouse, he saw Nasir's men pull Afi's body out of the SUV and drop it on the floor like he was a bag of garbage.

Tears formed in Qafar's eyes. He could only hope that he would be rewarded for the deeds he'd done against the infidels. His lungs started to lock up, filling with fluid. He coughed again and winced against the pain.

Nasir stepped close and pointed his gun at Qafar's forehead. "It's nothing personal, old friend." He squeezed the trigger.

Qafar toppled over backward. His lifeless eyes stared up at the opening in the ceiling as a single cloud passed in front of the moon.

16
Dar es Salaam

Sean looked through his binoculars at the busy pier. Men were rushing around, loading crates from trucks similar to the ones from Toli's compound.

Forklifts made quick work of the heavy payloads—removing the crates from the transport and placing them in a yellow square next to what appeared to be a huge commercial fishing vessel. Others were being loaded onto a couple of yachts, a merchant shipping vessel, and a smaller commercial fishing ship.

The driver hadn't been lying. Toli's men were using a variety of boats to avoid detection.

"Gotta give it to Toli," Sean said, "pretty smart to use fishing boats like that one. No one would suspect."

Tommy, Emily, and Fitz were all watching the same scene through similar lenses.

The driver was tied up in the back of the truck with a cloth strapped to his mouth so he couldn't scream. Sean had given him additional incentive to stay quiet by promising him a bullet in the throat if he made so much as a squeak. The driver nodded that he understood and had behaved himself thus far.

"So how do we stop them?" Fitz asked. "The workers aren't armed from what I can tell."

"But those guys on the watchtowers and on the ships are," Emily pointed out.

"Yeah," Sean agreed. "I noticed that."

"What is with all these dudes and AK-47s?" Tommy asked.

"Cheap and easy to get," Emily and Sean both answered at the same time. They glanced at each other with a smirk, and then went back to scanning the pier.

"There are too many of them," Sean said. "At least for the four of us."

"Agreed," Emily said. "I count forty, and that's just the ones we can see. There'll be more aboard the ships."

"If we can draw their attention somewhere else, we might be able to get on board the ships and disable them."

"What good will that do?" Tommy asked. "They'll fix them and be out to sea before dark."

"It could buy us some time, though."

"Time for what?"

Fitz interrupted. "There's a U.S. ship about a hundred miles off the coast from here. My guess is that's where Fletch and his men were taken. If we could get a call in to them, they might just be able to get here before these ships leave. That is, if we can disable them long enough for the Navy to arrive."

"I like it," Sean said. "Any objections?"

No one said anything.

"Good. So what are we going to use for a diversion?" His eyes wandered to the back of the transport truck.

Emily followed his gaze and snorted a short laugh. "So we're going to use the same gag again?"

Sean shook his head. "No. You don't do the same gag twice. You do the next gag."

"So what's the next gag?"

A mischievous glimmer filled his eyes. "Let's untie our friend in the back."

Sean climbed over the tailgate and sat on the bench in the cargo area. He looked down at the driver who was bound with his wrists behind his back. The man appeared as though he'd perspired half a gallon of sweat. His shirt was soaked, and moisture trickled down his forehead in several rivulets.

Sean turned to Fitz and asked for a bottle of water. He untied the driver's hands and then gave him the bottle. "Now don't do anything stupid like scream for help. Okay?" Sean wagged his pistol at the man.

The driver's head shook vigorously, and he gulped down the entire bottle in less than six seconds.

Sean went on. "Now, my friends and I have a little job for you to do."

"A job?"

"Yep. We want you to drive up to the gate and act like you're making your delivery as scheduled."

"But the crates? My truck is empty."

Sean waved his free hand in the air. "Don't worry about that. They aren't going to check. Just drive up to the gate and act cool. They're going to let you in. When you get inside, tell them that there were no more shipments when you arrived in Mbeya. We'll take care of the rest."

The driver wasn't sure. "They'll think I stole the boxes."

Sean could see he was dubious and reassured him. "By the time they start asking questions, my friends and I will be inside. You saw what we did to Toli's army, right?"

The man's head bobbed up and down rapidly. He remembered exactly what he'd seen and had no intention of crossing the Americans. Just in case, however, Sean gave him a little reminder.

"And if you for a second think about taking this truck and running away, my friends and I will chase you down and kill you. Understood?"

"Yes. Clearly." There was genuine fear in the driver's eyes. Sean was certain of that.

"Okay. Good. Let's get you set up."

Sean hopped out of the back followed by the driver.

They walked around to the cab and stopped. Sean pointed at the road that wound around a grassy median. It led down to the gate where there were men standing guard with assault rifles. "Take this street down to the gate, and do as I said. And don't worry. It will all be over soon. When it is, you can go free. We will be over there at that small building." He pointed to what looked like a storage facility made out of cinderblocks. "When I give you the signal, head to the gate."

The driver acknowledged the directions with a nod and climbed up into the cab. Sean stepped back and joined the other three.

The engined rumbled to life, and the driver looked down at them. He gave a thumbs-up.

"Time to get into position," Sean said to the others.

The four Americans jogged down the right-hand sidewalk toward the storage building and waited in the shadows at the corner behind a row of bushes.

"You sure this is gonna work?" Emily asked. "I mean, what if he takes off?"

Sean glanced at Tommy. "You cut the brake line, right?"

Tommy nodded. "Yeah. Second time he hits the brakes, nothing's gonna happen."

Sean smirked. "If he tries to get away, Agent Starks, he's going to have a very short trip."

He stood up and waved his hand so the driver could see. The man in the truck nodded and shifted into gear. He stepped on the gas, accelerated slowly around the curve, and began the descent down the hill. About fifty yards from the gate, he hit the brakes and slowed down a bit. The truck coasted by the four Americans crouching behind the bushes and continued rolling.

"Okay, let's go. Brisk but casual."

They stood up and started walking down the sidewalk at a moderately quick pace with weapons tucked away so no one could see.

The truck picked up speed as it neared the gate. The brake lights flashed over and over again as the driver tried to slow his speed.

Down at the foot of the hill, the guards at the gate were waving their arms furiously in a vain attempt to get the driver to stop. At the last second, they dove out of the way as the truck smashed into the blockade, plowed through it, and kept rolling onto the pier. The guards recovered immediately and rushed after the runaway truck. They slowed momentarily to fire their weapons and then took off again.

The gate had done little to slow the truck. It barreled ahead at full speed toward the edge of the wharf. There were more men standing between the oncoming vehicle and a shipping vessel. They ran to both sides, barely avoiding being crushed. The truck rumbled by and rammed the first boat in its port side. Workers and guards ran to the scene as smoke began billowing out of the engine. Before anyone got to it, a fire ignited and started burning.

One of the guards started barking out orders, and some of the men scattered to retrieve fire extinguishers.

The four Americans watched the entire thing transpire as they walked toward the gate. Once all the guards' attention was on the runaway truck, the Americans broke out at a dead sprint. Every eye was on the vehicle as it crashed into the shipping vessel with a huge bang. No one saw the four strangers run through the gate and behind the stacks of containers, parked machinery, and outbuildings.

Once they were completely out of view, Sean stopped behind the base of a crane and looked out at the boats.

"Looks like that one may already be out of commission," Tommy said.

"I cannot believe that worked again," Emily commented.

"One of these day's you'll learn to trust me," Sean replied. "That leaves four boats for us to take out. I'll go for the big fishing vessel on the end. You three take the others. Do whatever it takes to disable those boats. The easiest thing might be to tear up the controls, screw with the wiring, something like that. We'll rendezvous at the coffee shop we saw earlier. Sound good?"

The other three nodded, but Emily spoke up. "Are you sure we should involve a civilian?" She jerked her thumb at Tommy. "I mean, I know you two are friends and all, but shouldn't the professionals take care of this?"

Tommy raised both eyebrows, but Sean cut him off. "He saved our skins back at Toli's. Tommy can handle himself in a fight. You just take care of your boat. He'll be fine."

"What about you?" Tommy asked.

Sean winked. "I've got a little something special in mind for my ship."

Before Tommy could protest, Sean took off.

He skirted the front of a warehouse on the back of the property and then disappeared around the corner.

"Never been able to talk any sense into him," Tommy said.

"I'm starting to see that," Emily agreed. "I'll take the shipping vessel. Tommy, take that yacht. Fitz, you got the other one."

Fitz considered making a wise crack about never getting to go on a yacht, but he thought better of it.

The two guys nodded.

They split up and ran through maze of containers and equipment until they reached the last stacks of big metal boxes. Each American peeked out from their hiding places and watched as the last of the men guarding the boats ran down the pier toward the burning wreckage.

Some of the first responders were desperately trying to get close enough to hit the flames with their extinguishers. Suddenly, an explosion rocked the shipping yard and a giant ball of fire rolled into the air. A fuel leak in the truck's engine must have ignited.

More black smoke poured skyward, and the men working the scene doubled their efforts to bring the blaze under control. One man who'd been knocked over by the blast was being dragged away by two others to a safe distance.

Emily motioned with her finger for her partners to make a break for it. She watched them dart across the causeway and climb aboard, keeping a wary hand on her pistol just in case she had to cover them. When the guys disappeared onto the boats, she made her move and took off. No one was looking her direction as she sprinted over the landing, up the gangplank, and onto the ship. Once she was safely aboard, she went straight to the control room and ducked inside. She peeked out the windshield and saw what looked like nearly a hundred people milling around the destruction. Behind her she saw a toolbox attached to the wall.

She grabbed the box and pulled out a screwdriver that matched the screws on the console and set to work. She just hoped the others could sabotage their ships before the crews started heading back.

Sean ran hard toward the last boat. He stopped next to a crane and looked around the corner at his target. There were still a few people aboard checking their cargo.

That would make getting on the ship tricky. And if he was spotted, the men would sound an alarm. Or worse, start shooting at him.

Sean scanned the area for a solution but couldn't see a good way to get to the control room, or to the boat for that matter.

He looked at the crane next to him. Then he glanced at a short stack of twenty-foot steel containers a short distance away. One of the containers already had cables attached to the top. *If I can't get to the boat to disable it, maybe I can do it from here.*

He climbed up into the crane's seat and found the key still in the ignition. Not surprising considering how fast everyone ran toward the diversionary crash. He turned the key and revved the engine. Working the different levers took a minute for him to figure out, but he finally got the gist of what did what and swung the crane's long arm to the right, stopping it over the containers.

"Just like with that arm grabber at the arcade," he said.

Sean pushed on one of the levers and lowered the cable. When it hit the top of the steel box, he jumped out of the crane and sprinted over to the stack. With a full head of steam he leaped into the air and reached out to grab the box's top edge. His body hit the side and his fingers gripped the ledge, but he'd mistimed the jump and before he could pull himself up, he lost his hold and fell back to the asphalt.

"Good one," he said to himself.

He retreated another twenty feet and got another running start. Now he timed it better. He flew through the air and caught the top edge with a solid grip, palms pressing hard into the corner. Sean used his momentum and pulled as soon as his fingers hit the metal.

In his training he'd done obstacle courses that had similar wall climbs. He remembered those being more difficult to get over in spite of the current one taking two tries.

His muscles tensed as he pulled himself up. He swung his legs over the edge and rolled to the middle of the container. There he took hold of the hook and worked the two cables through it. The move took less than ten seconds.

He lowered himself back down to the ground and started running back to the crane. *Almost too easy.*

His thought came just before he heard a familiar sound. Automatic gunfire popped from across the pier landing. Sean looked to his side as he ran to the crane. One of the men on his target ship had seen him and was firing. A few random bullets pinged off the asphalt and other containers nearby. At that range, he'd be a tough target. Still, any idiot could get lucky.

And in the crane he'd be a sitting duck.

His original idea had been to swing the container over the vessel's control room and drop it. Now Sean doubted he had the time for such a precise maneuver. When he reached the base of the crane, he drew his weapon and answered the gunman's volley with one of his own. He squeezed off six shots that sent the man diving for cover behind the ship's sidewall. The rounds missed wildly, as Sean knew they would. From that distance, his pistol would be horribly inaccurate, despite the fact that he was a great shot. His intention wasn't necessarily to hit the target. He just needed to buy some time.

With the gunman down for a moment, he pulled himself up into the crane again and hit the lever to raise the cable. The hook jerked on the other end, and the cables attached to the container tightened. A second later the heavy metal box was rising off the ground.

Over the rumble of the crane's diesel engine, Sean heard the shooter firing again. Two bullets struck the top edge of the windscreen and splintered it into a glassy spiderweb. Sean ducked and yanked on one of the levers. The crane's long arm swung left, whipping the container around in a slow arch.

Sean could see the gunman's assault rifle still firing. More rounds struck the metal base of the crane, plunking into it harmlessly. Suddenly, the guy saw the container flying his way. Sean narrowed his eyes as if taking aim with his makeshift wrecking ball.

The container swung dangerously right toward the shooter, but he reacted too fast and dove down again. The metal box soared over him beyond the starboard side of the boat.

Sean couldn't see clearly out of the cracked windscreen, but he thought he saw a smile on the gunman's face as he popped back up and took aim again. Sean jerked one of the levers back, and the long arm slowed to a stop and then began moving to the right. The container's momentum carried it out high over water for another few seconds before it started swinging back.

The gunman took careful aim with his weapon, apparently realizing that his previous technique wasn't doing the job.

"Come on," Sean said.

The shooter set his feet and readied to fire. Sean ducked down to the floor as the man squeezed the trigger. The bullet zipped through the windscreen and the seat cushion. It would have hit Sean in the chest had he waited any longer. Now he watched through the narrow glass on the floor as the gunman started to adjust his aim.

He never had a chance to get off another shot. The container swung down over the boat and smacked into the gunman from behind with incredible force. The crane continued the box's momentum until Sean popped up and pushed the lever again to change its direction. Once more the container swung high into the air. When it started its downswing, the shooter slid off the front face and dropped to the ground at a sickening speed.

His legs snapped when he hit the ground, though he was already dead or unconscious.

Sean watched the metal box flying back at the ship. His timing had to be perfect, or he'd screw it up completely. And there was only going to be one chance at it.

The container whizzed through the air, thirty feet over the ground. "Almost there," Sean said to himself. "Almost there..."

He hit the lever that lowered the cable just as the metal box reached the edge of the pier. The cable slackened, and the box's flight path changed, sending it straight at the boat's control room.

Sean hung out of the crane and watched the container crash into the ship's bridge with devastating force. The entire cabin was ripped off the vessel. The men tending to the truck's wreckage heard the loud boom and looked back to see what happened.

They saw the container fly out over the harbor and drop back into the starboard side of the ship's hull with another massive crashing sound. For a moment, they were in stunned disbelief. The next, their eyes shot over to the crane to find who was responsible for the destruction.

The crane, however, was empty.

17

Dar es Salaam

The pier swarmed with activity. City police and emergency crews had responded to the chaos just minutes after the Americans made their escape. Fifty minutes later, an American destroyer made its way into the waters just outside the harbor, and word was that more U.S. Navy ships were coming to assist in apprehending any other vessels that tried to get out with malicious cargo.

Sean walked into the coffee shop and found the other three sitting in the back corner. The place smelled of fresh brewed Kenyan coffee and old wood. The latter was from the walls and floors being covered in darkly stained panels. It had an old feel to it, like the shop could have been around for two hundred years.

A man behind the counter greeted Sean with a toothy grin and asked what he'd be having.

Sean ordered a cup of coffee and took it over to where his companions were already sipping on theirs.

"What took you so long?" Tommy asked.

Sean knew his friend was going to say that. "So predictable. You know, after all these years of hanging out with me, I'd think you'd have come up with something original."

The two exchanged a laugh. "Well, I do have to say your little stunt back there with the crane was pretty original."

"You saw that?"

Tommy raised his shoulders and hands, palms facing up. "You didn't think I was just gonna take care of my boat and leave you behind, did you?"

Fitz raised his cup in salute. "I gotta admit, Tommy, you're pretty handy in a fight. You ever think about becoming an agent?"

"Sorry, guys," Tommy shook his head, "I've already got an agency of my own to run. And speaking of, I'm afraid I need to get back to the camp before the crew starts to worry."

"What are you working on?" Emily joined the conversation.

Tommy took another sip of coffee before answering. "The Tanzanians found an ancient temple near where our camp is set up. They had a team of their archaeologists working on it but had some trouble with one of the structures."

"What kind of trouble?"

"It's a little difficult to explain, but the temple is a monolith at its core."

"Like Stonehenge?" Fitz asked.

"Very similar to that. But early indications suggest this site is much older. Anyway, it turns out what they found was just the inner ring of this temple and that it extends out in a sort of spiral and into the surrounding hills."

"And by into the hills you mean underground," Sean said.

"Exactly." Tommy nodded. "The ancient people who lived there apparently built an intricate tunnel system into the hills and mountains. We believe it was for ceremonial purposes, perhaps burials. Once our engineers stabilized the tunnels, we were able to go in and begin recovering some of the artifacts. So far we don't have much, but it's likely we'll find more the deeper we go."

"Sounds fascinating," Emily said.

"It's pretty cool stuff. When you get to see something that no human eyes have seen for thousands of years, it's an incredible feeling."

"When you put it that way," Fitz said, "it sounds a lot more interesting than what we do. And safer." He chuckled at his own comment.

"It has its moments. But we encounter our own kinds of trouble. Thieves are always looking to rob excavation sites. Sometimes we have to deal with people who mean to destroy them altogether."

"Terrorists?" Emily asked.

"From time to time. Though we don't have that sort of situation happen often. All of our crews are armed at all times just in case, since our specialty is recovery and transportation of priceless artifacts."

"So you're like the armored trucks that go to the bank and pick up the money."

Tommy smirked. "Kind of. We get in and dig around in the dirt too." He turned to Sean who'd been unusually quiet for most of the conversation. "Speaking of, now that you've solved this whole thing, why don't you come back out to the dig with me and have a look around? We might even find something down in the tunnels."

Sean glanced at Emily, almost as if to ask for permission. "The director doesn't have anything else for us right now, does he?"

"Not that I know of. I figured we would head back to the States in the morning. But if you want to hang around for a few days, I'm sure that would be fine. We never get another assignment right on the back of another one."

It *had* been too long since Sean had hung out with his friend. The idea brought back memories of the old days when they were kids, running around the foothills outside of Chattanooga.

Sean finally nodded. "You know what? Yeah, I think I will stay and hang out for a few."

The look on his friend's face brightened instantly. "Awesome. When we get back, I'll show you around the temple site and then maybe take you down into the cave."

"Been a long time since I've been in a cave," Sean said. "Not sure when I'll get to do that again in the future, so I'm looking forward to it."

"Not me," Emily cut in. "Going underground is not my sort of thing. But you two boys enjoy your catch-up time together. Fitz, you coming back with me?"

"I've gotta get my gear from the camp, but I'll be reporting back to Axis as soon as all that's cleaned up." He turned to Tommy and Sean. "Carpool?"

The two friends laughed. "Yeah, that's fine."

"I need to get my things from the camp too," Emily said, realizing her gear bag was still there. "I guess I'll ride back with you guys and help Fitz get his stuff back to the airport."

"Aww, thanks, Agent Starks," Fitz said in a sarcastic tone.

The ride back to camp was quiet for the most part. The Americans had rented an SUV from the airport and on the long ride chose to just look out the windows quietly and enjoy the scenery. Exhaustion had set in by the time they reached the camp, and with the arrival of darkness the group said their goodnights and settled in for some rest.

The next morning, with everything packed in the SUV, Emily and Fitz said their goodbyes, leaving Sean and Tommy alone in the makeshift dwelling.

"All's well that ends well," Tommy said as they watched the other two agents drive away.

"I really hate it when you say stuff like that." Sean didn't look at his friend as he spoke.

Tommy frowned. "Why do you say that?"

"I dunno," Sean said with a shrug. "Just a weird feeling, I guess."

"About?"

"This whole scenario. Toli, how we took him down, how we stopped the missiles from leaving the country. Something about all of it doesn't seem right. Like it was too easy."

"Easy?" Tommy laughed. "Buddy, nothing about any of that was easy. We almost got killed at least twice. And I'd say you probably three or four times."

"Yeah, I know. Maybe I'm just paranoid or superstitious. I can't put my finger on it, but something's off. I hope I'm wrong. But when you said what you did about it all ending well, I got this sick feeling in my stomach, like when a pitcher is throwing a no-hitter and someone on the bench mentions it. It's bad luck."

The SUV disappeared around a bend of tall grass, kicking up a cloud of dust as it rolled away.

"First of all, I don't believe in jinxes. And secondly, if you were so worried, why'd you let those two leave? I mean, if there's something you need to investigate, they should have stuck around with you."

"No," Sean shook his head. "It's probably nothing. Like you said, Toli is dead, and the missiles are being confiscated. I'll be fine. Let's take a look at that temple you were telling me about. All the time I spent studying history in college, I never really got to get out and see that sort of thing in person as much as I'd like to."

"Well, my friend. You're in for a treat. Follow me."

18

Cairo

"What do you mean the shipment was lost?" Khalif roared in spite of a considerable effort to stay calm. "Find it!"

Ahmed cleared his throat and lowered his head for a second. He'd been afraid to deliver the bad news but also knew if he didn't do it immediately, his employer would be even angrier at him for waiting.

"It's not lost like that, sir. The Americans...they've taken possession of the shipment."

Khalif turned around and walked over to the window. The sun was rising into a clear sky to the east. A gentle breeze brushed across his robes. He put his hands on the railing and took a long, deep breath. Then he sighed and turned around slowly, putting his hands behind his back.

"Get me the American senator," he said.

"Right away, sir." Ahmed bowed but hesitated to leave. "Also, we have confirmation that Toli is dead. Apparently he was killed by an American strike force."

Khalif cocked his head to the side. The loss of Toli didn't pull on his heart strings, but it did present a problem. He needed answers.

A moment later, Ahmed handed the phone to Khalif.

"This better be good, Omar. Do you have any idea what time it is over here?" The senator was beyond annoyed at the middle-of-the-night call.

Khalif paced back and forth in front of the balcony. "Why am I hearing about a special forces unit killing Toli?"

"Now hold on just a second. We told your boy they were coming. Toli knew all about it. Last we heard, the unit sent to take him out had been captured. We were going to work out a deal with him. You're telling me he's dead?"

"Don't play stupid with me, Harold. You had to know what was going on."

"Look, Omar, I'm telling you, I've kept my hands out of this one as much as possible. If Toli couldn't handle his business when we were basically handing it to him, that's not on us."

Khalif stopped pacing and looked out over the city. The smells of spices, garlic, onions, and bread began wafting through the district.

"Toli's death is of no consequence to me, Harold. What bothers me is the incident that happened in Dar es Salaam."

"What incident?"

Khalif fought to keep calm. "Five of my boats were taken by American and Tanzanian forces. The shipments were confiscated by your Navy. I want to know why. And don't tell me this is the first you're hearing about it. You're a senator of the United States. You hear everything."

The senator sighed. "Yes, I heard about your little problem at the shipyard."

"My problem?" Khalif's temper took over. "It is not just my problem, Harold! I have reports from some of the men that there were Americans sighted on the premises when the ships were attacked. I want to know who they are and why."

"Okay, first of all, you need to calm down. Yes, I heard about the Navy confiscating the missiles. But I swear to you, I didn't know anything about an operation to go after your shipments."

"Lies!"

"Hold on, now. Why in the world would I go through all the trouble of helping you get those weapons just to turn around and take them back from you? Huh? Doesn't make any sense."

He was right. It didn't make any sense. That was probably what bothered Khalif the most about the whole scenario. There was a possibility. "Perhaps you thought you could sell me those weapons and then take them from me so I would have to buy more. Is that your game?"

The senator laughed. "Now you're just looking for a conspiracy, Omar. You know I wouldn't double-cross you. We both have too much to lose."

"Indeed."

"Yeah. So before you go making accusations, maybe you'd like to know just who you're dealing with."

"Yes," Khalif said, "I would like to know very much who these miscreants are."

"We have an agency here that operates outside of my knowledge on occasion. I've never actually liked the idea of it because they could go rogue, which is what I believe happened in the case of your shipments. I don't know which agents were involved, but if I had to guess, I'd say it was someone from that group. I already confirmed that CIA wasn't involved. They told me they had nothing to do with it. And I believe them."

The information was helpful but incomplete. Khalif wanted names. He also knew he would never get that intel from the man on the other end of the line. "I wonder if these agents of yours are still in Tanzania. If they try to interfere further with my affairs, they will be killed on sight."

"I have no idea if they're still around or not. Most likely, they came home and are debriefing. But just to be safe, make sure your men are on alert at all times. The last thing I need is someone to stumble on your little operation and find American missiles in the hands of the Pakistani military."

"I understand your concerns. Now understand mine: See to it that there is no more American interference. That shipment was a considerable loss but not a total one. We already have many of the missiles in place. I would appreciate a little effort on your end to keep your dogs chained."

The senator's tone turned defensive. "Hey, you have to do a better job of protecting your assets too, pal. It's not my fault you had a bunch of inept guards keeping watch. If I were you, I'd bring in some professionals to handle things. Not these two-bit morons you found out in the desert."

While Khalif didn't appreciate the tone the American leader had taken, he did present a fair point. Too much had been lost. And for his plan to work, he couldn't afford to lose any more missiles. It was time to call in more help.

The senator interrupted his thoughts. "On a more pleasant topic, good job taking out Qafar. The media is going crazy for it over here. I'd bet you're probably trending on social media right now as some kind of heroic leader for getting rid of him."

"You're welcome."

Khalif ended the call and set the phone on a nearby end table. He folded his hands behind his back and stared out at the city once again. "Ahmed?"

"Yes, sir."

"See to it that our facility is reinforced immediately. If these Americans happen to stumble upon it, we can't have any more incidents like what happened yesterday. Understood?"

"Yes, sir. Right away."

"This is awesome." Sean stood with his hands on his hips, staring out at the dig site. "You guys have done a lot of work."

He and Tommy were standing on the lip of a huge, circular hole in the ground. Within the confines of the manmade crater, a circle of titanic cones were propped on their ends, one next to the other. As Tommy had mentioned previously, the megaliths spiraled out until they came to an end in the side of the hill where the ancient tunnel entrance cut into the rock.

Tommy hesitated on accepting the compliment. "Well, most of the excavation was already done when we got here. The first group on site was headed up by Dr. Brandau out of Cairo, but he was supervised by a few people from here. Anyway, it was pretty much like this when we arrived." Tommy pointed at the temple complex. "We've mostly been trying to secure anything valuable and get it back to the government as intact as possible."

Sean continued to stare out at the scene. Workers of several nationalities were busily sifting through dirt, brushing away at stone, and carrying heavy buckets away. "So what did they find that the Tanzanians needed your help with?"

Tommy's poker face cracked, and he laughed out loud for a second. "You picked up on that?"

Sean turned to his friend, still wearing a stone-cold look on his face. "We've known each other a long time, pal. I know when you're trying to hide something. Throw on top of it the fact that I know you don't usually get a call for an excavation. The Tanzanians found something, and they either couldn't get it out or they didn't want to risk moving it. So they called the one agency in the world that specializes in that sort of thing."

"We do have that niche pretty much cornered."

"You've also got the art of stalling cornered."

Tommy laughed again and this time Sean's stoic facade cracked.

"Seriously, man," Sean prodded, "what's going on? Whatever you found must be pretty important for you to keep it so hush-hush."

Tommy took a deep breath and sighed. "I was gonna show you anyway. Just wanted to keep it a surprise or at least somewhat suspenseful."

"Okay. I'm officially intrigued. You gonna show me, or we just gonna stand here like a couple of lost tourists all day?"

Tommy twitched his head to left. "Come with me."

The two friends made their way over to a wooden ladder that led down into the pit. Once they'd descended to the bottom, Sean gained a new appreciation for how astonishingly massive the megaliths really were. He was six feet tall, but the giant stones were easily double his height.

"These were carved by hand?" Sean asked. He touched the closest one with his fingertips, feeling the smooth surface of the rock.

"Yes. Unless you subscribe to the *aliens did it* theory. We figure they were put here a little over ten thousand years ago, but the time frame is a bit sketchy. One thing we do know is that this rock is not found around here. Whoever placed these stones had to drag them over a great distance."

"Sounds like a lot of work to stack a bunch of rocks."

Tommy led the way through the maze as they continued their discussion. "Yeah, it had to be an incredible undertaking. Obviously, this place must have had some kind of sacred significance to them. Some cave drawings in the tunnel allude to some kind of creation story. It's remarkably similar to the ones found in Australia."

"Interesting."

Tommy slowed his pace as they neared the tunnel entrance. He looked over at his friend, putting a hand on his shoulder. "You know, if you ever get tired of government work, you could always come work for me."

Sean bellowed. "Work for you?"

"What's so funny about that? It's not like I would be your boss or anything. But you've always had a love of history and stuff like this. It's right in your wheelhouse. And whatever the government is paying you, I'll match it plus 10 percent."

Sean's head twisted to one side and then the other. "You know they pay me pretty well, right?"

"Money isn't a problem, my friend."

He was right. It wasn't a problem.

Tommy's parents had left him a fortune when they died tragically. He and Sean were in high school when it happened.

The Schultzes' plane and their bodies were never recovered. Sean and his parents had been instrumental in helping him with the grieving process. With the money he'd been left, Tommy decided to start an archaeological agency in Atlanta, just a few hours south of Chattanooga.

Later, he founded a historical center as part of the agency's complex. It served as a museum of unknown history, much of which centered around artifacts and relics found in the Southeastern United States.

"I appreciate the offer," Sean said. "Tell you what, if I get tired of working for Uncle Sam, you'll be the first to know."

Tommy grinned. "I'm going to hold you to that."

The two reached the cave entrance and paused.

"Don't get your hopes up," Sean replied. "I just got started."

Tommy changed the subject. "Watch your head. Whoever built this either wasn't very tall, or they wanted to play a trick on people taller than them. It opens up on the inside, though."

He bent down and stepped inside the tunnel. Lightbulbs burned brightly along the wall, all attached to a cord that ran outside to a generator.

Sean followed close behind. "You guys aren't messing around." He noted the lighting and the wooden steps that had been put into place for the first thirty or so feet into the tunnel.

"It was pretty muddy up here near the surface, so we installed this walkway. Well, the original team did. Once we get down into the mountain, the sediment is gone and it's primarily bedrock."

The two walked down the pathway until they reached the point where it ended. As predicted, the floor ahead was stone, chiseled from the mountain rock. Tommy pointed up to the ceiling at a collection of drawings. There were bizarre-looking animals and people. The legs were thin—like stick figure drawings—attached to plump figures. Some of the animals had horns.

"We figure they must have had some kind of cattle based on these images here." Tommy pointed at one of the horned beasts.

"Early agricultural civilization?"

"Sure looks that way." Tommy motioned for Sean to keep following. "Come on. You have to see this."

The ground leveled off, and the two made their way through a part of the corridor that curved from right to left and back again.

"The archaeological team believes that this part of the passage is curvy because it represents a river."

"Rivers were extremely sacred to ancient peoples. Probably because if they didn't have water they would die."

"Right. Come on. You gotta see this."

Sean pointed at a split in the tunnel. "Which way we going?"

"To the right. That way was cut off by a cave-in. We may try to clear it out at some point once we're sure it's stabilized."

Tommy took the path to the right and walked another twenty feet. He stopped suddenly in a giant chamber carved in the shape of a pyramid.

Sean nearly stumbled into him but caught his balance and stopped short.

Floodlights bathed the room in yellowish light, all focused on a central object.

"That's...that's impossible," Sean said.

Tommy slapped him on the back. "That is exactly what I said when they told me what they'd found."

"It can't be. The timelines are too far apart."

"Again. What I said."

Sean gazed at the huge object with an absentminded stare and stepped toward it, as if in a trance. The floodlights reflected off it, casting a more golden hue to the room's artificial illumination.

"So what you're saying is you may have found something that will change our understanding of ancient history." Sean stopped near the base and continued looking up.

"To be fair, I didn't find it. I'm just the one hauling it out of here. That's something we're still working on. But yeah, what you're looking at—for all intents and purposes—appears to be a sculpture of the oldest god in Egyptian mythology."

"Nun," Sean said, almost in a whisper.

"That's what it looks like."

The two Americans stared up at the golden sculpture. The likeness of the deity was close to eight feet tall and held a narrow boat over its head in two hands. The clothing, hair, and facial features were all reminiscent of images Sean and Tommy had seen of Nun.

"I mean, there are a few minor differences from what I can tell. But come on, that has to be it."

Tommy agreed with Sean's sentiment. "Creators of various sculptures, especially of deities, often had subtle differences between each one. We suspect that, often, that sort of thing happened just because the craftsmen weren't a factory."

"Kind of like the way records used to be made. They had to record each one separately. As a result, every record had slight differences in the sound."

"Exactly." Tommy crossed his arms and gazed on the image.

"This is big news, man. I mean, this connects ancient Tanzanian culture as the forerunner of Egyptian mythology."

"I know. Kind of mind blowing, right?"

Sean nodded. "So what's the plan? You guys pull it out of here and give it to the Tanzanian museum?"

Tommy snorted a laugh that echoed in the pyramidal chamber. "Yeah, something like that. It's the first part we're struggling with. We'll figure it out. That's what we do."

"Good luck with that. This thing is a monster. I wonder how they got it in here."

"Also a good question. It would have been impossible to bring the entire piece in all at once. That means it must have been done in sections. Further cross section analysis of it will give us that answer, and along with it the answer to removing the thing."

The two stood for a moment, admiring the astounding work of art. Sean kept looking at it while he spoke. "Figure it was a place of sacred importance, huh?" He quoted Tommy's line from earlier.

"Yep."

They lingered for another minute before turning around and heading back down the corridor.

Tommy started talking about some other items of interest they'd discovered during their short time on site as they walked toward the fork in the passage.

"So that part was pretty exciting," Tommy finished his sentence about a jar they'd found in pieces near the statue.

Sean cut him off as they rounded the turn leading back to the surface. "Wait. Did you hear that?"

Tommy shook his head. "Hear what?"

Sean took a step into the darker tunnel straight ahead and listened closer. "It sounds like diesel engines. It's faint. You can barely notice it."

Tommy listened closer but still heard nothing. "I think you're hearing the generator from up above. Come on, there are a couple more things I want to show you."

"There it is again. Can't you hear it? It sounds like dump trucks or something." He wandered cautiously into the dark tunnel. He stopped a few feet in and turned around. "You have a flashlight?"

"Yeah." He pulled the light out of his back pocket and handed it to Sean. "But I already told you, there's nothing over there. It's blocked off. You can't go more than a hundred feet before you get to the cave-in."

Sean ignored his friend's counsel and switched on the light. He pointed the beam into the passage ahead. The circular light flashed around on the walls, ceiling, and floor, showing an empty space.

"Do you mind if we check it out anyway?"

Tommy rolled his shoulders. "Be my guest. But there's nothing back there."

Sean was already moving forward into the tunnel, so Tommy had to catch up before he was either left at the split or consumed by darkness. He stayed close so he could keep an eye on where he was stepping.

The corridor bent around to the right, and soon the lights from the main shaft disappeared. Except for the flashlight, they were in pitch black.

"Kind of an eerie feeling, not having those lights around," Tommy commented. His voice was unsteady.

"Shh." Sean stopped moving. "There it is again."

This time Tommy heard it too. "That's weird. It's definitely not the generator."

"Right? That's what I was saying. It sounds like diesel trucks." Then he had a thought. "This tunnel doesn't run under a road or something, does it?"

"Nope. Nothing but empty mountain here. Above us is just trees and rock."

They kept going until they reached a point where huge slabs of broken stone were piled up on the path, blocking the way through. Sean stopped and leaned in—shining the light in and around the nooks and crannies—hoping to get a glimpse through to the other side. But it was completely shut off.

"See?" Tommy said, "I told you. No way through. That happens in these cave systems sometimes."

Sean looked up at the ceiling and back down at the rubble. Something didn't add up. "That happens in natural caves, Schultzie. Not usually in something like this."

"Are you saying that someone did this on purpose?" Tommy shot his friend a sidelong glance.

"Hard to tell for sure, but this doesn't look like it happened naturally." He inspected the edges of the wall. "I don't see any traces of explosives, but that doesn't rule it out."

"Yeah, but like I said, the archaeology team said this cave-in has been here for a long time. Maybe someone was looking around in here a hundred years ago and accidentally set off some dynamite or something."

Sean scratched his head. "You said that the other archaeology team told you this had been here for hundreds of years."

Tommy nodded. "Admittedly, I thought it was probably more recent too. But I thought maybe an earthquake or something."

"Does this region get a lot of those?"

"Couldn't say. But probably not."

"Right. Who did you say the director of the archaeology team is?"

"Dr. Brandau. But he took over for another guy."

That last part perked up Sean's curiosity. "Wait, what other guy?"

Tommy wasn't sure where this was going, but he sighed and explained anyway. "I don't remember the guy's name. He was already gone when I got here."

"Gone?"

"He died, Sean. Had a heart attack in his bed while he was sleeping."

"Really?" Sean elongated the word to emphasize his doubts.

"Oh come on. You're not saying someone killed that guy in his sleep to keep this cave-in a secret, are you?"

Sean spun around and shined the light on his friend's face. Tommy tried to block it out with his hand.

"I'm not saying that's what happened. But it's certainly plausible that the archaeologist in question may have ventured down that passage, seen what was on the other side, and was told not to tell anyone."

"If there *is* something on the other side. And even if there is, it just sounds like dump trucks. Maybe there's a quarry close to here."

Sean nodded. "Yes. A quarry. That would make sense. Let's get back up to the surface and take a look."

He didn't say anything to his friend, but Sean already knew there was no quarry. He'd gone over the map of the area several times for the mission. Not once did he see anything that even remotely resembled a quarry. Something else was going on. A man had possibly been murdered in his sleep, and this cave was cut off.

Another thing bothered Sean. Why hadn't they taken any of the gold from the statue? If whoever caused the cave-in knew about the passageway, they certainly would have explored deeper into the tunnels.

Unless they were told not to.

20

Mbeya

"I really don't think there's anything to see over that hill, Sean," Tommy whined as they climbed to the top of the low mountain ridge.

"Honestly, I can't believe you haven't come up here just to look around. This view is pretty impressive."

Tommy's breath was coming in big gasps. He clearly hadn't been keeping up with his exercise regimen.

"I've...been busy. You know...working and stuff. Didn't really have a lot of time for sightseeing."

Sean reached the crest and suddenly hit the deck. Tommy was several yards behind but instinctively crouched down when he saw his friend get down on his belly.

"What is it?" he asked, squatting next to a scraggly bush.

Sean peered down into the valley. He couldn't believe what he'd seen. And he immediately realized what had happened.

A gravel road wound its way up the next hill and out toward the west. A transport truck—eerily similar to the ones Toli had been using—rumbled down the road and into a large tunnel cut into the mountain. Just before it reached the bottom of the drive, another truck appeared at the mouth of the entrance and passed, heading up the hill.

Tommy crept up to where Sean was eyeing the activity and saw what had caught his attention.

"Those look like the trucks from Toli's compound."

Sean twisted his head slowly to the left. "No, really?"

"Yeah, but those can't be his trucks. He's dead. And his little army is scattered."

Tommy was right. And his comment only reinforced what Sean had already figured out.

"Don't you see what's going on here?"

Tommy was oblivious. Sean could see it on his face. His friend was good with riddles, history, and a number of things that other people wished they could do. But street smarts wasn't necessarily Tommy's thing.

"Toli was a cover," Sean said, turning his attention back to the gravel road.

The realization started to sink in. "Wait a minute," Tommy said. "You're telling me that whole thing with Toli, the missiles we found, the ships in the harbor, all of that was just an elaborate cover-up to keep us from seeing this?"

"Maybe I'm just being paranoid," Sean said. "But what are the odds that the exact same trucks Toli used to move those missiles are within miles of his compound? What could they possibly be delivering or removing from that tunnel?"

Tommy squinted against the bright sunlight. "I don't know. Maybe they're drilling for diamonds or something and those trucks are hauling away the dirt and rock."

"No," Sean shook his head. "They'd use dump trucks for that sort of thing."

"You don't think?"

"Yeah. Like I said, Toli was just a cover-up. It was a shell game. A really elaborate shell game. Whoever is behind all this wanted us to find Toli. They wanted us to find those missiles. Maybe they didn't want to lose those shipments. But I have a bad feeling the real mother lode is in that cave."

"So that's why they blew the tunnel."

"And why they killed that archaeologist who was first on the job."

It was a sobering moment. But the major question still lingered.

"If Toli wasn't the one behind all this," Sean said, "who was?"

"I don't know. But there's only one way to find out."

Tommy saw a familiar look in his friend's eyes. It was a look that had gotten them in trouble when they were younger. More than once.

"Nuh-uh," Tommy protested. "We are *not* going down there."

There was no deterring Sean's resolve. "If there are more missiles in those trucks and in that cave, a lot of people could be in major trouble if we don't do something about it. You want to go back to the camp and keep figuring out how to get that statue out of the cave, fine. But I have a job to do."

He was right. As usual. There was no arguing with Sean's rationale.

"Fine. But how are we going to get in there? There's a guard at the tunnel entrance. Looks like he's got a gun."

"So do I," Sean said, showing off his sidearm.

"Yeah, but I don't. I left mine back at the camp."

Sean pointed at the guard. "Well, you can have his once I take him down."

Tommy didn't like where this was going. "And just how are you going to do that?"

Seventeen minutes later, the two Americans crouched behind a collection of shrubs growing over the entrance to the tunnel. They watched as the next truck rumbled down the gravel road toward them.

"So what's your plan?" Tommy whispered. "Something about dropping down on that guy? You'll break your legs."

Sean had underestimated the distance between the top of the tunnel entrance and the ground beneath. From the previous vantage point, it didn't look like it was quite twenty feet. Now he realized it was between twenty-five and thirty. Tommy was right. He would break his legs, even if he did time the jump right and land on the unsuspecting guard. And there was also the problem of Sean's fear of heights. The young Axis agent had serious issues if he got above twenty-five feet.

Another idea popped into his mind as the truck rounded the last curve and turned onto the straightaway heading to the entrance.

"New plan," Sean said. "And you're not gonna like it."

Tommy followed his friend's gaze and shook his head. "No. Come on. That's just as bad. The truck is moving too fast. You'll miss it."

"Nah. They slow down before they go through the opening. And it's only eight or nine feet to the top of the cargo bed cover."

"Even if you make it, the driver will hear you when you land."

"The thing's made of canvas, Schultzie. He won't hear a thing. That diesel motor is too loud anyway."

The truck was bearing down on their position. If he was going to do it, Sean had to be ready soon or he'd miss the chance.

"I think this is a bad idea, man. There's got to be another way."

Sean ignored his friend's protests and inched his way out from behind the bushes. The truck's brakes squealed, slowing it as it arrived at the entrance. The cab passed underneath. *Now or never,* Sean thought.

He jumped over the edge, hit the back of the canvas top, and nearly rolled over the edge. His fingers grabbed at the edge of the fabric roof and squeezed. The muscles in his forearms tensed as his legs flew over the side and onto the back bumper of the truck.

Tommy leaned out over the tunnel lip and looked down to make sure his friend hadn't hit the ground. To his surprise, the guard was still standing there, looking out at the gravel road. And there was no sign of Sean. The only problem was, Tommy didn't know how he was going to get down.

Suddenly an arm wrapped around the guard's neck from behind. The man struggled for a moment, dropping his weapon in a vain attempt to pry the threat away from his throat. His fight only lasted thirty seconds before he started to give in to unconsciousness. His arms flailed for a few seconds more until the body went completely limp.

Sean dragged the guard over to a huge bush off to the side and hid the body from sight then reappeared a moment later holding the man's assault rifle. He raised it for Tommy to see and then motioned at a little path on the side of the entrance that led down to the ground.

Another truck's engine groaned, and Tommy ducked back into his hiding place. He swallowed and watched the truck leaving the cave. When it reached the curve, Tommy crept back out of his spot and over to the steep path.

Once he was on the ground, Sean handed him the guard's weapon. "Be careful with that. If you keep your finger on the trigger, it will ride up pretty hard. Not to mention it's one of the loudest guns you'll ever shoot. So only use it if you're ready to have a little ringing in your ears for the next few days."

"Thanks. I've actually shot one of these before. Back when..."

"Get down," Sean said and shoved his friend back behind the bush.

Tommy tripped and fell on top of the guard, their faces just inches away from each other. Sean dove next to him and waited.

Another truck came into view and rolled past them into the cave.

"Is this guy dead?" Tommy asked. He was too afraid to move but desperately wanted to get away from what might be a corpse.

"Possibly," Sean said. "I didn't bother checking. I just know he won't be getting up for a while."

"And by a while you mean, like, forever?"

Sean rolled his shoulders. "Not sure. We need to go. Come on."

He stood up and trotted over to the entrance with his pistol at the ready. He stopped at the corner and peeked inside. Lights hung along the sides of the walls, dimly illuminating the interior. A path ran along side the road—Sean assumed for guards or other workers to move in and out of the cave.

Tommy joined him at the entrance. "What's the plan? Storm the cave, take the missiles, that sort of craziness? Because I have to say, I don't like our chances."

"Hopefully we won't have to fire a single shot. We need to find out where those trucks are going, not start a small war. Get in and out as fast and as quietly as possible."

"So pretty much the opposite of what we did back at Toli's fortress."

"Right."

Sean turned into the tunnel and ran down the side, keeping close to the wall. He chased the red tail lights of the last truck that passed, trying to keep pace. Tommy had trouble keeping up but pushed himself to stay right behind.

Up ahead, two bright orbs appeared on the other side of the narrow road. Another truck was heading toward the front of the cave. Sean had noticed little recessions cut into the rock every thirty feet or so. Now he realized what their purpose. If a person was walking along the road and two trucks met at the same place, they could get crushed into the wall.

The grooves were cut deep enough for three average-sized people to squeeze.

"Quick, in there," Sean said as he looked back at his friend. He ducked into the little alcove.

Tommy had just passed one of the cavities and had to turn around to get to it, but he jumped out of sight just before the two trucks passed each other. A few moments later, the exiting truck rolled by.

Sean kept his back pressed into the stone, hoping the driver didn't look to his side. The tunnel wasn't well lit, and the little recessions were somewhat shaded. Still, he wasn't sure they were in the clear until he saw the truck reach the mouth of the cave and continue beyond. Satisfied the driver hadn't noticed them, Sean and Tommy stepped out onto the narrow walkway and pressed deeper into the tunnel.

They didn't have to go far before the corridor started to brighten. Along with more and more light came an increase in noise. Sounds of trucks, machinery, and men yelling echoed off the walls. The two friends hurried around a bend in the road, and as they came around the turn, saw where all the noise was coming from.

Forklifts were busily rolling from one point to another, carrying wooden crates to four trucks parked in a loading area. The crates were a spot-on match to the ones found at Toli's compound.

A man climbed up into the cab of a truck on the far left. A moment later, he pulled out of the loading bay and onto the road leading out of the tunnel. Sean and Tommy were in the open, and there were no more recessions in the wall for them to use. If the driver saw them, he'd alert everyone in the cave. And the two Americans would be trapped.

Sean broke out at a dead sprint toward two forklifts that were parked against the wall directly ahead. He didn't need to tell Tommy to hurry. He pumped his legs as hard as he could to keep up. The truck stopped suddenly, and for a moment Sean thought they'd been spotted.

His shoes skidded to a stop behind the forklifts. Tommy nearly ran over him as he reached the hiding spot.

Sean peeked around the back end of the machine and saw the reason the truck driver stopped. One of the other workers had flagged him down. The man ran up to the driver's side door and held up a piece of paper. The driver reached down and took it before resuming his exit.

"That was close," Tommy said while panting for air.

"Yeah. I thought he saw us for sure. We were lucky."

Tommy watched as the truck rumbled by and around the bend in the tunnel. When it was gone, he turned back to Sean. "I'm not seeing any more trucks coming in." Then he looked around at the giant room. "What is this place? An old mine of some kind?"

"Most likely. The original use couldn't have been for storing illegal weapons. Plus from the looks of it, all of this was done decades ago."

The tunnel opened into one massive cavern. Scaffolding rose almost to the ceiling in a few corners of the room where floodlights shined down on the work area. Metal catwalks lined the walls and crossed the floor in two places above the loading area. Giant steel shipping containers were stacked in the back of the cavern. An old dump truck with a flat tire was parked along the wall to the left. The thing looked like a relic from a 1970s construction company.

Sean watched the scene with keen interest. He counted ten workers, plus four men with guns identical to the weapon Tommy now possessed. All of the men, unlike the guard at the front, wore masks over their faces like bandits.

There were only a few crates left. Tommy's point about no more trucks coming made sense. Almost all the crates were gone. That meant the two Americans had to come up with a plan, or the missiles would be gone forever.

Tommy must have been thinking the same thing. "What should we do? Looks like we don't have much time to make our move."

Sean noticed several Toyota pickup trucks parked at the back of the loading area. They must have belonged to the workers. He instantly plotted a path around behind all the machinery and supplies.

"We can sneak around behind everyone if we go that way," he pointed at the course he was considering. "We go through there and wait by those pickup trucks. They must be transportation for the workers."

"So we're gonna steal one of their trucks?"

Sean didn't answer the question directly. "We wait until the last group is leaving, and we steal that one. Then we follow them to wherever they're going."

"Yeah, but when we get there—wherever *there* is—they'll see us and most likely try to kill us."

"I didn't say it was a perfect plan. But it will buy us a little time to figure out what to do next."

"Fair enough. Let's do it."

21
Mbeya

Tommy and Sean peeked out from under their hiding place. They'd managed to sneak around to the pickup trucks without being seen. That part of the plan was easier than expected. What they didn't consider was where to hide once they'd made it to the trucks.

The answer presented itself when Sean looked into one of the truck beds. There was a canvas tarp in the back along with a few tools and rags.

The two Americans climbed over the tailgate and hid under the tarp, keeping their weapons ready as they looked out at the workers as they finished loading the last transport.

"What are we going to do if they look in here?" Tommy hissed.

"I guess we'll have to shoot our way out."

"Kind of an awkward position to carry out an attack like that, don't you think?"

Sean cast a sarcastic glance over at his friend. "Look on the bright side. We'll have the element of surprise. No way they'll expect to find a couple of guys with guns in the bed of their truck." He noticed several of the workers and the gunmen heading their way. "Get down. Showtime."

Tommy did as told and tucked back under the cover. He mouthed, "Showtime? Really?"

Sean mouthed a silent retort. "Shut up."

Tommy's lips creased as they heard the men's voices getting closer. Then they heard the truck doors opening. One of the men barked out some orders to someone else.

"Farsi?" Tommy asked by moving his lips but keeping quiet.

Sean acknowledged with a single nod. Farsi wasn't something Tanzanians typically spoke. Not that he knew of, at least.

The engine revved to life along with the others. The sounds of the vehicles shifting into gear came next, and then suddenly the truck lurched forward.

The Americans didn't dare say a word, but they both looked at each other as if to say, "Here we go."

The convoy made its way down the tunnel and out of the mountain. When they passed through the entrance, the darkness under the tarp brightened significantly. The truck reached the first turn on the winding road and swung around sharply. Tommy nearly rolled on top of Sean, who braced his friend with a quick hand to the chest.

Sean fired his friend warning glare that suggested he brace himself a little better.

At the top of the climb, the truck straightened out for a moment before the two hidden occupants felt it tilt downward to begin its descent on the other side of the mountain.

Once the truck reached flat land below, it made a right turn and picked up speed. The ride was much smoother and quieter, signaling they'd turned onto a paved road. The tarp flapped louder as the truck drove faster.

"How long we gonna sit back here?" Tommy asked. He was fairly certain the men in the truck couldn't hear him, but just in case, he kept his voice as low as possible.

"We aren't," Sean said.

"What do you mean, we aren't? Let's just sit back here and wait 'til we get to wherever we're going. Then we can climb out, sneak around, and call in the cavalry."

"Yeah, unless this truck isn't going where all the transport trucks are going. We may already be going the wrong way."

Tommy hadn't considered that. "Then what do we do? Hijack a speeding pickup?"

"Something like that."

Before Tommy could protest further, Sean peeked out from under the tarp. It was impossible from his angle to see if they were still with the other vehicles. If he stood up any more, he'd be in full view of the driver and anyone else in the cab.

"Wait," Tommy said, but it was too late.

Sean flung back the tarp and rose to his knees. He pointed his weapon at the truck's back window and fired a shot into the base of the passenger's skull. Then turned and did the same to the driver.

For a second, the truck lingered in limbo while the driver's hands still clung to the wheel. Sean knew that wouldn't last long. He'd hoped that the truck would slow down, but as luck would have it the driver's body slumped forward, pressing his foot down harder on the accelerator.

Sean grabbed the side rail to regain his balance and climbed out on top of it. The driver's weight shifted, and the wheel pulled to the left. That wouldn't have been a terrible thing if they had reached the plains, but the road out of the mountains ran right next to a deep ravine.

The truck veered left, and Sean instantly recognized the danger. He was only going to get one shot.

He reached into the front window and grabbed underneath with his left hand, bracing himself with the right. Then he swung his weight over the top of the truck and crouched.

The left side of the pickup scraped against a metal railing along the road. Less than two thousand feet ahead, the railing ended.

Sean wrapped his fingers underneath the window and started to lower himself down when he heard several successive gunshots from the road behind.

They hadn't been the last truck in the convoy after all. A masked gunman was leaning out of the pickup to the rear, emptying his magazine. Firing a weapon from a moving vehicle was difficult, and most of the bullets sailed harmlessly by. Two struck the tailgate, which immediately drew Tommy's attention.

"Shoot back!" Sean yelled.

Tommy raised his weapon and squeezed the trigger once, twice, three times. The first two shots missed, but he corrected and put the third through one of the headlights.

The other driver hit the brakes momentarily and caused his gunman to lose his balance. The man almost fell out of the window but slapped a hand against the front edge and saved himself.

Sean looked down the road ahead. The other truck was too far in front to see what was happening. And he also realized they'd almost reached the end of the guardrail. With less than a thousand feet to go, he gripped the underside of the window once more, crouched down, and swung through the opening.

His feet hit the passenger in the back, and he landed awkwardly on the driver. He scrambled to regain his balance and grab the wheel, jerking it to the right just before the truck ran off the road and into the ravine.

Tommy tumbled to the other side of the truck and slammed into the side. He didn't have time to ask his friend what he was doing. More gunshots boomed from the truck behind. He risked a look over the tailgate and saw they were closing fast. Another volley thumped into the tailgate and bumper. Tommy still clutched his weapon and popped up with his back against the rear of the cab. He took aim at the gunman and fired. The round sparked off the roof of the other truck, and again the driver hit the brakes. This time, the other shooter slid back into the cab. Tommy could see he was reloading. Now was his chance. He lined up the driver in his sights and pulled the trigger.

Inside the truck, Sean struggled to get the driver's body out of the way. He reached over and grabbed the door handle, pulled it, and then shoved the dead man out. The moment he did, the guy's foot came off the gas pedal, and the truck slowed. Sean maneuvered his legs around and stepped on the accelerator again.

The tailing truck jerked suddenly to the right at the same time Tommy's truck started slow down. The combination of his truck's momentum change and the target moving rapidly caused the shot to zip by, missing by a foot. A moment later Tommy saw what the other driver was dodging as a body rolled by on the road.

He looked back through the cracked rear window and saw Sean in the driver's seat next to the other corpse.

"Would you mind holding it steady?" Tommy shouted. "I'm trying to save our necks!"

More rounds pounded the back of the truck.

"Sure, I can give them an easier target if you'd like!" He yanked the wheel to the right and back to the left.

Tommy wavered one direction and then the other before he stabilized himself with one hand on the end of the truck bed as he crouched low to keep out of view. "Come on, man! Give me one second here!"

"Hurry up and finish them off then!"

Tommy snorted. He positioned himself on one knee and popped up from the floor. He looked down the barrel and immediately located the gunman, the driver, and another larger target. The sights locked on the front of the truck, and Tommy fired. It only took him a split second to bring the weapon back to level and fire again. The two rounds pierced the truck's grill and ripped through the radiator. Steam instantly spewed out of the hood.

The driver panicked and jerked the pickup left and right to see past the smoke. It slowed to a stop, completely engulfed in steam pouring out of the engine block. The two occupants got out to assess the damage. But Tommy wasn't through. He took aim one last time and squeezed the trigger. The front right tire ruptured, and the corner of the truck dropped in seconds. The men scattered, running behind the truck to take cover.

By the time they stepped out from hiding to return fire, the truck with the Americans in it was gone.

Sean glanced back in the mirror to make sure the other vehicle was out of sight. Satisfied they'd been left behind, he slowed to a stop.

"Hurry; get up here!" he shouted.

Tommy didn't need to be told twice. He kicked a few shell casings as he hopped over the side of the truck and onto the ground. When he opened the door, the passenger's body fell out onto the road.

"Ugh," he said and stepped over the man.

Before the door closed, Sean stepped on the gas again. "We gotta catch up with those other trucks. If we lose them..."

"I know. We lose the missiles for good. You said that already."

Sean glanced over at his friend with a smirk. "You know, you're pretty good at this spy stuff. I could put in a good word with my boss if you're interested in joining."

Tommy laughed and set the assault rifle between his legs. "No thanks. I'm good."

"Just as well. We only keep, like, eleven agents active at any given time, and we're full."

"Sounds like you're worried I'd take *your* job."

Sean let out a loud "*Ha!*"

"No, but that was some good shooting back there. Well done."

"Thank you. Now let's hurry up and finish this before my crew starts to worry. Besides, we've got a gold statue to extract."

"We?" Sean shot him a curious look.

"Yeah. It's the least you can do for me saving your butt from Toli. And for taking out that truck back there."

He wasn't wrong. And Sean knew it. "Let's just say I'll take a little more time off to hang around. First things first. I need to call the office."

22

Songea, Tanzania

To Sean's surprise, the convoy ended up going south to the city of Songea. The town was larger than expected. He figured there must have been a few hundred thousand people in the immediate area, though it was hard to gauge. Most of the city was rundown, like many cities in that part of the world. While growth had been fast, development had been slow.

Roads were in disrepair, and the majority of the buildings reminded both Sean and Tommy of a shanty town in South Africa.

"Have you ever been to Cape Town?" Tommy asked.

"No," Sean shook his head. He'd followed the truck in front at a safe distance just in case they took a closer look in the mirrors. Before they'd arrived in the city, Tommy grabbed some rags out of the truck bed, and the two men wrapped them around their faces and heads to help conceal their identities. Those would only work for so long, though.

"It looks a lot like the slums there," Tommy went on.

Signs of poverty were everywhere. Some of the roads were dirt and split off the main street into little collections of multicolored homes that were barely better than mud huts.

"I wonder why they picked this place," Tommy rattled.

"Probably because it's obscure. Whoever is behind all this has done a good job of throwing us off the trail. At least so far. This is just one more move in keeping with that plan. And I have to say, I'm impressed."

The last line wasn't a lie. Sean hadn't expected the mission to go this far. He figured they'd go in, take out Toli, and liberate the hostages along with a few hundred kids. Apparently, no one knew how far the rabbit hole actually went. Intelligence had given him nothing about someone else pulling the strings. So as far as the government and his agency was concerned, he was flying with both eyes closed.

The truck in front sped up as the convoy neared the outer edge of the city. Sean increased his speed as well, carefully navigating the throngs of pedestrian traffic, motorcycles, and mopeds that were so prevalent in the burgeoning town. The streets were lined with sagging trees that reminded the two Americans of weeping willows back home in the South.

Lifeless faces passed by, staring at the truck as it rolled through. The city's citizens appeared malnourished and tired, all of them. If there was a nicer part of town, Sean hadn't seen it.

The number of homes and people grew more and more sparse until there were only occasional houses in the middle of fields. The sidewalks ended and were replaced by tall grass growing out of control along the side of the road.

Tommy figured out where they were going at almost the exact same time as Sean. He saw the outline of a few airplane hangars in the distance, though no planes were taking off or landing at the moment. The airport terminal was nothing more than a beige, one-story building with a dark green roof. *Songea Airport* was painted on the roof in bold white letters. A midsized white plane with twin turbo-prop engines was sitting in front of one of the hangars. There was a collection of other smaller planes parked in various spots close to the runway. All of them looked like they'd seen better years a long time ago.

Then something caught the Americans' eyes on the other side of the airfield. A large cargo plane was sitting out in front of an open hangar. Parked next to it were four transport trucks. And more were turning onto the airport road leading to the airstrip.

Even from several hundred yards away, Sean and Tommy could see people loading the plane, scurrying around both on foot and with loaders to get the cargo in place.

"I don't mean to put a damper on all this," Tommy broke the silence, "but don't you think now might be a good time to start thinking of a plan? I mean, we're about to jump into the hornet's nest here."

One of the transports in their convoy turned off the road and onto the thoroughfare heading to the hangar. A moment later, the next one followed.

Sean said nothing, keeping his hardened gaze steady on the truck in front of them.

Tommy's head was on a swivel as he looked at his friend for a response and then watched the line of trucks slow down and turn into the airfield. "Did you hear me? Sean? I said we need a plan. You're not actually going to drive in there? They'll kill us within ten seconds."

"Relax," Sean answered. "We're disguised. And I'm not planning on getting out of the truck."

"What?"

The pickup directly ahead of them veered onto the side road.

"When we get in there, I'm going to park us off to the side. We don't have enough ammunition to take out all those guys, even if we wanted to."

It was a thought Tommy had already considered. "Yeah, I know. So why are we going in there? We should wait for Emily."

Sean had used his SAT phone to call Emily on their way to Songea. He'd only been able to give her their current location and the direction they were headed. Fortunately, her plane had stopped for fuel in Johannesburg, but getting back would take time. And unless he called, she wouldn't know where to go. If he whipped out his phone, it would raise suspicion. So for the moment he had to play it close to the vest.

"Hey, I said, why don't we wait for Emily?"

"She has no idea where we are right now. Only which way we were going. I was going to call her when we got here, but that might get attention we don't want. Know what I mean?"

He spun the wheel to the left and fell back in line with the other trucks.

Tommy grabbed the bar on the door and squeezed it like Sean was driving a hundred miles an hour. "I hope you're sure about this. Just gotta ask, and it's not because I don't trust you. But if we're not calling for backup, how exactly are we going to take out all these guys?"

"We're not."

"Okay..."

"We need to stop the plane. Not the men on the ground. We have to get aboard that cargo plane and keep it from taking off. Or at the very least, land it somewhere until the cavalry arrives."

Tommy was silent for a second but his wide-eyed stare said it all. "Are you crazy? That plane is loaded down with missiles. So you want to not only get on board an airplane packed with illegal missiles, but you want to take it over and possibly land it if it's already in the air?"

"Sounds about right."

"Do you even know how to fly a plane?"

Sean thought for a second. He'd flown one before. Landed one, not so much. As far as Tommy was concerned, he didn't need to know that bit of information until after the fact.

"Yes, I've flown a plane before."

Tommy was still dubious. "When?"

"We're swinging around to park. Just trust me. It's gonna be fine."

"Trust you? I'm still a little hazy on the how we're getting on the plane part."

Sean didn't answer. He spun the wheel and stayed behind the same pickup he'd been following since leaving Mbeya. The line of transport trucks circled around the plane and parked in a row next to the others while the pickups drove over to the side of the hangar.

There was no way Sean was going to risk parking next to the others, so he kept going—passing the hangar—and continued around to the other side. He steered the truck into the empty parking area and drove around to the last available spot before pulling in.

"You think they're not going to notice that?" Tommy asked as he grabbed the rifle from between his legs.

"Maybe," Sean said. "From the looks of it, they're in too much of a hurry to worry about one of their worker trucks parking on the wrong side of the hangar." He pulled out his pistol and checked the magazine. "I don't have many rounds left."

"Yeah, so doing this as peacefully as possible would be a good decision."

"I agree completely."

"Yet somehow I have a bad feeling that isn't what's going to happen."

Sean's eyes squinted above the bandana across his face. "When have I ever led you into a bad situation where we had to fight our way out?"

"Not including the last forty-eight hours?"

"Obviously."

"Well, there was that time when we were in middle school where you picked a fight with Jerry McTavish and his friends."

"Okay, probably not a good time to be rolling down memory lane. It was rhetorical. Just keep your eyes open."

Tommy stared out the window.

The high sun beat down on the truck, and now that the breeze from driving was gone, the temperature inside climbed rapidly.

They'd only been sitting in the truck for a couple of minutes when one of the guards appeared around the hangar corner. He stared at the truck with a curious expression.

"We've got trouble," Tommy said, getting Sean's attention.

A second later, the man with the gun started shouting at them and motioning with his hand for them to come.

"Looks like he wants us to get off our butts and do some work," Sean said. "Even with these masks, they'll see we're Americans as soon as we get close."

"So what do we do?"

The guard's expression turned irritated, and he started stalking toward them.

"Follow my lead," Sean answered.

He reached down and pulled the lever that opened the hood. The latch clicked, and the hood popped up. Then he opened the door, got out, and hurried around to the front. He threw the thing open as Tommy scurried around and leaned his weapon against the bumper.

Sean propped the hood up with the little bar inside the seals and started looking around, as if there was a problem with the engine.

The guard was closing rapidly, yelling something in Farsi at the two men he must have believed were slackers.

"You understand any of that?" Sean asked under his breath.

"Nope. I was hoping you did."

"I know a little Arabic, but that's about it."

"Same here."

The man stopped ten feet away from the truck and continued yelling, pointing at the truck. From his tone, it sounded like he was asking what the problem was.

Tommy shrugged but kept his face turned away. Sean did the same, leaning over as far as he could to keep his head as much out of view as possible. His blond hair would be a dead giveaway if it snuck out from the bandana he had on his head.

The guard raised his voice and started speaking faster. Sean and Tommy didn't dare look at him. Even with their heads and faces covered, their eyes and the surrounding skin would belie their identities.

For a moment, Sean wasn't sure if the guard would come closer or not. From where the guy was standing, taking him down would prove difficult. Even as Sean had the thought, the guard stepped forward, shouting orders at them they didn't understand.

Tommy could feel him close in. Sean saw him with his peripheral vision.

Saliva shot out of the man's mouth in tiny bursts as he continued barking. Then he reached out and put his hand on Tommy's shoulder.

He spun the American around. It only took a second for him to see the two men weren't who they were pretending to be. He never had a chance to raise an alarm or even brandish his weapon.

Tommy clocked him squarely in the nose with a jab and then knocked him out with a roundhouse to the jaw. The guard was unconscious before he hit the ground.

Sean had stepped over next to his friend to assist and now stared down at the man. Tommy had always been a bruiser. Handy in a fight, though often sloppy. He frequently got hurt almost as badly as his opponents.

"Quick, let's get him in the back of the truck," Sean said.

Tommy grabbed his arms. Sean took the feet. They carried the guard over to the tailgate and with a few grunts dumped him into the truck bed. Sean picked up the assault rifle off the ground and checked to make sure there were plenty of rounds in the magazine and one in the chamber.

"At least we picked up a few more bullets."

"Still won't be enough with all those guys. Again, I'm curious to know exactly what it is you're planning to do to get on that plane."

Sean peered out at the runway. "First of all, nice shot. That guy was out cold. Remind me not to pick a fight with you. Second, you're right. I don't like our odds. But maybe we don't have to get on the plane. Maybe we just need to take it out."

"And just how do you plan on doing that?"

Sean glanced back over at the truck and then at his friend.

"What are you thinking?" Tommy asked.

"Third time's a charm," Sean said.

Tommy's face creased in a devilish grin. "I like it."

Sean started the truck and backed it out of the parking space. He spun the wheel around and aimed the hood at the back of the plane. He rolled down the window and said to Tommy, "Go around to the back of the hangar and steal one of the other trucks. Bring it behind the back wall and be ready to punch it. We should have a minute to get away while they're distracted."

Tommy nodded. "Gotcha."

He took off and disappeared around the corner.

Sean waited for nearly a minute to give his friend time to find their escape vehicle. He also made sure the crowbar he'd found behind the seat would wedge tight enough between the pedal and the seat. It wasn't perfect, but it would work.

Certain he'd given Tommy enough time, he shifted the pickup into gear, made sure the truck was lined up, and stepped on the gas. The engine growled, and the truck lurched forward.

He had a clear patch of runway for eighty yards to the plane. He just hoped the vehicle's alignment wasn't off. If it veered off course, the plane would get away, and the men loading it would immediately turn their attention to him.

It was a risk he had to take.

He grabbed the crowbar and shoved it down into the floorboard between the seat and the pedal. The speed slowed slightly, but it would be fast enough to disable the plane.

Sean flung open the door and dove out as the truck rolled out from behind the hangar and toward the aircraft.

He rolled to a stop and ran as hard as he could back toward the rear of the building. Gunfire erupted from around the front, but no bullets whizzed by him or struck the tarmac nearby. The gunmen were shooting at the truck.

A matching pickup appeared around the corner of the hangar with Tommy behind the wheel. He drove over the curb and onto the blacktop, jostling around inside like he was off-roading.

Sean didn't look back at the plane until he was in the passenger seat.

The truck was rolling at a steady pace, probably thirty miles an hour, headed right for the belly of the aircraft. Bullets were plunking into the doors, the side of the truck bed, and the front left quarter panel. The windows and windshield were completely shattered. But it kept driving forward and was only twenty yards away.

Neither of the Americans dared say anything for fear of jinxing their luck.

Unfortunately for them, it wouldn't have mattered.

With only ten yards to go, one of the gunmen's bullets struck the front left tire. The rubber exploded, and the truck suddenly veered sharply to the left, narrowly missing the back of the aircraft and rolling harmlessly down the tarmac toward the lot where the other pickups were parked.

"Ugh," Sean said. "We were so close."

The torpedo truck's hood popped open and smoke started billowing out of it. The hail of bullets had finally pierced a crucial part of the motor and disabled the vehicle.

Four of the guards and two workers ran toward the smoking pickup to find whoever was responsible for the intrusion.

"Now what?" Tommy asked.

"Now we have to catch the plane."

23

Songea

The plane's engines were already running when Sean launched his attack with the other truck. With the loading bay door closed, the aircraft began inching its way forward.

"What are you going to do, again?" Tommy asked. He shot his friend a dubious, sidelong glance.

"Step on the gas. And pull up next to the plane."

Tommy definitely didn't like the sound of that. "Um, no? Then they'll all start shooting at us. I'd prefer to leave quietly."

"We have to stop that plane. If we don't, a lot of people could die. So if it's all the same to you, punch it and let me worry about the shooters."

The aircraft turned out onto one of the lanes leading to the runway, already picking up speed.

Tommy didn't wait for his friend to ask again. He pressed the pedal down to the floor and steered the truck toward the plane.

"Get as close to the rear wheels as you can," Sean said. "I'm going to try to climb up through the landing gear."

"Wait!" Tommy almost shouted as he turned in behind the aircraft. "You're gonna what?"

"Just do it!"

Sean climbed out the window and swung his leg around the edge of the truck bed. He threw his weight over it and landed in the middle on a pile of rags and tools. The wind blew hard in his ears as he climbed up to a crouching position on the driver's side and readied himself for what was almost certainly a suicidal move.

Up ahead, the plane made its final turn on the approach to the runway. Meanwhile, more gunfire popped from the hangar as the guards and workers realized what was going on. The Americans were out of range for the moment, but the men would give chase.

Tommy closed the gap to the aircraft, reeling it in rapidly until they were only forty yards away. He had to slow down to make the sharp turn onto the runway but punched the gas through the apex. The tires squealed on the blacktop as Tommy pulled through the curve. Sean gripped the side of the bed, keeping his balance until Tommy straightened out and lined up with the plane.

"Faster, buddy!" he shouted. "We're gonna lose it!"

The plane hadn't even paused at the end of the runway. The pilot gunned the throttle, speeding the aircraft down the tarmac faster and faster.

"Giving it all I can!" Tommy shouted back.

The truck's speedometer showed it was nearing ninety miles per hour. The engine whined loudly, protesting the demands of the driver.

Already at top speed, Tommy had a head start on the plane and had closed the gap to twenty yards to its rear right tires. Now that gap was closing slower as the plane matched the truck's speed.

"Come on, Tommy!" Sean yelled.

The wind ripped off the bandana on his head and tore at his eyes. He had to squint hard to stay focused on the target.

Tommy jerked his body forward and back, as if that tiny bit of momentum would get them there.

The gap was only five yards. Sean reached his left hand out and got ready to make the jump. He planted his right foot on the top of the truck bed rail and braced himself as best he could.

"Almost there!"

Then the gap increased, first by a yard, then two, then twenty. The plane pulled away as the twin engines roared. In less than ten seconds, the aircraft reached takeoff velocity and started to lift off the ground. Sean climbed back into the truck bed and watched as the plane tilted up and took flight.

Tommy knew there was no point in trying to keep pace so he pulled back a little and slowed their speed. Sean's heart sank as the aircraft soared into the air and banked to the right.

He'd failed. Or had he?

His eyes caught movement behind and to the right. "Tommy?" he shouted.

"Yeah!"

"They're coming! Time to get out of here!"

Tommy looked back in the rearview mirror and saw the line of pickups speeding around the turn. He noticed a maintenance thoroughfare on the left up ahead and tapped the brakes.

Sean felt the truck slow and smacked his hand on the roof. "I'm thinking faster is probably better, buddy!" he yelled.

"Trust me!"

Tommy slammed on the brakes and whipped the truck to the left, then stomped the gas pedal again. Sean was thrown from one side of the truck to the other. Fortunately, he wasn't standing up and rolled to a stop against the bedrail. Tommy heard his friend being tossed around in the back and looked in the mirror to make sure he was okay.

"Everything all right back there?"

Sean recovered and braced himself. He glared at his friend through the back window.

"A little heads-up would have been nice!"

Tommy's teeth flashed in the mirror. He jerked the wheel to the right, and Sean lost his balance again, falling over into the bed.

Now he was irritated. "Quit doing that!"

"Do you want to get out of here or not?"

Sean looked back and saw the other trucks still in pursuit. They were at least three hundred yards behind, but that could change.

The access road leading out of the airfield approached on the left, and Sean knew exactly what his friend was thinking. He braced himself against the right bedrail and squatted down as Tommy leaned into the turn and spun the wheel.

The tires squealed, and the truck swayed. The rear end fishtailed for a second, but Tommy corrected and guided the vehicle toward the exit. A pair of armed guards were rushing to get the chain-link gate closed. One was standing in the middle of the road, waving his hands over his head in a feeble attempt to stop the Americans.

The other pushed hard on the gate, rolling it out toward the other side. Tommy didn't let up. He pressed his foot harder on the pedal. The truck sped at the guard who suddenly realized he was in an extremely compromising position. Twenty feet before the pickup reached him, he dove out of the way and rolled to the side of the road.

The gate was almost closed, but Tommy had no intention of letting that deter him. His eyes narrowed, and his knuckles whitened, fingers gripping the wheel tighter. "Might have a little debris back there, Sean! You should probably cover your head!"

"What?" Sean shouted back. He looked up through the back window and realized what his friend was talking about. "Whoa!" He ducked down just before the hood of the truck smashed into the gate.

The pickup shuddered but won the battle, crashing through the weak fencing with devastating force. The hinges ripped from the poles, and the gate broke free. It stuck to the grill for a few seconds before it fell under the front tires. The truck bounced over the warped, twisted metal and sped away to the main road.

Sean rose up from the truck bed and looked back at the remains of the gate, then through the window at his friend. "Nice work!"

Guns popped from the guards at the entrance, but they were already out of range. A moment later, the other trucks appeared still in pursuit.

"We've still got trouble, though!" he yelled at Tommy again.

Tommy flashed a glance in the rearview mirror and noticed the line of trucks in pursuit. Just ahead, the road split off in two directions. One was the way back into the city. The other led out to the mountains. It was a no-brainer. Driving back into the city would not only slow them down and allow the enemy to catch up, but it would put innocent people at risk.

Tommy spun the wheel to the right, and the truck's tires skidded across the asphalt. He corrected the turn and pounded the gas again. The engine grumbled as it sped away.

Sean watched the other trucks follow, still several hundred yards back. If all things were equal, they wouldn't be able to catch up. He stole a quick look through the window and saw Tommy was heading into the mountains. *Good idea,* he thought. *We can lose them there.* Then he saw the dark clouds forming in the distance. Right in the direction they were heading.

As if reading his mind, Tommy shouted back. "You might want to climb up front if you can. Looks like we're gonna get wet! And by we, I mean you!"

Sean shook his head. "If they catch up, I'm gonna need to be back here to fend them off! Just keep going. Maybe we can lose them in the rain!"

Tommy steered the pickup through the straights and curves of the flatlands, past the farms, ponds, and outcroppings of forest. They passed small villages with dozens of huts that looked like something from an ancient time. People were sparse, but the ones they passed stared in wonder at the high-speed chase zipping through their little part of the world.

Suddenly Tommy slammed on the brakes.

The truck's tires skidded and bumped on the road in a desperate attempt to stop. Sean was pressed into the head of the bedrail at the sudden change of momentum. He peeked over his shoulder, wondering why Tommy would do something like that.

Then he saw. "Oh, you have *got* to be kidding!"

A local herder was leading a flock of a few dozen sheep across the road. They were completely blocking both lanes with no way to get by. Sean looked back down the road.

The trucks behind them were still coming, and now they were closing the gap rapidly. One of the men in the lead pickup leaned out the window, holding a Kalashnikov to his shoulder and preparing to fire when the target was in range.

"Tommy! Get us out of here!"

"I can't get around! There are sheep everywhere!"

The oblivious shepherd smiled and waved at the Americans as if everything was fine. Then he looked beyond their truck and saw the approaching vehicles, along with the gunman. His clueless smile immediately turned upside down, and he started smacking the ground with his shepherd's rod in an effort to get the animals moving faster.

The last of the sheep entered the road, which gave Tommy a small bit of space between the left lane and the shoulder.

"Hold on!"

Sean barely had a second to grab the rail as Tommy gunned the pickup around the animals. The left tires kicked up red dust when they hit the shoulder, riding precipitously close to the drop-off into a five-foot-deep ditch. While the ditch wasn't life threatening, getting stuck in it certainly would be.

Tommy deftly guided the truck back on the road and kept his foot to the floor.

In the back, Sean rechecked his weapon. The men in the lead pursuit truck opened fire. They'd pulled within a few hundred feet and were well within range. Of all the rounds the gunman fired, only one struck the Americans' pickup. The red taillight exploded in an eruption of plastic and glass.

Sean steadied himself and took aim. He couldn't waste a shot since they had a finite amount of ammunition.

The gunman ducked back into his seat to reload, and Sean squeezed the trigger. The first shot splintered the windshield into a giant spiderweb. The driver jerked the wheel left and right to make for a harder target, but he overcorrected and lost control. The truck veered off the road and into the ditch. It slammed into the embankment so hard that both occupants were thrown violently through the windshield.

As if nothing happened, the next pickup in line took its place. Sean had counted five trucks before. *One down. Four to go.*

He pressed his back into the headboard of the truck bed and firmed the weapon's stock against his shoulder. Another gunman popped out of the window of the new lead vehicle and started firing. He was more accurate than the previous shooter and put two rounds firmly in the Americans' tailgate.

Sean breathed evenly, just as he'd been trained to do. Situations like this could cause a person to panic. When that happened, the first thing to change was their breathing. Erratic breaths could alter a shooter's aim by fractions of an inch. Those fractions added up to several feet over a given distance.

He felt the trigger tense against his finger as he lined up the driver in his sights. Just as he squeezed, Tommy wheeled the pickup to the right. Sean's round missed far to the left, sending a plume of red dirt into the air. He looked over his shoulder and saw they'd reached the foothills leading into the mountains.

The road ahead curved back and forth like an S. Lush green trees flew by on both sides as Tommy steered to the left, then right, and then back again. The easily distracted Sean had a fleeting thought about how much fun the road would be for one of his motorcycles. A gunshot from the truck behind them brought him back to the danger at hand.

He planted his feet as firmly as possible against the left wheel well and pushed his back hard against the bedrail. The gun's barrel wavered one direction and then the other as the turns in the road dictated its momentum. Instead of fighting it, Sean let it move.

Just like shooting clays, he thought.

The target passed through his weapon's sights once, twice, and a third time. On the fourth, his finger twitched and pulled the trigger. The bullet smashed through the windshield and struck the driver in the chest. A second later, the pickup drove off the road through the curve and crashed into a tree.

Tommy saw what happened in the rearview mirror. "Good one!" he shouted back at his friend.

Sean didn't reply to the compliment. He still had three more targets to go.

The next truck in line repeated the same process the other two had used. They closed in, and the gunman in the passenger seat steadied himself to fire. The road straightened out for a moment, and Sean took quick aim at the other shooter.

"Rain coming!" Tommy yelled.

In the blink of an eye, the world around them dove headfirst into an all-out downpour. There was no subtle sprinkle leading into a rain shower. Just a sudden, unapologetic deluge.

The gunman climbed back into the cab for a moment to wipe his eyes. The windshield wipers went back at forth at a furious rate, sending sheets of water off to the side with every pass.

Tommy was forced to slow down due to poor visibility, and to keep better traction. Fortunately, the other trucks had to slow for the same reasons.

Sean kept his weapon trained on the next vehicle and lined up the sights with the grill. Huge drops of water dripped off the muzzle and barrel. His hair and clothes were soaked. But his aim was steady. He let the weapon move and breathed with the movement of the truck. As the sights passed by his target, he squeezed the trigger twice.

One round missed, but the second plowed through the front of the truck, piercing the radiator. Steam poured out of the hood, and the truck's speed fell off. The last two in line passed it, and soon it was out of sight.

"Two left," he said to himself. Sean shook the rain from his face and hair and lined up the next truck.

These guys, however, had no intention of going down the way the others had. The last pickup in line pulled up next to the other one as they entered a long straightaway.

Both gunmen popped out of their windows and opened fire. Most of the shots were wildly off target. They were at a major disadvantage trying to fire into the wind-driven rain. It was unlikely they could see anything, and if a single raindrop struck them in the eye, it would have felt like being hit by a pellet from an air rifle.

Sean—on the other hand—didn't have that problem. But the sheer volume of rounds being fired by the gunmen presented serious danger. Any idiot could get lucky if they squeezed off enough shots.

As the pursuit entered a long curve, one round shattered the side mirror on the Americans' truck. Another ripped through the metal frame on the passenger side of the cabin.

Instinctively, Sean ducked for cover until they were through the turn. A deep ravine appeared on his left. The chase was climbing the mountain quickly, in spite of having to slow down due to the downpour.

The shooters to the rear retreated to their seats to reload, and the driver of the truck from the back returned to his lane.

Then—just as suddenly as it had begun—the rain ended. Warm, steamy air washed over the truck, and sunlight radiated down on the mountain. The little advantage Sean possessed was gone. *No more potshots*, he thought.

The road wound to the left and then made a sharp turn back to the right, climbing toward the summit.

The driver in the rear swerved into the other lane and pulled alongside the other truck. Their shooters simultaneously reappeared in the windows and readied their weapons.

Sean slid to the back of the truck and braced his feet against the tailgate. He pressed his shoulder into the butt of the weapon and aimed at the front right tire of the truck to his right.

Two birds with one stone.

The shooters opened fire, but so did Sean. He pulled back on the trigger and held it, unloading the contents of his magazine at the oncoming pickup.

One of the rounds struck through the bumper and into the rubber. The tire ruptured instantly, causing the pickup to lurch to the right. The driver couldn't regain control fast enough and he plowed into the other vehicle.

His comrade didn't expect to be sideswiped and was unprepared for the blow. He fought the force, trying desperately to steer left, but the oncoming curve was too sharp.

Both trucks sailed off the road and over the edge. Sean watched them go airborne until they disappeared in the trees of the steep valley below.

He tossed the weapon into the truck bed and crawled back to the front. He smacked the cabin roof twice. "Hey, slow down. They're gone."

Tommy nodded and pulled the pickup off to the side of the road where the shoulder broadened to create a makeshift overlook.

Sean just sat in the back for a minute and collected himself. Tommy hopped out and rested his arms on the bedrail. He looked back at the empty road and then at his friend.

"Good shootin', Tex."

Sean's head bobbed once. "Thanks."

"But what are we gonna do about that plane?"

Sean's gaze remained on the tailgate. "I memorized the tail number. We'll track it down. Just as soon as I find a towel."

"Senator, I'm growing very tired of this annoying interference from your government." Khalif spoke into the phone with a cool, even tone, dipped in venom.

"And I'm growing tired of this conversation, Omar. I warned you to handle your people better. What happened now? Another shipment get lost? If those missiles end up in the wrong hands, you better make sure no one knows where they came from. I've got a lot to lose if you screw this up."

Senator Thorpe did little to hide his irritation.

Khalif was in his study. Beige linen curtains hung from iron rods over the windows, blunting the sunlight pouring into the room and giving it a sort of permanent dusk feel. He leaned back in his Corinthian leather chair and pressed his head into it, drawing a deep breath. The leather's scent filled his nostrils before he sighed.

"I have taken every precaution, Harold. If your people continue to pursue this, I assure you they will not return to America."

"Fine! Kill them. Whatever you have to do. Just make sure they can't trace any of this back to me. You hear?"

"I understand, Senator. But you made assurances—assurances that the United States would leave me alone. And while I have taken extra measures to make sure my plan succeeds, I am disappointed that you have not held up your end of the bargain." He twirled a finger around and around in his mustache.

Thorpe laughed. "What do you mean, I haven't held up my end? I got you what you wanted. You know what? Stop calling me. You're right; we are finished. I got you what you wanted. You paid me. As far as I'm concerned, our deal is completed. Okay?"

Khalif nodded, staring absently at the glossy finish of his gigantic oak desk. "Yes, Senator, our deal is complete. I will no longer require your assistance. You may consider our business relationship at an end."

Thorpe hesitated. "Okay then. Good. Glad to hear it. So you're not going to call me anymore with these stupid questions or requests?"

"No. I will not be calling you anymore. We have everything we need. There are just a few loose ends to tidy up."

Thorpe didn't like the sound of that. "What do you mean, loose ends?"

"Mmm, for starters, the agents that are causing so much trouble for my men. I'll have to kill them."

"Like I said, fine by me. The fewer loose ends, the better."

Khalif's eyes wandered to the ceiling fan overhead. Its blades were carved to look like palm leaves. "Did you know, Senator, that those agents killed several of my men earlier today in Tanzania?" Before Thorpe could answer, he went on. "Apparently, they discovered my depot outside of Mbeya and traced the trucks to Songea, where a large shipment was being loaded onto a plane."

"So? How many times do I have to tell you to get your act together? Stop hiring amateurs, and you won't have those problems anymore."

"I have to say, Senator, I am going to miss our little conversations. Especially your helpful advice. I assure you that only the best will be handling my most important tasks."

"Good. Now if you don't mind, I'm going to have a quick bite to eat before I head back to the office. If there isn't anything else pressing you'd like to tell me, I bid you good day."

Khalif's eyes lowered, and his gaze lingered on the doorway across the room. "In ancient times, Senator, when situations like this arose, men were called upon to do things they wouldn't normally do. They had to take measures into their own hands to create a shift in power, or to even the score."

"What in the world are you talking about?"

"The great leaders of the ancient world had to take what they wanted, often with their own hands. On occasion, they called upon a trusted friend to handle more delicate matters. Take you for instance."

"Me? Just what are you getting at, Omar?"

"You have provided me with a supply of weapons—weapons that will wreak havoc on one of America's allies. And in exchange, I paid you handsomely."

Thorpe was confused and hesitated to reply for a moment. His tone escalated rapidly to raw agitation. "Now wait just a minute. What are you talking about, America's allies?"

Khalif ignored the question. "But that deal wasn't good enough for you, was it, Senator? You had to be the cowboy, the hero that put a stop to a madman's plans. So you went and brought in those agents to save the day." He clicked his tongue several times.

"Listen, Omar, I don't know what you're getting at, but if you use those weapons against our allies, I can't stop the thunder that will come down on you. You'll be on your own. As for the agents, I have no idea how they found your facility. But I wasn't the one who put them on your tail."

"Do you know what I like the most about you, Senator?" He didn't wait for a response. "It's your predictability."

Silence came through the earpiece as Thorpe waited for Khalif to finish his thought.

"You take your lunch at the same time every day. And on this particular day—every single week without fail—you happen to eat lunch at home. Your consistency is admirable."

"So what?" Thorpe said with a nervous tremble in his voice.

Khalif imagined the senator's head was on a swivel, twisting around to make sure no one was watching him. He could hear Thorpe's footsteps on his hardwood floor. The man was likely checking every room in case of an intrusion. Soon he would call for his security guard, a highly trained government asset that would—in all likelihood—be standing outside the front door, oblivious to what was happening inside.

"I find it important," Khalif went on, "a routine in place. Take me, for instance. I wake up at the same time every day. I have my coffee and breakfast, take a shower, and then immediately attend to my morning prayers."

"Okay, Omar." Thorpe tried to end the conversation. "That's great, but I have to go now. Nice talking to you. Do me a favor. Lose my number. Don't want anyone tracing our conversation."

"You won't have to worry about that, Senator. Just like with some of the crooked leaders from history, your time is at an end."

Before he could retort, Thorpe gasped. Khalif heard muffled grunting that quickly turned into frantic, muted screams. A loud clack and a rattle shot through the earpiece, a signal that the senator had dropped his phone. Then just as suddenly as the struggle began, it ended. The noises faded away, and Khalif was left with silence.

A familiar voice broke the quiet a moment later. "It's done," Ahmed said.

"Good. Return here at once. I have another assignment for you."

He ended the call and set the phone down on his desk.

Ahmed was one of the deadliest men he'd ever come across. His ability to move in and out of areas undetected was extraordinary. He'd no doubt used his stealth to sneak into Senator Thorpe's mansion, kill his guard, and then take out the primary target.

Adept at many forms of killing, for this particular assignment Ahmed had chosen a rare toxin that would cause cardiac arrest in the victim. Just a small prick in a freckle or mole would deliver the poison into the blood stream. From what Khalif had heard, it was an excruciating way to go. Luckily for the dying person, the toxin worked incredibly fast, causing the heart to stop in less than a minute. For a smaller or older person, it worked even faster.

The senator would be found on the floor of his home within the next day or so. Khalif imagined what the media headlines would look like. They would—no doubt—mention all the good and wonderful things Thorpe had done for his state, the country, and maybe even the world.

There would be a huge memorial service. And then eventually the gears of American government would start turning again. Soon, Thorpe's memory would be forgotten.

Ironic, Khalif thought, *that the man who sold out his country and people he believed in protecting would be honored as a kind of hero.* If the media knew what he'd done, Thorpe would have been thrown out with the rest of the trash.

But not even the senator had known what he'd done. Thorpe believed he was just making a quick buck with a company he'd been in bed with for some time. He never dreamed he was funding one of the largest terrorist operations in history.

An operation that was almost ready to begin.

"You know, all this would be a lot easier if I was there." Emily's voice was laced with agitation.

"You're the one who was in a big hurry to get back to the office." Sean spoke coolly into the phone.

He wanted to put on a dry T-shirt and a fresh pair of khakis, but he and Tommy were still twenty minutes away from the camp.

"We completed the mission."

"We *thought* we completed it. But Toli was just a front. Someone else is behind all this. And the missiles we found are just the tip of the iceberg."

Emily was stuck in the Nairobi airport—not exactly the other side of the world, but not close either.

"What do you need me to do?"

"Is Fitz with you?"

"Yeah, he's here."

Sean breathed a sigh of relief. "Good. Write down this sequence. You ready?"

There was a brief pause before she said, "Yes. Go ahead."

He rattled off the sequence of numbers and letters from the plane and then asked if she needed it repeated.

"No, I got it. What are we doing again?"

"That's the tail number from the plane we saw in Songea. It left with a shipment of missiles just like the ones we nabbed in Dar es Salaam. We need you and Fitz to find out where that plane went. Get the location, and call me back."

"So you want us to find an airplane that flew out of Songea to somewhere in the world? That doesn't narrow it down at all."

He ignored her sarcasm. "Listen, just tell Fitz what to do. He should be able to hack into one of the systems in the area. From what I understand, their security isn't all that. Once he's in, he should be able to sift through and find the one we're looking for."

"And what if he can't?"

"Well then, the world is going to be in a lot of trouble. If what we know about those weapons is correct, a lot of people could die."

Emily paused for a second. She hesitated to say anything, but Sean needed to know. "Sean, we had the warheads from the missiles analyzed. They're armed with a potent nerve gas called X38. Each warhead has the capability to kill anything within ten city blocks. And that's just in the first thirty seconds. Inside of two minutes, anyone within fifteen blocks will be dead."

Sean's eyebrows furrowed. "Where in the world did these guys get something like that?"

"We don't know. When we were told they had some kind of bioweapons, we figured it was the usual: anthrax, some kind of viral substance, but we had no idea it was anything like this. They could wipe out more than 50 percent of New York if those missiles were detonated over the city."

Another thought occurred to him. "Except we don't know what the target is. It might be New York. But that would be too obvious. And no one would dare try to hit that place again, not after September 11."

"Why? Because of increased security?"

He shook his head. "No. Like I always say, don't do the same gag twice. You do the next gag. Criminals and terrorists think the same way. How many times do you rob a bank?"

"Once?"

"Right. Not because you can't. But because you've already done it. New York isn't the target."

Emily sighed. "Then where?"

"I don't know." Sean scratched his head. "But I have a feeling if we can track down that plane, we will find out. Get Fitz on it, and call me back."

"Okay. Will do."

Sean ended the call looked over at his friend. "They're in Nairobi."

Tommy nodded. "What are we going to do if they can't find the plane?"

It was a question Sean had already considered. "Planes can't just disappear anymore. Not easily, anyway. They have transponders. Radar and satellites track them. And then there is information that has to be filled out on the ground; flight plans have to be filed."

Tommy recalled the shanty-like airport in Songea. "Not to burst your bubble, but I'm not sure that airport we saw really does a bang-up job at keeping records of such things."

Sean snorted. "Good point. But the other stuff is trackable. Even in this part of the world. Fitz will find it."

"And then what are you going to do? Go after the missiles?"

Sean noted the way his friend had worded the sentence. It insinuated Tommy wasn't going to come with him. He understood. Tommy had already done more than enough to help out, especially considering he wasn't a government agent. It wouldn't be fair to ask him to come along on a mission that was likely going to be extremely dangerous.

"That's my job, Schultzie. It's what I do."

Tommy shook his head. "Like I said before, the offer still stands. If you ever get tired of dodging bullets, give me a call. I could use someone like you in a security capacity."

"I appreciate it."

"You know where to find me," Tommy cocked his head to the side and winked.

The two pulled into the camp and found it just as they left it. A few of the site workers were milling around a campfire between some of the tents and buildings. When they got out of the truck, Tommy made his way over to them. He let everyone know he was okay and that he'd had to take care of some logistical stuff in the city that had to be done immediately. Everyone seemed to accept the explanation without fuss.

Sean went inside the building where all his things were and took a quick shower. The sun had dipped below the horizon by the time he got out. Twilight quickly gave way to darkness. He checked his phone to make sure Emily hadn't called while he was cleaning up, but there was nothing.

He pulled on a clean T-shirt and had one leg through a new pair of pants when the phone started ringing. "Of course," he said.

Sean bounced on one foot in an attempt to hurry the process of pulling the other leg through the pants and nearly fell over onto his back. He wavered for a second before steadying his balance. Leaving the button and zipper undone, he grabbed the phone and answered.

"Go."

"Is that how you always answer the phone?"

"Do you want me to go back to calling you Emily?"

"Fine. We got a fix on the plane. It landed at a small airport along the border with Mozambique. We made a few calls. There's a SEAL team en route right now to intercept."

"That was fast." From call to call, it had taken just over an hour for Fitz and Emily to figure out where the plane had gone. "I'm impressed."

"There was a Navy ship in the Indian Ocean, just off the coast of Mozambique. We were lucky. The SEALs should be there within the next hour. If there's anything on that plane, they'll find it and take out anyone who gets in their way."

Finally, things were turning their way. With another shipment of weapons lost, whoever was behind all this would likely rear their ugly head. And when that happened, Sean wanted to be there to knock the head back down. Permanently.

"Good work, Agent Starks. Please tell Fitz I said the same to him."

"Will do. So what's next for you? Finally coming home? Or is there some other trouble you're looking to find?"

Sean's lips creased. "I think I've had my fill. And I could use some home cooking. The food out here isn't great."

"Tell me about it. Nairobi isn't much better."

"Tell the director I'll report in day after tomorrow to debrief."

"Sounds good, Agent Wyatt." She paused for a moment and then said, "Oh, and Sean...good job on this one. You saved a lot of people's lives. That X38 is extremely dangerous. Seriously, if you and your friend hadn't done what you did, there would be major consequences."

Sean nearly blushed. Not from the compliment, but from her calling him by his first name. "Thanks. Get some sleep. You've earned it."

He hung up the phone and plugged it into the wall charger. Outside the little bedroom window he watched the flames dancing from the fire, licking the air with multicolored orange tongues. Tommy was sitting by the fire pit, talking to one of his workers. From the looks of it, he was getting the lowdown on the day's activities. He slapped the guy on the back and laughed at something the man said. It was a hard life, being on dig site after dig site. The days could be long and hot. The work, grueling. But in the end, they loved it.

Tommy's invitation dug away at the back of Sean's mind. He shook it off and collapsed onto the bed, disregarding the fact that he was fully clothed. It didn't matter.

Exhaustion was taking over, and he was willing to let it. He needed some rest. As he closed his eyes, Sean's consciousness drifted into visions of golden statues and caves with strange writing on the walls.

Sean awoke in the darkness to the sound of his satellite phone ringing furiously on the nightstand. He snapped out of bed and grabbed it.

"Hello?" he said, rubbing his eyes.

"That was quick." Emily's voice crackled through the earpiece. She sounded more tired than he felt.

"I'm a light sleeper. What's up?" He picked up his watch and checked the time. It was just before 5 a.m. local time.

"We have a problem."

That was never a good thing to hear, especially at such an early hour of the day. And definitely when it was from a high-level government agent.

"Why did I have a feeling you were going to say that?"

She didn't answer his question, instead getting straight to the point. "The SEALs found the plane at the airfield in Mozambique."

"That's great news, Em...Agent Starks. What's the problem?"

"It was empty."

Sean frowned and put his face in his free hand. "Empty? What do you mean, empty?"

"There were no missiles. There weren't even any crates. If that was the plane you saw leaving Songea, there was nothing on it."

Sean felt a sickening feeling creep from his stomach into his throat.

"I'm sorry. For a second there it sounded like you said the plane was empty."

He still didn't believe it. And at such an early hour, wrapping his head around pretty much anything was a difficult task.

"Are you sure you got the tail number right? You didn't mix up a letter or a number?"

"Agent Starks, there may be a lot of things I screw up in life, but remembering number-and-letter sequences is not one of them. Call it a gift."

He wasn't being cocky. It was the truth. Sean didn't exactly have an eidetic memory. But with certain things, he was fairly close. License plates and phone numbers were easy. More complex sequences were a little harder but only when they reached fifteen or more characters. As a result of his ability to memorize those sorts of things, he'd done extremely well on that part of the IQ test in graduate school.

"You're certain?" Emily double-checked.

Sean wasn't offended. "Positive, 100 percent."

"Then they must have unloaded the cargo and taken off."

It didn't make sense. Why would they fly the missiles to Mozambique just to unload them? They could have driven them there. It's not like it was a twenty-hour journey. With the time it took to load and fuel the plane, get it ready for flight, and up in the air, they would have been halfway to their destination.

"Something doesn't add up," he said.

"You think?"

"No," he shook his head and stood up. His feet began pacing mindlessly back and forth across the room. "Flying such a short distance. The logistics involved, everything it takes to get an aircraft ready to fly; it's too much time. Why would they spend so much time doing all that unless...."

Sean stopped in mid-sentence. A chill shot through his blood, raising the hairs on his skin.

"Unless what?" Emily prodded.

"Unless they wanted us to see them do it," he murmured.

There was a three-second pause before Emily said, "What? Why would they want that?"

Sean stopped in place, and his head rose and fell slowly. "That's it. They wanted us to see the plane take off. Don't you see? They knew we found the underground storage facility. They even knew we would follow them all the way to Songea. The shootout, the car chase, all of it was a ruse."

"I'm sorry. What?"

"It was all a setup. Whoever is running this thing knows every move we're going to make."

Sean's head spun. The puzzle pieces whirled around like a blizzard. There was a piece missing, but he couldn't figure out which one.

"How is that possible?" she asked.

Sean froze in place. "Are you close to Fitz right now?"

His question came out of the blue. "No. He's in his own room. I called him before I woke you."

"How well do you know him?"

"I don't. I've only worked with him a few times before this mission. You don't think..."

"That he could be a mole? Yeah, it's possible. I'd say anything is possible right now."

Emily hesitated for a moment. "What if there isn't a mole and the people behind all this are just being really careful? If Fitz was a traitor, we'd be dead already. He could have killed us and left us in the middle of nowhere. And no one would be the wiser."

"Point taken. Please don't tell him I said that."

She let out an irritated grunt. "Maybe they're just outthinking us."

That part wasn't too far off. Whoever was moving the missiles appeared to be a master chess player. Sean was brilliant in several areas, but he'd always struggled at chess. It wasn't his forte. Right now he felt like a pawn up against a board full of queens and knights, and someone else was moving him around.

Emily interrupted his thoughts. "The people responsible for all this must have a ton of money. I mean, the funding necessary to make all this possible would be astronomical."

Valid point. But they were getting nowhere. Whether someone was watching their every move or not didn't matter. The most immediate concern was that the missiles had disappeared, somewhere between Songea and the airfield in Mozambique. That last thought caused Sean's head to lift instantly.

"Wait. What if the plane didn't unload at the airport in Mozambique?"

The question caught Emily off guard. "What do you mean? Where else would it have unloaded? They wouldn't have had time to stop somewhere else first. Based on the information we obtained, that aircraft flew straight there."

"Right, I get that," he said. "But what if instead of unloading the cargo at the airport, they dropped it mid-flight?"

"I don't understand. Why would they do that? Unless..."

"Unless they knew we were coming. Or at least thought we would."

They keep playing the shell game, he thought.

He went on. "They could have dropped the cargo with parachutes on the way to Mozambique. From there, new trucks could have picked up the crates and taken them to who-knows-where."

Sean hurried over to his gear bag and pulled out a map of the region. He carried it over to a small desk and opened it onto the surface. Next, he drew a huge circle around the location of Songea and then neighboring Mozambique.

"Sounds like a bit of a stretch." Emily said, breaking the silence.

"No. That has to be it. They let us see the plane leave. They knew we would track it down. And they knew we would seize it. That means the plane dropped its cargo somewhere between here and here." He pointed at the map as if someone else was in the room with him.

"Here and where?"

"Sorry. I have a map, and I just drew a line between the two airports. The question is, where did the missiles go once they left the cargo plane?"

"Kind of a big question."

He stood back and stared at the map. "If the crates were dropped off in mid-flight, that means someone had to be waiting for them on the ground or be there shortly after to pick them up. There's an area on the map that would be perfect for that. It's a nature preserve, so no one would be around, at least not many people anyway."

"They'd still have to get the weapons out of the country, though."

"Which means they'd need an airport."

"Or an airfield," Emily corrected. "Check on your map for any smaller airfields in the vicinity. Doesn't have to be much. Just a strip where a plane could take off and land."

He leaned over the map again and scanned the area around the line he'd drawn. Nothing jumped out immediately. On his second pass, however, he noticed something. "It looks like there's a small airfield just outside of Kandulu. If they dropped the cargo in the Niassa Reserve, it could have been picked up and taken to a new plane in no time."

"And no one would be the wiser."

"Right." Sean's brain was running at light speed. "Get Fitz to find all the flight paths of any aircraft leaving that airstrip in the last twenty-four hours. We can narrow it down to a list of likely candidates and go from there. Call me back when you have something."

"On it."

Sean ended the call and stared at the map. On top of the innumerable ideas flashing through his mind, one kept popping out at him and smacking him in the face. "Whoever is pulling these strings is being awfully careful," he said to himself.

Terrorist groups *were* careful. They planned things well and executed them to near perfection. But this was something else. Even the most organized terrorists left breadcrumbs now and then. The person or persons behind this plan had more cover-ups in place than he'd ever imagined.

That could mean only one thing, at least in Sean's mind.

Whoever it was had a lot to lose. And Sean wanted to make sure they lost it.

They would have to be wealthy and well connected, possibly with political allies. Sean wondered if it was someone who had their fingers in American pockets. He shook off the thought. He knew there was corruption and conspiracy around every corner. Sometimes he found it best to just not think about it.

After running through a short list of potentials, he wrote off every one. None of the most wanted terrorists in the world had the finances to carry out this sort of intricate operation. It had to be someone bigger, a fish that none of the other fish would mess with. Someone whose pockets were deep but had a hidden agenda, a thirst for chaos.

No faces came to mind.

He sat back down on the edge of the bed and waited, hoping that Fitz and Emily would find what they were looking for.

He didn't have to wait long. Only thirty minutes later, Emily called him back.

Sean answered on the second ring.

"What have you got for me?"

"Well," she stalled, "I have good news and bad news."

"I don't like the sound of that."

"Yeah. You're not gonna like any of this news either. The good news is that we found the plane."

"You're sure? How did you narrow it down so fast?" he asked, impressed.

"That part was easy enough. Only one plane has flown out of that airstrip in the last twenty-four hours. For the most part, it's unused. If your hunch is right, it's safe to say the goods were picked up and loaded onto a plane there."

"Great. What's the bad news?"

She hesitated to answer for a few seconds. "It's where the plane went. We tracked it to a place where Americans have had trouble in the past."

He already had an idea of what the answer might be before she said the words.

"It landed in Somalia."

27
Nairobi, Kenya

The next day, Sean woke early and drove back to Dar es Salaam. From there he took the relatively short flight to Nairobi to meet up with the other agents.

Tommy had stayed behind with the IAA team. After all, he had a major agency to run and a big contract with the Tanzanian government. An engineer was flying in from Sweden later in the day to take a look at the golden statue and run some scans that would show whether or not the thing could be taken apart.

Sean understood. It wasn't Tommy's fight. Plus he wasn't a government agent. The fact that he'd been involved in the first place could have gotten the other three in a heap of trouble. They'd agreed it was something that wouldn't be put in their reports.

Sean especially didn't want his friend coming along, given the destination.

Americans didn't exactly have a great history with carrying out missions in Somalia. The story of the Black Hawk helicopters that were shot down over Mogadishu in 1993 sent chills through people who read the book or watched the movie. Lawlessness abounded in much of the city, and the surrounding countryside mirrored that culture. Still did to this day, in fact.

People did as they pleased, stealing, raping, and murdering with reckless abandon. The chaos had been brought about by local warlords seizing power. As their reach grew, so did the mayhem until the city was bathed in a constant stream of crime and violence.

There were pockets of civilization. The mosques carried out the ritual prayers five times each day. And in the business sector, new buildings were being constructed on an almost yearly basis.

Where the money went was a mystery. One thing was certain. It wasn't being reinvested back into the community.

Just before he got on the plane to Kenya, Tommy called to wish his friend a safe journey and good luck. They talked for a few more minutes before Sean was called to board.

Once he was in Kenya, Sean found himself sitting on the edge of Fitz's hotel bed and staring at a laptop. Fitz was in the desk chair near the computer, and Emily sat up straight on the twin bed next to Sean.

The room was sparsely decorated in drab colors that could have come from the 1970s. It was the best the Americans had been able to find on such short notice. But they weren't on vacation, so what the room looked like didn't matter.

Fitz pointed at a map on his screen and then zoomed in. "This is Mogadishu."

"I can see that," Sean said. He couldn't ignore the inner smart aleck.

Fitz sighed and kept going. "Anyway, it's not like it used to be. When those Black Hawk helicopters were shot down, everything was a mess. Now there are emerging boroughs where the people are taking back the city. They're a long way from being civilized, but it's headed in the right direction."

"That's good to know. So maybe we won't have as much trouble as we suspect?"

"Not so fast," Fitz held up a finger. He then pointed at an area on the edge of the city, close to the airport. He zoomed in on an aerial photo of a large building with a tin roof.

"We believe this is where the missiles are. It's in an area that is still run by a bunch of different gangs. And they pretty much kill anyone they don't recognize, without asking any questions."

"Okay. Noted. But I have to ask, Fitz. How do you know that's where the missiles are?"

"We don't," Emily answered for him. "But that warehouse has been abandoned for nearly a decade. It's a wonder the thing is still standing."

"Building codes aren't really their specialty in that part of the world," Fitz added.

Emily kept going. "Notice anything unusual outside the warehouse?"

Sean leaned in. "Those look like transport trucks."

"Right. Now what would trucks like that be doing outside an abandoned warehouse?"

Sean's lips creased. "Very nice deduction, Sherlock."

"It took us a few hours of scouring the surrounding area of the city," Fitz explained. "Not the most exciting work, but it paid off."

"We hope," Emily said.

"Unless the two of you have a better lead than this, it looks like our only shot. Now the only problem is getting into Somalia. Tension between the Somalis and the Kenyans has been a little rough of late. I doubt we can stroll up to the border and simply drive across."

Emily shook her head. "No, you'll need to do it a little more clandestine than that."

Sean raised an eyebrow. He couldn't help but notice the way she'd phrased the sentence. "You? What happened to we?"

Fitz answered for her. "It's better if you go alone. One person can move with a lot less notice than two. Plus she's a woman."

"Hey!" Her faux protest brought a grin to Sean's face.

Fitz finished his thought. "An American woman in Mogadishu would be like seeing a hundred-foot unicorn walking around in Central Park. You don't want that kind of attention."

"I could wear a disguise," she interrupted. Her eyes fired darts at him.

"I know you could." He stumbled through his words, trying not to sound like a chauvinist. "But the other part of it is that if you were caught... Let's just say the kinds of people who live in that area do awful things to women."

"I knew the risks involved when I took this job. I can handle it."

"Yet you agreed to let me go it alone," Sean jumped in.

"Only because he's right about one person moving more easily than two," she answered. Then she switched gears. "We will take a fishing boat around the border. You'll be dropped off on a beach where you'll meet a man who is going to take you into the city."

That part sounded a little sketchy to Sean. How did they have a connection in Somalia? *I guess for the right amount of money,* he thought.

"Who is this *guy*?" he asked.

"Someone we've used before. He's a rebellious sort," Fitz explained. He read Sean's reaction and explained. "Don't worry. He'll do as told. While he's got bravery in spades, he's afraid of Americans for some reason. He won't double-cross us."

"If he's so afraid, why is he working with us?"

"Because we pay him better than any job in his ragged-out country ever could," Emily answered.

"Yeah," Fitz agreed. "He won't have to work for a year. And what we pay him wouldn't get a studio apartment in a small town back home."

Sean still wasn't sure about using hired help, especially from a place full of untrustworthy people. But he didn't have much choice.

"Fine. So we have the way in. Then what? I go in, find the missiles, and bring down the warehouse?"

Emily and Fitz exchanged a sideways glance.

"No," Emily said. "Though that would be an efficient way of taking out the warheads, it could also contaminate the area, killing tens of thousands of people. Yourself included."

"And then there's the head of the snake to consider," Fitz added. "If we destroy those missiles, we lose the guy who was behind all this. He'll rear his ugly head again at some point and start all over again. And next time he'll be even more careful. We can't afford to blow this one."

"So what then?" Sean eyed them both.

Emily reached into a gear bag next to her feet and pulled out three circular discs, each about the size of a bottle cap. She held them out to him. Each one had a tiny button embedded on the side.

"These are fresh from R&D."

Sean took one out of her hand and inspected it, holding it up in the light and twisting it around. "Tracking device?"

She nodded.

"State of the art," Fitz said. "Actually, ahead of state of the art by about three years. That beacon has a signal five times stronger than anything currently being employed by our government."

Sean raised a dubious eyebrow. His eyes shifted to Fitz. "Really? How'd you get your hands on it?"

A clever grin crossed Fitz's face. He shrugged. "Let's just say I have a friend who does a little contract work with DARPA. Maybe I'll introduce you sometime. You two would get along great."

"Good to have friends in the right places." Something puzzled him, though. "So why did you get three of them?"

Fitz's confidence waned. "They're small, for one. So if you had them, say, in a pocket or something, you could lose one pretty easily."

"On top of that," Emily continued for him, "the lithium batteries inside these things aren't entirely stable. Sometimes they peter out without warning or reason. So to make sure we get a reliable signal, try to place all three with the missiles. If possible."

"Ah, so there is a catch." He carelessly tossed the device to Emily. She snatched it out of the air with ease. "Nice."

"Please be careful with those," Fitz said. "They are very expensive and very rare."

Sean turned to him. "So rare that we're about to put them on some terrorist missiles that may or may not be blown to bits in the next few days?"

"Point taken."

Emily took over again. "Once the tracking units are in place, get out and meet up with your ride. He'll be there for up to six hours. After that, his orders are to get out."

Sean pouted his lower lip. "Should be enough time, unless he drops me three hours away from the target."

"You'll be dropped off less than a click from the warehouse. There's a good bit of activity in that area: pedestrians, delivery trucks, car traffic. Though we advise you not to linger. You need to get in and out—"

"As quickly as possible," Sean finished her sentence. "Yeah, I get the gist. So when are we doing this?"

Fitz answered the question. "We're leaving in ten minutes. So get ready."

28

Coast of Somalia

The waves slapped against the side of the little fishing boat in a mesmerizing rhythm, one after another. Sean had only been in the boat for a few minutes, and he already found himself swaying back and forth in time with the sound.

He and the others had taken a surprisingly luxurious yacht from the port of Mombasa and gone north, staying far enough away from shore to keep any watchful eyes unsuspecting, but close enough that when Sean launched the wooden dinghy attached to the side it wouldn't take him more than twenty or thirty minutes to make land.

"Sure you don't want to trade?" he'd joked with Emily. The yacht was lined with plush, creamy leather and glossy wood appointments. There was a fully stocked bar in a living room that approached five hundred square feet. He spotted Fitz eyeing it and had to remind him they were working. Fun could come later.

"We'll be waiting for you here," Emily said. "These are international waters. Your boat should have enough fuel for you to get to the shore and back. But just in case, there's a little canister of spare fuel tucked under the tarp near the front."

Sean steered the boat via a rudder-like stick attached to an old outboard motor. It sputtered and groaned like it could die at any second. He hoped he wouldn't have to resort to using the oars that were stowed away on the floor.

He pulled the stained, tattered scarf a little tighter around his face. He'd gotten sunburned once off the coast of Tampa while fishing for tarpon. Exposure to too much UV wasn't the only reason he was completely covered from head to toe in raggedy clothing. His body perspired constantly underneath the layers of clothing. The Somali sun beat down on the little vessel and trapped the heat inside like a convection oven.

Sean didn't dare take off any of the clothing. He had to look the part of a fisherman, but he also couldn't allow himself to be recognized as an American. If that happened, to say people would become suspicious would be the understatement of the decade. From what he understood, keeping covered would actually cause his body to cool itself, kicking the hypothalamus into gear to maintain a constant temperature.

That didn't mean it was a pleasant temperature. And he wondered how so many desert nomads dealt with it on a daily basis.

The tiny vessel rose and fell between the swells, churning its way toward a place Sean had never considered visiting. Every once in a while, a big splash would wash over the boat, and he'd have to scoop it out with a bucket sitting next to his feet.

He wiped the perspiration from his brow, put the bridge of his hand against his forehead to shield his eyes from the bright sun, and peered into the distance. The white sand beaches of the coastline were a thin strip on the horizon. There were no long stretches of palm trees. Only an outcropping of one or two here and there. And unlike the coastlines of the United States, there were no high-rise condominiums, hotels or multimillion-dollar homes. There wasn't even a bungalow to be found. The only buildings within sight were a collection of colorful huts huddled together a mile or so north. The huts stood a few hundred feet back from the shoreline and looked like they'd been built several decades ago. The vast emptiness of the shore was a stark contrast to the way things were back home, and a reminder of how different life was between the First and Third Worlds.

Fishing village, he thought. As long as he kept covered, he should fit right in. Unless, of course, everyone preferred to do their fishing with nothing on but a pair of shorts. Sean had seen his fair share of those kinds of fishing towns. Their no shirt, no shoes, no problem way of doing things could, in fact, present a *huge* problem were anyone to notice him.

At present, there was no one in sight. Sean kept the throttle maxed out, just in case. The sooner he could get out of the open, the better.

Reaching land seemed to take an hour, when in reality it was probably closer to fifteen minutes. Sean shut the motor off a few seconds before the keel dug into the sand. He grabbed a canvas bag and slung it over his shoulder. It was a replacement for his gear bag, which would clearly not be in keeping with his authentic fisherman appearance. Inside were his usual tools, pistol, extra magazines, and a few other things he thought he might need. And then, of course the tracking beacons were stored with care in their own little pouch.

He reached back and pulled the spark plug cap away from the motor. It was a simple yet effective way to keep any potential thieves from getting away with his escape vehicle. At the very least, it would slow them down and give them reason to reconsider. Sean had learned that most people—when presented with even the slightest challenges—tended to give up more often than not.

He grabbed a rope from inside the craft and dragged the boat until it would go no farther. The tide was low at the moment, but later on in the day it would rise again. When it did, his little boat would be at risk of drifting out to sea.

The dinghy was equipped with a small anchor—nothing more than a thirty-pound kettle bell tied to an old rope. The makeshift anchor would probably be maxing out its potential just keeping the boat in the general vicinity, much less in one spot. But it was better than nothing.

Sean scanned the beach to the north and south but only saw a few fishermen milling around near one of the buildings. No one had paid any attention to him. Not yet, at least.

Best not to stick around and give them the chance.

He stalked across the packed sand that gave way to softer tread up away from the waterline. When he reached the bushes that lined the beach, he ducked down and broke out at a run. His contact was to meet him somewhere nearby. He shoved his hand into the bag he'd slung around his shoulder and pulled out a pair of binoculars. He crouched low to keep out of sight and turned one way and then the other until a pale blue Toyota Land Cruiser passed through his view. He froze and brought the lenses into focus.

The old SUV was parked in the shade of a scrawny tree about four hundred yards away. Sean stuffed the binoculars back in his bag and breathed a sigh of relief. He was concerned the little boat may have veered off course in the currents, but the little vessel had done its job and kept him remarkably close to his landing zone.

He clutched his rudimentary gear bag close to his side so it wouldn't make a noise as he ran through the brush patch toward the SUV. The terrain was sandy and full of finger-like roots sticking up everywhere. On more than one occasion he nearly tripped.

When he reached the clearing where his contact was parked, he stopped at the edge of the bushes and waited. The dark-skinned man in the driver's seat was smoking a cigarette. He took in a long puff of smoke and exhaled out the window. Sean could see the sweat pouring off the guy's high forehead.

That was him, all right.

Sean recalled what he'd read in the dossier. They only knew the man by one name. Kanu. Going by a singular moniker had its advantages in a place where anonymity could save your life. Sean had no intention of pressing the issue with the guy who was his in *and* out of one of the most dangerous places in the world.

He stood up from the bushes and walked cautiously toward the vehicle. It took Kanu a moment before he realized someone was approaching. When he did, however, his instincts kicked in.

Kanu pulled out what looked to be a Desert Eagle .50 caliber and pointed it through the window at the approaching American.

The smell of cigarette smoke and salty air filled Sean's nostrils as he raised his hands slowly and pulled down the scarf covering his mouth and nose. "You must be Kanu," he said in a cool tone.

There was a brief pause as the man stared out of the SUV like a wild animal in a corner. His eyes were wide, tense, ready to strike.

"And who are you?" he asked with a thick accent.

Sean kept his hands where Kanu could see them. "I'm Sean Wyatt. Heard you're my ride into town."

Kanu hesitated for another ten seconds, sizing up the stranger. Sean's explanation was apparently good enough, and the man lowered the weapon. He placed it on the center console and motioned for the American to get in.

Sean slid into the passenger seat and stuffed his bag on the floor.

Kanu started the engine and looked over. "Yes, I am Kanu." He eyed Sean's outfit with a curious expression. "You look ridiculous."

Sean chuckled. He liked Kanu immediately.

"We figured it would be best if I kept a low profile. Americans aren't really appreciated over here."

Kanu backed the SUV away from the tree and steered it out onto the dirt road. "True. But I hope you brought something more flexible to wear. Would be unfortunate to try to run for your life in that outfit."

Sean nodded. "I've already got it on. This was just for the local fishermen if I ran into any."

"Did you?"

Sean felt a little embarrassed, like he'd done something stupid. "No. Just saw a few up the beach, but they didn't notice me."

"That's because they're done with most of their work before this time of day. They go out early in the morning." Kanu belted out a long laugh. "You could have been wearing shorts and sandals."

"Hilarious." Sean pulled the wrapping off his head and started removing the outer layers of clothing.

He wore a lightweight combination of clothes underneath. Black cargo pants and a loose-fitting shirt made from a new material that was supposed to wick away perspiration from the body. At the moment, it wasn't living up to the hype.

Kanu reached into the ashtray and pulled a cigarette out of a half-full pack. After putting it in his lips, he took a lighter from near the pack and—as he turned the vehicle onto a paved road leading north—let go of the wheel, pressed his knee against it to steer, and cupped his hands to his mouth to light the cigarette.

A cloud of white smoke circled around his head for a second before swirling out of the open window.

"Smoke?" he asked.

"No, thank you. Never got into it," Sean said.

Kanu shrugged.

Sean eyed the pistol between them. "That's a big gun. A little over the top, don't you think?"

The driver took a long drag from his cigarette. The tip burned bright orange. Then he let the smoke out through his nostrils. "In this place, intimidation can save your skin. I've never had to fire that weapon because it intimidates anyone standing at the other end of the barrel."

"Good thinking."

It *was* an impressive piece, however impractical. Sean couldn't imagine a scenario where he'd want to be firing that weapon. He'd used one once at a gun range. A friend had bought it after seeing it in a movie. The price tag alone was enough to make Sean take a pass on owning one. But when he fired the small cannon, he was convinced he would never need one. Its recoil was unmanageable, the end on the heavy side, and keeping it balanced without firing was a chore.

Of course, with a .50-caliber round, one shot was likely all you'd need if your aim was on. The damage it caused to any human target was absolutely devastating.

"We drive on this road for an hour and then take one of the side roads into the city. This one will be blocked by one of the warlord's men. They don't take kindly to strangers, as you mentioned earlier. It would be best for us to avoid them."

No kidding.

Sean didn't bring up the fact that his driver was overstating the obvious. The less interaction they had with one of the warlord's men, the better. The problem was those types were all over the place around the outskirts of Mogadishu. And while Kanu apparently knew a back way into town, Sean wasn't entirely convinced that would be clear either. He didn't have a choice. It was Kanu's way or no way.

Conversation between the two was sparse. Sean got the feeling the man didn't want to chat. It wasn't that he was unfriendly. But keeping an anonymous persona also entailed not saying too much. To anyone. Perhaps Kanu also respected the fact that he was hosting an American government agent. There had been no lies or half truths when the transportation arrangement was made. Kanu wasn't stupid. Americans wanting to get into Mogadishu, unnoticed, and then out again just as efficiently? That reeked of some kind of special mission. So yeah, the Somali driver didn't mind keeping things quiet, for both parties.

Kanu smoked like a chimney and during the course of the hour drive, went through most of the contents in his cigarette pack. Sean didn't judge. He imagined living in such a dangerous area came with more than a few vices. If he lived there, he'd probably have to smoke constantly just to keep his nerves in check. The truck's ancient air conditioning unit didn't work. It blew air out through the vents, but it was the same warm, dusty air coming in from the windows.

The outline of the city appeared on the horizon about an hour into the drive. Sean could make out a few of the long, skinny towers that sounded the ritual prayers to the citizens five times a day. More buildings came into view, blurred by the heat waves rippling off the earth's surface.

"Hold on," Kanu said.

He slowed the SUV and jerked the wheel to the left onto a rough dirt road that ran parallel to the city. Deep ruts carved through the road in some places from erosion during wet seasons. Kanu's vehicle bounced and jolted through the terrain, but he kept up their speed. Sean glanced back in the rearview mirror at the clouds of dust the SUV was kicking up in their wake, but Kanu seemed unconcerned so he didn't bring it up.

As far as Sean was concerned, the guy knew what he was doing. Best to trust his expertise. After all, they were playing in Kanu's sandbox now.

The SUV hit a huge hump in the road and went airborne for almost two seconds before it crashed back to earth with a thud. The occupants jostled around, but Kanu kept his hands on the wheel, guiding the vehicle through a couple of quick turns.

"You take this shortcut often?" Sean asked.

Kanu nodded. At least it looked like a nod. His head may have been bobbing from the bouncy road. "Yes. Two, occasionally three times a week."

"And they haven't caught on to your little shortcut?"

"The warlords don't want any trouble. People who take the main road into the city won't put up much of a fight. But someone who knows these roads could be trouble. Smugglers use them all the time. And smugglers are usually well armed. Best to save their bullets and men for the less troublesome travelers."

Good point, I guess. "Makes sense." Sean wanted to question why Kanu was in such an all-out hurry if he wasn't worried about anyone following. He figured it was because they were on a tight schedule, so there was no point in complaining about it.

They reached a long bend in the road that eventually straightened out and headed right for the western side of the city. The terrain smoothed somewhat the closer they got until it transitioned awkwardly from dirt to rough asphalt.

Sean looked back at the odd road construction. "I guess they decided to only pave so far." He turned around and faced forward.

Kanu cast him a sidelong glance. "The government doesn't have much money, and what it does have rarely goes to fixing things properly."

"Sounds like the local warlords are taking taxes of their own."

"Yes. But it is changing. Their numbers grow smaller by the day. And their territory is shrinking. Perhaps someday order will be restored to the city. For now, we must take precautions." His eyes flashed down at the hand cannon.

Kanu slowed the SUV as they approached some of the outlying homes on the city's periphery. Most were shanties—rickety structures of concrete and corrugated metal that looked less like homes and more like stand-alone storage units. Children played in a dirt lot near the street. They ran back and forth, kicking a round ball that looked like it was made from leather bookmarks all stitched together.

"You should cover up," Kanu said. "Don't want anyone seeing an American in my truck."

Sean caught the selfish spin on his driver's comment and let a grin cross his face before he pulled the black mask over. He took a quick look in the mirror. With the mask on he either looked like a ninja or a terrorist.

Kanu twisted his head to the right and examined Sean's disguise. "You look like someone who is up to no good," he said. "You'll fit right in."

29

Mogadishu, Somalia

Sean knew how rough Mogadishu could be, but his knowledge was secondhand, delivered to him by American media outlets and pamphlets he'd read before departing on the mission.

Nothing he'd heard did justice to the level of absolute desperation and poverty of Mogadishu's slums.

The buildings—some painted in faded colors, others in brilliant white—looked like they might collapse at any moment. Every person who passed on the streets and sidewalks had the look that they were eyeing the Toyota, hoping it might—at any moment—break down and present them with fresh prey. Their vapid eyes gazed on the passing vehicle like they were zombies—lifeless and uncaring.

"They are a starving people," Kanu said, breaking the silence. "They're hungry, but they are also starved for education and work."

Sean's first thought was how desperate they looked. Kanu's comments only added to that impression.

"Nothing will change until the warlords are removed from power," Kanu went on. "But the people have to overthrow them. It can't come from the outside."

Sean agreed with a solemn nod.

He was about to say something about the nobility of a revolution when Kanu cut him off.

"This is where I will drop you off." He pointed at a junkyard half a block away. "It is right next to the warehouse you're looking for."

When the Toyota reached the next intersection, Kanu turned right and eased the vehicle into an empty parking spot. He turned off the engine and pointed at the fence surrounding the junkyard.

"There is a side entrance to this place not far from here. The door hangs open most of the time. It's locked with a chain and padlock, but you can squeeze through easily enough. From there, you can access the warehouse lot on the other side."

"Sounds easy enough." He wanted to ask why Kanu knew so much about this side entrance but decided to let it slide. No point in angling for inconsequential details.

"Just be sure to stay out of sight. I'd stay close to the fence and use the junk piles for cover."

Thanks for the tip. Wasn't planning on running through the middle of the thing and yelling at the top of my lungs.

"Anything else?" Sean asked. He kept his snarky thoughts to himself.

Kanu shook his head. "No. I'll be waiting here for you. If you aren't here when the time is up, I will leave you. This area isn't a place you want to be after dark."

"You'd leave me after all we've been through?"

Kanu's blank stare showed he wasn't amused by the comment.

"Okay then."

Sean grabbed his pistol and shoved it in a side holster then covered it with the bottom of his shirt. Next he took the three homing beacons and secured them in one of the side pockets on his pants. Two spare magazines went into his back pockets.

He gave one last look around outside. None of the onlookers they'd seen before were around. The junkyard must have been one of the few places no one hung out.

"See you in a few," Sean said.

He hopped out of the SUV and trotted across the street, looking both ways to make sure that no one noticed him. The road was still oddly vacant, like a ghost town. Back to his right, another husk of a manufacturing facility stood against the blue sky. All the windows were shattered, the walls covered in graffiti, and the gutters on the roof had rusted.

Sean turned his attention to the fence surrounding the junkyard as he veered onto the sidewalk and kept moving. It was chain-link fence and, judging from its appearance, had been put there at least thirty years before. There were big dents in it, likely from where a vehicle had struck. Some of the supporting poles were rusted or bent. But the outward-tilting barbwire on the top still presented enough of a threat to keep the general public away.

His eyes looked ahead, searching the long metal facade for the opening Kanu had described. He stole a glance back over his shoulder and heard the Toyota's motor grumble to life. Kanu waved and turned out of the parking spot and back out onto the main road.

Sean didn't think his ride was leaving. He figured Kanu would circle for a while, maybe find a safer place to park—if there was such a thing in this city.

He pushed ahead, quickening his pace.

There.

The breach in the fencing was just as Kanu described. The chain-link door was technically hanging by two hinges, but the top one had pretty much given up the fight long ago. And as Kanu had said, it was locked with a chain and padlock, with more than enough of a gap to get through for an average-sized person.

Tommy probably couldn't squeeze through this thing, he thought with a smirk.

Sean gave one last look around the street and ducked under the chain, slipping easily through the space.

On the other side, he found mountains of crushed cars, parts of machinery he didn't recognize, and components that must have come from some of the old factories around the area. Like the street he'd just left, the junkyard was abandoned, devoid of any activity. He half wondered if the area was contaminated. It was an eerie thing to consider.

Sean had heard of places where chemical spills rendered large portions of cities completely uninhabitable. Most of those stories came from Third World countries much like Somalia. But nothing in the dossier said anything about that, so he chose to believe things were desolate because of the warlords and the floundering economy.

After he reconnoitered the space within seconds of stepping through the fence, Sean darted to the right, keeping low until he reached the first pile of junk. Dead ahead, the fence came to an abrupt halt and was replaced by a concrete block wall. According to the map he'd memorized, the warehouse would be at the other end of that wall, just beyond the far corner.

He sprinted from one junk pile to another until he was only fifty feet away from the corner. The wall was only nine feet high, but he'd need to use something to get over it. That part wouldn't be the problem. He found a beaten-up ice chest in the pile next to him and carried it over to the wall. It would give him just enough of a boost to reach the upper edge.

Standing next to the concrete barricade, the real issue vocalized itself quite literally.

He could hear men barking out orders on the other side. Engines running on propane—likely forklifts—were zooming back and forth. Once on top of the wall, he'd be a sitting duck.

There had to be a better way in.

Sean went through the overhead view of the warehouse grounds in his mind. The corner where he'd considered going in should have been the best option. But that was based on the notion that the place was not in use, which it clearly was. And—no doubt—the men on the other side were armed and ready to kill on sight.

The wall extended away from the corner in the other direction, but that would lead to the warehouse entrance. A direct entry wouldn't be any good. Even if he made it beyond the first set of guards, the alarm would be raised, and he'd end up either dead or captured.

He stepped back to the junk pile and into the meager shade it provided. From the second Sean stepped out of the SUV, the sun had started baking him. While his black outfit would help him look more like someone not to be messed with, it was a terrible choice for the blistering Somali heat. Then an idea struck.

He'd been thinking about things too linearly. The odd layout of the walls came to a sort of X at the corners, which was where he planned to go in. But if he scaled the junkyard wall away from the corner and traversed the lip to the other wall, he could switch over and traverse to a point where there was less activity. It would be extremely difficult. It was, however, his best option.

Sean grabbed the ice chest and hauled it five yards away from the corner. He stepped up on the wobbly metal cooler and—after steadying his balance—made the short jump up. His fingers grabbed the edge, and within a second he'd pulled himself up to the top. In a single motion, Sean swung his legs over the other side, and he let himself hang from the wall. He was only a foot off the ground, but if he fell, getting back up would be a tough trick.

In an instant, he saw the small area in which he hung was a vacant lot, surrounded by the warehouse wall, the junkyard wall, and the fence that extended between the two.

So yeah, if I fall here, I may not get back out. Not without a lot of cuts from that barbed wire.

He was only going to get one shot. His fingers gripped the gritty concrete surface. He planted his toes against the wall and started sliding to the right. The corner was close yet so far, and he didn't hear any indication that he'd been spotted. He shuffled one hand to the right and then the next, using his feet to help redistribute the weight.

In the corner, his forearms were already burning, and he had to make a tricky transition. Sean let go with his right hand and quickly moved it over to the other wall. His fingers grasped the edge, and he started to let go with his left, but suddenly his right-hand fingers slipped on some debris. A surge of panic shot through his body as he felt the ledge slide out of his grip.

Instinctively, he squeezed as hard as he could with his left hand. His torso swung against the first wall, and for a moment he was hanging with one hand. He felt his back muscles on the left side straining. His fingers rapidly lost strength. To compensate, he fired his right hand back up and grabbed the first ledge again.

Now the fingertips on his right hand stung, and he noticed a few specks of red on the gray block.

That's gonna hurt for a few days.

Sean winced and inched closer to the corner to make the transition easier. He shifted his weight and reached over again. This time, he ran his hand across the top to make sure any grit was removed before putting his faith in the ledge.

The muscles in his forearms were nearly exhausted. He'd have to move fast or risk being trapped. He grabbed the next ledge and quickly brought his left hand over. His right foot slipped on the first try, but then he got a toehold on a seam between the blocks. He resumed shuffling five inches at a time, making the same painful movement over and over again.

It took every ounce of focus and discipline Sean could muster, and after three minutes of the grueling exercise he was a good thirty feet away from the corner and nearing the warehouse wall. He had nothing left in the tank save enough for one last pull over the wall.

He dug deep and hauled his legs up to the ledge. Luckily, he discovered the top of the wall ran along behind the warehouse wall. He hurried to the shaded spot and sat on the lip, allowing his legs to dangle over the side. The hiding place gave him somewhere he could stay out of sight long enough to recover.

Sean's fingers barely worked at first. The effort of holding up his body for so long had strained the muscles and tendons to their limit. He kept flexing them until the feeling started to come back, which took several minutes. His breathing returned to normal much faster. When he could work his fingers normally again, he rechecked to make sure his pistol was tucked firmly in its holster. Then he checked the homing beacons in his pocket.

They were still in place.

He'd put them in a little case to keep them from jostling around or falling out of his pocket. Given the ridiculous maneuvers he'd just executed, that idea had been on point.

Break's over, he thought.

He shifted his weight and stood up, pressing his torso into the warehouse exterior wall. Next he shuffled along the ledge until he reached the corner and cautiously peeked around.

That's not so bad.

Sean counted twenty men with assault rifles plus fifteen workers rushing around on foot and in forklifts. And there—about ninety feet away—were six crates, the same ones he'd seen in Tanzania.

They were being loaded onto more transport trucks. And unless Sean missed his guess, they were likely heading to another plane.

One of the strongest points Sean had as an agent was his uncanny ability to work through tough situations and reach a solution in a short amount of time.

Now that skill was being put to the test. He was far outnumbered. No matter how good he was with his pistol, by the time he'd taken out the first few guys, the others would rally and mow him down like it was the Saint Valentine's Day Massacre.

He needed to distract the men in the warehouse long enough to slip the beacons into three crates.

The thought occurred to him to shoot one of the men nearby. He wouldn't have to kill the guy, just hit him. Everyone in the courtyard would rush to see what happened and immediately be put on full alert. They'd comb the premises to find the shooter. More than likely, they'd fan out to work more efficiently. The problem with that was that the crowd would gather close to his position, cutting off his way into the warehouse and cornering him with no way to escape.

No good. Too risky.

He sighed and examined his surroundings. Nothing helpful. Or was there?

A sturdy drain pipe ran up the exterior wall to the roof about ten feet above. Sean shuffled over to it, careful to keep his weight leaning in. He ran his hand around the rusted metal and found just enough of a gap between it and the wall where he could wedge his fingers.

If his memory served correctly—and it usually did—there were some holes in the warehouse roof, probably a result of a lack of maintenance over the years. If he could get to one of those spaces, there could be a way in. That or it would be a huge waste of time.

And time was running out.

30

Mogadishu

A stupid tune ran through the back of Sean's mind as he climbed the drain pipe. As he put one hand over the other, the nursery rhyme he'd learned as a child danced in his ears.

The itsy-bitsy spider went up the waterspout.

He'd never liked that song. Things didn't end so well for that arachnid. And he liked it even less considering he was the spider climbing the waterspout.

The burning in his forearms returned much more quickly than before, but before the muscles reached a critical level he hoisted his legs over the edge and onto the roof.

Sean rested for a moment with his back on the hot roof before rolling onto the balls of his feet. When he did, a sudden and terrifying realization hit him. He was fairly high off the ground, and the roof pitch rose gradually until it reached the top.

He swallowed and stared up at the corrugated surface. The roof had seen better times—like forty years ago. To say it looked unstable was a massive understatement. Throw on top of it Sean's irrational fear of heights, and his original idea got more appealing by the second.

"No," he said quietly. "You have to push through this."

His fear of heights was something Sean had fought his entire life. He wasn't sure where it came from, though while he was in college his mother told him a story about pushing him out of a swing when he three years old.

Whether the phobia came from that traumatic childhood moment or not, he would never know. What he did know was that anytime he stood in a place more than twenty-five feet high his balance wavered and everything felt less safe. It wasn't just for him. If he noticed someone standing close to a ledge, he worried incessantly that they would fall, and found it nearly impossible to relax.

Standing on the warehouse rooftop, all those issues came to a head. He crouched low to keep a lower center of gravity and started moving toward where the roofing came to a point high above the warehouse floor.

After only a few steps he got down on his hands and bear-crawled forward until he reached a point where one of the ceiling panels had fallen in. He stopped and lowered down until he was lying on his chest. He eased himself a few inches forward and peered down through the gap.

Seven trucks were parked side by side in the warehouse. The final two had tailgates down, being loaded by the workers.

Directly below him—about ten feet down—a rickety catwalk stretched across from one side of the warehouse to the other. It connected in the middle with another walkway running down the center. Off to the side, the catwalk was attached to a set of stairs that led to a lower walkway and another staircase to the floor.

That would be his best bet to get down to the trucks. And there were fewer men inside the warehouse than out. He counted six with guns and four workers. Definitely more manageable numbers. Still not good, but it was something he could work with. Especially if he could get the drop on them.

Unfortunately, drop was the operative word.

To make it work, he would have to hang from the ceiling and let himself drop to the catwalk below. This presented a few new problems.

If he missed the catwalk, he'd obviously die. Best-case scenario: He'd survive the fall to the floor below with a broken neck and pretty much every other bone in his body. Then there was the possibility that he could stick the landing on the elevated walkway. If he did and it wasn't stable—which was the prevailing appearance—his weight could rip it from the housings, and the whole thing would drop to the floor, bringing him back to broken neck and other bones or dying. Probably both.

Of course, he could make it to the catwalk unnoticed, sneak down to the bottom, take out the men, plant the homing devices, and escape unharmed.

Facing the three scenarios, that last one was—at best—33 percent likely to happen.

Sean didn't like the odds, but he had no choice. There was no other way in that gave him a better chance of success.

He drew in a long breath and shook his head. Another hard swallow coursed through his throat.

"Become a government agent," he said to himself. "That will be exciting. And you'll make a difference in the world."

I need to stop listening to that voice.

Sean took a few more quick breaths to build up his courage and then swung around so he was sitting on his butt.

"Okay. Now or never, Sean. Just don't look past the catwalk, and you'll be fine."

He gave a quick nod as if to confirm his decision and then pushed backward, placing his hands on the edge of the roof where the tile had ripped free. It wasn't a very good place to grip, and he'd only be able to hold it for a second.

Have to do it fast, he thought.

Two more breaths. Then he pressed his palms into the roof, lifting his body over them. He hovered for a moment and then extended his legs out over the opening and started lowering them. As his bodyweight got heavier, his fingers started to slip on the roof surface. He squeezed harder to make sure he got his feet as close to the catwalk as possible before letting go. He looked down to make sure they were lined up and then released his grasp.

The drop wasn't far, but it felt like it lasted ten seconds. When his fingers let go, his body's momentum kicked forward ever so slightly, causing his feet to go out from under him. He struck the grated metal walkway with his tailbone, and the entire structure shuddered.

The first thought that ran through his mind after the incredible pain from his butt was that his fate would be option two, the catwalk falling to the floor.

He winced as the walkway shook and wiggled. Then the vibrations slowed until it was still again.

Fighting off the pain, Sean rolled onto his side and looked down at the floor. None of the men below had noticed a thing. With all the noise of the trucks, forklifts, and people shouting orders, his loud landing was lost in the chaos.

He struggled to his feet and grabbed onto the railing. The floor below might as well have been a mile away. His tailbone radiated a horrible, throbbing pain, up through his spine and down through his legs. The agonizing sensation actually tore Sean's concerns away from his fear of heights momentarily. He held the pouch as he limped forward toward the wall. His eyes remained on the men below until he arrived at the adjacent catwalk.

His next concern was anyone who might be sitting in the truck cabs. From his vantage point, he couldn't see anyone, but that didn't mean much. The near angle cut off part of the truck's interior, so getting a view beyond the dashboard was difficult.

For the time being, he was safe. Down on the lower grate could be a different story.

He kept moving toward the closest staircase. With every step, the pain in his lower back dissipated until by the time he reached the stairs it was gone. He drew the pistol from its holster and kept it close to his shoulder, ready to aim and fire should the need arise.

As he descended the steps, he kept an eye on the men with the assault rifles. On the lower landing, he found a stack of old boxes just under the stairs and took temporary refuge behind them. He stayed low and crawled to where he could peek around one of the boxes and get a better view of the trucks.

Just as he'd hoped. They were empty. The drivers must have been running double duty, loading and delivering.

Guess they've never heard of a union.

The gunman at the corner of the closest truck twitched and looked back over his shoulder. Something had gotten his attention.

Sean ducked back behind the boxes and evened his breathing. He pivoted around and crept back to the other side of the stack and looked around. The guard was bending over, examining something on the floor. He stood up and held a rusty bolt into the light. His head cocked to the side for a moment before he tossed the piece of scrap out of the way. He returned to his station and continued keeping watch, his head turning one direction and then the other.

A forklift appeared through the main entrance, apparently in a hurry. One of the wooden crates burdened the front loader. Suddenly—out of nowhere— one of the other forklifts appeared on the other side of the last truck in line and nearly cut off the other machine. The driver with the crate brought the forklift to a panicked stop, and one end of the crate slid off the left fork. It hit the ground with a thud.

Everyone in the building, including Sean, grimaced for a second. It must have been no secret what the missile warheads were carrying. The last thing any of the workers wanted to do was set off the device. If the explosion didn't kill them, the nerve gas would.

Nothing happened. Of course nothing happened. The weapon wasn't armed. Even so, dropping it or jostling it too much was probably a bad idea.

While the gunmen and workers scurried over to the fallen wooden box, Sean tiptoed over to the next set of stairs and made his way to the floor.

The two drivers were yelling at each other in what Sean assumed to be obscenities. He couldn't understand the language they were using. Not that it mattered. His job wasn't to translate angry terrorist speak.

He ran behind a pair of fifty-gallon steel barrels and ducked down for a moment. Then he sprinted to the farthest truck in the line and ran around the front to the driver's side.

Before he could stop, his shoulder barged into someone standing next to the wheel.

Sean staggered back for a moment and then looked up at the mammoth he'd run into.

The man was smoking a cigarette and turned around slowly. His dark, hollow eyes glared down at Sean like he was nothing more than a fly buzzing around a bull.

The man was close to seven feet tall. His rippling muscles bulged out of the tight V-neck shirt he wore. Sean raised his weapon to shoot, but the giant knocked it away with a sweep of his hand.

Sean watched his gun hit the floor and slide until it stopped next to a plastic barrel.

He turned his attention back to the truck driver just in time. The man reached out with both hands to grab the American. Sean ducked out of the way and rolled to the side. The move saved him from being crushed, but it also put the driver between him and his gun—a fact that the giant didn't seem to consider.

The big man lurched forward with fists raised. He fired a jab. Sean parried it to the side and then a second, but blocking the heavy-fisted punches was no easy task. The giant leaned back, and Sean knew what was coming next.

A gargantuan boot swung his way, and he turned to the side and tried to jump clear. He almost succeeded, but the big man's heel struck Sean in the ribs with enough force to send him flying six feet.

There was no time to pay attention to the stabbing pain coming from his ribs. Sean rolled to his feet again and prepared for the next attack.

The huge driver stalked to his prey, again taking a stance like an old-school boxer. Sean knew if he kept playing defense, the giant would eventually break him down, and then it would be over.

Another jab shot by his face, then again. Sean ducked and weaved, swiped his hands at the man's wrists as the punches missed. Then the driver faked a jab and swung a roundhouse.

Sean realized too late he'd overcommitted his defenses. All he could do was turn his head as the huge fist struck between his cheek and jaw.

It hit with brutal force and sent the American reeling backward. The warehouse started to nosedive in Sean's vision. He squinted and reached out his hands to grab onto something, anything, that would help him stay on his feet. If the big man pinned him to the ground, he'd be a goner.

His fingers wrapped around something against the wall, and Sean realized what it was.

An axe.

The giant lumbered at him and raised his right fist like a hammer about to squash a bug.

Sean squeezed the axe handle and lifted it from the hooks holding it to the wall. He sidestepped the big man's hammer punch and raised the axe over his head. With no time to spare, he aimed for the man's side and swung as hard as he could.

The blade whipped through the air in a dramatic arch and stopped suddenly as it struck. But it hadn't struck the target.

The giant had seen Sean's move and blocked the blow with his hand, grabbing the shaft of the axe below the base only a split second before it delivered a mortal blow. The big man's thick fingers squeezed, and he easily jerked the weapon free from Sean's grip.

Sean took a step back. His eyes darted left and right, scouring his surroundings for another weapon. There was nothing. Then he remembered his pistol. He was between the driver and the firearm.

He turned and took off toward the weapon. It was twenty feet away, but it may as well have been a hundred yards. Just two yards from the gun, Sean started to dive for it, but he heard a loud grunt and glanced over his shoulder in time to see the giant throw the axe.

The blade zipped through the air—end over end—at Sean's head. He flipped over onto his side, the sharp metal edge missing his neck by less than an inch.

The good news was that he'd dodged the axe. The bad news was the heavy weapon hit his gun and knocked it over to the wall and far out of reach.

Sean was going to have to win this fight fair and square.

He stood up and rolled his shoulders. *Never show fear.*

The giant grinned and stepped at him again with the same boxing-style attack he'd used before. Sean knew one thing before the big man threw his first punch: no way he'd expect a quick counter.

Bullies liked to rely on intimidation. They used their size as a way to strike fear in their opponents. That fear caused bad decisions. Bad decisions led to pain.

Sean had already made a few of those, and the pain was evident. Time to fix that.

The giant fired out a jab, but this time Sean twisted his body, grabbed the big man's wrist, and yanked him forward. The driver was thrown off balance and stumbled, leaning over at the waist. Sean continued his spinning motion, swinging his right leg around to give momentum, and jumped. He twisted in midair and hovered for a second over the giant.

The big man had recovered and started to raise up, but Sean dropped down onto his back and hammered down with his fist as hard as he could—striking the man at the base of the skull.

A gasp escaped the driver's mouth, and his body twitched. Sean wrapped his legs around the man's torso and his left forearm around the neck, squeezing with all of his might. His opponent wobbled, the effects from the first strike causing him to nearly lose consciousness.

Sean didn't give him a chance to recover. He clenched his fist and pounded the same spot on the back of the giant's head again. The massive body weakened further and dropped to one knee. The man braced his fall with his hands. One more time, Sean mustered all his strength and raised his fist high. He leaned back to get all the power he could behind it and drove his knuckles into the man's head.

Instantly, the body went limp and dropped to the floor, trapping Sean's feet beneath the heavy torso.

He wrested his left hand free from the giant's throat and then wiggled one foot loose, then the other. His breath came in quick gasps, and for the first time since his battle began he realized how exhausting the fight had been. He spotted his weapon over by the wall, but his first order of business was making sure no one had seen what was going on.

The entire struggle had happened behind the farthest truck in the line, away from where the forklift incident occurred.

Sean scrambled to his feet and rushed over to the back of the truck. He leaned around the tailgate and saw the men had just secured the wooden crate and were resuming their normal activities.

He ducked back behind the side of the truck and lifted the canvas top—snapping one of the buttons that held it in place. He reached up, grabbed the side, and hauled himself into the back.

The cargo area was dark, but enough light snuck through the cracks to let him see what he was doing. The crates were nailed shut.

He would have killed for a crowbar, but after a quick look around realized the truck was without one. Unless it was in the cabin. He didn't have time to look.

The long crates were stacked two high and in three rows. He climbed on top of the closest one and wiggled the end of the lid. To his surprise, it wasn't sealed as tightly as he suspected. With a slight tug, he opened the lid wide enough to get one of the homing beacons inside. Sean opened the cargo pocket on his pants and pulled out the little container. He removed one of the devices, pressed the button, and slid it into the crate.

After mashing the lid down with his weight, he moved to the next one. It took considerably more effort but he eventually managed to get a wide enough opening for another beacon. Again, he activated the signal and put it in the wooden box.

Then he heard men's voices outside the truck. They were getting closer.

Sean was trapped in the back. If someone looked in the cargo area the mission would be compromised. The same could be said if someone saw the unconscious giant lying outside the truck's cab.

He needed to move the body but wasn't sure if he could manage it. On top of that, if that guy was the driver, who was going to drive this truck?

Sean was starting to realize he hadn't fully thought things through.

Sean had to act fast. He still had one beacon left, but by the time he got the last crate open he worried the men outside might already be all around.

Another gut-wrenching thought occurred to him. What if he was putting all his eggs in one basket? By placing the homing devices in crates in the same truck, he was taking a big risk. If something happened to this truck en route to wherever the missiles were going, the rest would be lost, as would the mastermind behind everything.

The voices grew louder, drawing ever closer.

No time to change course now, he thought. Two beacons would have to do the trick.

He climbed back out of the truck and ran around to the front. No time to move the giant's body. Sean stayed in front of the truck's hood and waited, watching as three men appeared around the back and kept walking, heading toward a door in the corner. One of them was tapping a pack of cigarettes while another had already fitted one in his mouth, preparing to smoke.

Taking a smoke break?

Sean wondered why they didn't just smoke in the warehouse, and then he remembered the missiles. They must have been paranoid about setting off the warheads.

These guys really don't know anything about what they're moving.

As soon as the door closed behind the three smokers, Sean dashed out of his hiding place and over to the big man on the ground. He grabbed him by the wrists and grunted.

The dead weight was easily over three hundred pounds, but it felt like a ton. Dragging went slowly. At one point, Sean considered rolling him. But he didn't need to get him far. Another stack of boxes was close by.

Once the body was near enough to the boxes, Sean stopped moving him and started stacking them in front. Relocating the empty cardboard proved much easier than dragging the huge man. By this point, Sean believed the guy was dead. There were no signs of life, and the man's skin was starting to get a little cold in spite of the heat inside the warehouse.

Sean's outfit was soaked in sweat. His mouth felt like he'd eaten a pile of chalk.

He'd just finished hiding the big body when the side door opened again and the three men returned. Instinctively, he ducked down behind the boxes next to the prostrate corpse.

One of the men split off from the other two and walked straight toward Sean's position. Sean looked over to his right and noticed his pistol lying against the wall less than ten feet away. His head snapped back to the left. He watched the man continue walking his way. Sean readied himself to dive for the pistol if he had to. It would be a last resort. At least that's what he told himself.

The guy stopped next to the driver's side door. He never bothered to look around for anything suspicious. Instead, he simply opened the door and started the truck's motor.

So that's the driver.

Sean glanced down at the body next to him, wondering who he was. Not that it mattered. As long as he wasn't driving the truck with the beacons, the mission still had a chance to succeed.

The truck backed out of its spot and wheeled around behind the others. Soon, all the engines rumbled to life, and the warehouse filled with diesel fumes. Sean waited patiently until the convoy and all its escorts were gone before he left his hiding place.

Moments before, the building had been a beehive of activity. Now it was like a tomb.

He spun around and ran over to where his pistol still lay on the ground. After picking it up, he gave it a quick once-over while trotting over to the building's mouth.

At the main entrance, Sean stayed close to the wall and looked around the corner. The last of the workers' pickup trucks disappeared around the concrete wall, leaving the entire lot empty.

They sure left in a hurry.

Sean started to have second thoughts about the mission. What if they'd been wrong? What if each truck was going to a separate location? It was possible.

He reassured himself that even if the latter were true, he and his comrades could at least track that shipment. From there, they could get more intel from someone at that site.

People had a bad habit of talking too much, especially when inflicted with intense pain.

He shook off the idea. Whoever was shipping all those missiles was planning something big. Sean didn't know what it was. Based on the number of missiles, he guessed someone was planning a sort of military strike. That meant it would be tactical, localized, centered on one or just a few select targets.

Sean jogged out to the street and looked both ways. It was just as empty as the warehouse property. He heard someone scream in the distance but couldn't pinpoint the sound's point of origin. It was one of the many random, bloodcurdling sounds in a town with a penchant for atrocity. The less time Sean spent there, the better.

He picked up his pace and made a left at the next intersection, ran to the next block, and then cut to the left again. He found Kanu smoking a cigarette, sitting a few parking spaces ahead of where he'd been before.

The Somali saw Sean approaching and started the SUV. He flicked his smoking cigarette onto the ground then reached over to the passenger door and flung it open. Sean hopped in, and before his butt hit the seat Kanu punched the gas and sped away. The door slammed shut from the force. As he made the first turn, Sean nearly toppled over onto him. Fortunately, he'd grabbed the handle over the door and managed to stay in the passenger seat.

"Something wrong?" Sean asked.

Kanu didn't reply immediately, which caused Sean to think the answer was yes. Once they were out of the city and back on the bumpy dirt road, he slowed down a tad.

"It's best if we don't hang around too long. Did you do what you came to do?"

Sean finally got his breathing back to normal. "Yeah. Taken care of. Was a little harder than I expected."

"I don't need details about it."

This guy sucks at chitchat.

"Right. So yeah, done deal. I guess we'll head back to the beach then?"

"Yes," Kanu said with a nod. "I will take you back to where you left your boat. Then we will part ways."

Sean pressed his lips tight together before he spoke. "Okay then. Sounds good. I appreciate the help."

The rest of the journey was made in silence except for the rumbling of the tires and the occasional flicking sound Kanu's lighter made when he lit a cigarette. The man was visibly on edge, though Sean wasn't sure what had him so nervous.

The yellow sun faded to orange as it neared the silhouette of the horizon to the west. Out to the east, Sean could see the abysmal darkness of night merging with the ocean beneath. Occasional whitecaps broke the deep blue surface.

They passed through a fishing village—the same one they'd seen before. It was little more than seven or eight buildings lining both sides of the road. A few more were farther off to the side, toward the coast. Some decorative lights hung under one of the roofs and wrapped around the building. Such decoration was common for places that served alcohol, so Sean immediately assumed it was a bar.

They drove another ten minutes before Kanu pulled off the road and stopped the SUV in the clearing where they'd met earlier in the day.

"Thanks for your help," Sean said. "I appreciate it."

"You are most welcome. I suggest you get back to your boat as quickly as possible. Strange things happen at night. It's not a good idea to be out."

Sean thanked him for the cryptic advice and grabbed his stuff. He stayed low as he crept back through the bushes toward the beach and his fishing dinghy. There was still enough light that he didn't need his flashlight, but that would change soon if he didn't hurry.

And then there was the issue of guiding the fishing boat out into the sea again. He'd rather not do that in the darkness. The yacht would have plenty of lights on. But if the current took him too far off course, he'd never be able to spot it. It was yet another part of this whole plan they'd not fully thought through.

He heard the SUV spin out on the rocky soil as Kanu drove away. Sean barely looked back over his shoulder. His focus was on getting back to the yacht.

The tide had come in while Sean was in Mogadishu. He knew it would and had taken the chance of leaving his little boat on the edge of the water anyway. It wasn't like he had a choice. Now, as dusk turned to night, the tide would be near its lowest point.

He arrived at the edge of the bushes where the grassy dunes turned to white sand. He closed his eyes for a brief second and said a little prayer that the dinghy was where he left it.

Sean stepped out of the shrubbery and scanned the beach. The boat wasn't where he dropped anchor. But it hadn't gone far. It had drifted fifty yards to the south, a little farther on the beach than he'd intended. He wasn't going to complain. Sean was just relieved the thing was there.

He hurried across the sand to the boat and tossed his stuff inside. Then he removed his sweat-infused shirt and threw it in as well. The cool evening breeze wafted over him. Before he started hauling the boat back into the water, Sean waded out until he was knee deep and then fell back into the foamy waves. A couple of seconds later the next wave crashed over him. The cool water felt amazing as it washed over his body. He'd been so hot and sweaty all day; it was the next best thing to a cool glass of sweet iced tea on a blazing July afternoon.

Sean felt the sand under his feet as the water pulled at his body to carry him out to sea. *Break's over.*

He didn't have time to waste, but washing off had only taken thirty seconds. He sloshed back over to the boat and grabbed the rope with the kettle bell on the end. Lifting the heavy weight with both hands, he carried it out into the water until the rope went taut.

The boat lurched forward a few inches.

Sean tugged with the weight again, pushing it ahead. Once more the dinghy crept its way toward open water. It took an exhausting five minutes of labor until the boat was finally tossing in the water, free of the land beneath. Sean reached back and pulled on the starter cord.

Nothing happened.

He yanked on the cord again and got the same result.

"Come on."

He repeated the process over and over, but the engine never even turned over. There wasn't even a sniff of it starting.

He spun around on the bench and opened the gas cap. Still plenty of gas inside. A terrible thought occurred to him. If the motor wouldn't start, he'd be stranded.

In Somalia.

Not good.

Sean glanced down at the oars in the boat's bottom. *You gotta be kidding me.*

"Why isn't this thing sparking?" he said out loud.

Then he remembered. He'd pulled the spark plug wire out of the plug. His own sabotage had slowed him down.

"Idiot," he murmured as he plugged the wire back into the threaded cap.

He pulled the cord again, and the motor sputtered a few times before catching its rhythm. No doubt he'd flooded it in his ridiculous attempts to get the thing running with no juice. Fortunately, that didn't keep it from working.

The boat started to ease away from shore, and soon he was out in the open ocean. The little craft rose and fell with the swells as it had done on the way in to shore. He steered the rudder carefully with one hand, holding a compass with the other to keep his line as straight as possible.

Minutes turned into an hour. The shore turned into a distant line on the horizon, and the black sky above sparkled in a billion places with the icy diamonds of the stars. It wasn't often Sean got to see the creamy residue of the Milky Way. He lived in places that had too much light pollution. Out here, though, the only light was coming from the heavens.

Well, the heavens and a luxury yacht about four hundred yards off the port bow.

"That's a sight for sore eyes," he said.

Sean adjusted the rudder to line up with the bigger boat. It took another fifteen minutes to cover the distance. When he was close to thirty yards from the yacht, he throttled down to slow his approach. He realized something he'd suspected before. The interior lights of the ship were doused, making it impossible to see inside.

That would have made sense if Emily and Fitz were trying to keep the thing invisible. But why would they leave all the exterior lights on if that was their plan?

Sean narrowed his eyes as he drew closer. He thought he saw some movement through one of the tinted windows, but it may have just been his imagination. Then again, he should expect movement. It was doubtful his friends were inside the ship trying to sit perfectly still.

A sudden flash from the rear deck sent him diving to the floor. Immediately a thunderous boom rolled across the waves and the little boat.

Who was shooting at him? Did Emily not see it was him?

He started to rise up from the boat again, but the weapon fired a second time. He dove clear again, but the bullet struck the motor squarely in the side. Seconds later, smoke poured out of it. It took less than twenty seconds for the thing to lock up and shut down.

"What the?" Sean whispered. "Why are they shooting at me?"

For a brief second, he caught a glimpse of the man holding a weapon near the back of the boat. If he'd wanted to, the guy could have cut Sean down on the first shot. If he was accurate enough to hit the motor like that, a human target would be easy.

That meant whoever was on board the yacht wanted him alive.

He pushed away concern for Emily and Fitz and rummaged through the sack he'd taken ashore.

The yacht's engines roared to life, and the larger boat started to come about. They'd be on him in seconds.

His initial thought was to grab his gun and the two spare mags. In the tight quarters of the yacht, it would be too easy to hit a friendly. So he grabbed something else.

The yacht drew closer.

Sean punched in a few numbers on his SAT phone and slid it back into the sack. He wrapped his sweaty shirt around it just in case.

He sat back on the bench and put his hands up. Even though he couldn't see the guns pointed at him, he could feel them.

The yacht's gears shifted, and the vessel slowed until it came to a crawl next to Sean's dinghy. A man appeared on the deck with a submachine gun slung over his shoulder. For some reason, he was wearing sunglasses. Another man stepped out from behind him wearing a light gray sport jacket and matching slacks. His white button-up shirt had the top three buttons undone, showing off his tanned chest.

Hard to tell in the dark, but he looked like he was from the Middle East, as did the other guy.

"I'm surprised you're not trying to shoot your way out of this," he said in a heavy accent.

Sean couldn't place it, but he was definitely from the Middle East.

"Mama didn't raise no fool," Sean answered. "Your boy in the back is a crack shot. I figure he'd take me out before I even got the gun to my hip."

Suit folded his hands in front of his waist and nodded. "True. And wise of you to not test him."

Sean's first thought—when the initial shot was fired—was that pirates had taken their boat. Those types scoured the seas around the Somali coastline, wreaking havoc on smaller trade vessels or the occasional tourists who'd gone astray. Now he could see these guys were not pirates. Or if they were, they weren't like any pirates he'd ever heard of or seen.

"So what am I supposed to do here?" Sean asked. "I'm assuming since you didn't shoot me you don't want me dead. Not yet at least. Should I tie up this boat and come aboard?"

Suit grinned like the devil and moved his head back and forth. "Very good, Sean. You will tie to the back and come aboard. If you do anything foolish, we kill your friends. They're being held by two of my best men inside the cabin. So I recommend you do as I say."

"I *was* doing what you said before you said anything." Sean thought the line was clever, but he could see it was lost on his captor. "I hope you didn't do anything stupid like hurt them. Because if you did, that's not gonna work out so well for you. Whoever you are."

Suit responded first with an icy stare that could have cooled even the dismal Somali heat. "Your friends are fine. We wouldn't want my employer's prizes to be damaged before the show."

The show? Prizes? This guy was a little overdramatic. Especially in that suit.

"I don't suppose you're going to tell me what all this is about, are you?"

"In time," Suit said. "All in good time."

32
Cairo

The yacht made its way to a port just outside of Mombasa. From there, the prisoners were transferred to black SUVs and taken to a small airport where a private jet awaited.

Sean had been impressed by the interior of the plane. Creamy leather and light wood appointments were everywhere. He hid his admiration easily enough, since it might be his last flight in this lifetime.

When the captives were seated and secured in place, the men with the guns took their places, one opposite each American. Suit hung around in the back near a bar that only featured water, juice, tea, and coffee.

"Don't suppose I could ask for a whiskey," Fitz joked.

The gunmen said nothing. And they still wore their sunglasses.

"How do you guys see with those things on?" he prodded. "I mean, it's dark outside for crying out loud."

"I hope you're not going to be like this the entire flight to Cairo," Suit said.

"Cairo?" Sean chimed in with an unusually loud voice. "What's in Cairo?"

"A grand surprise," Suit answered. "Now I suggest you three get some rest. We will be there in around four hours. This will be your best chance to sleep."

Sleep? How are we going to sleep? Sean wondered.

Emily had remained unusually quiet, but he could see the gears spinning in her head.

"You okay?" Sean whispered to her across the aisle.

"Yeah." She gave a nod that was as curt as her answer.

"Mad that they got the drop on you?"

"A little."

Sean knew it. He'd be ticked at himself, too.

"Don't beat yourself up over it. We'll be dead soon."

She frowned and looked at him like he was crazy. He returned the look with a stupid grin that may well have confirmed his insanity.

"What is wrong with you? You do realize they really are going to kill us, right?"

"Yep." He rocked back and forth in the seat. "Or we're going to kill them. Either way, this is going to end badly for someone."

"Well, if you ask me, it's going to be us."

The conversation had ended there, and no one said anything else during the flight. When the plane landed in Cairo, the prisoners were moved to the back of a white van and shoved onto the floor. All the doors were locked from the outside, and the tinted windows were covered by metal screens that gave Sean the impression this wasn't their first abduction.

The ride was less than comfortable and a major contrast to the luxurious seating of the private plane.

"Never been to Cairo," Sean said. "Always wanted to check it out."

"You realize you're going to die here, right?" Emily asked.

"You know, you could be a little more positive," Fitz interjected

"Yeah, Em...Agent Starks, look on the bright side."

"Which is...?"

Sean chuckled. "I don't know yet, but I'm sure there is one."

He stole a quick look out the nearest window. It was early morning and still dark outside.

"Looks like a nice area out there, though."

Emily leaned against the van's interior wall and put her head against the grating. "It's the Garden District. Wealthy elite live here."

"There you go," Fitz said. "We'll be killed in a nice place, which means probably not put in a dumpster."

She sneered at him but said nothing else.

Silence settled over the van for the next five minutes. Only the bumps in the road and the engine invaded the quiet space. Sean stole a glance at his bag stuffed between the driver and passenger seats. The men who'd taken the boat relieved him of it and did a rudimentary check of the contents.

He'd watched as they removed the gun and two magazines. Then he had a quick laugh at their expense as they started to remove the smelly shirt and then hurriedly put it back.

They'd returned the weapon and magazines to the bag as well, keeping it a safe distance from the American agent. Salvation was only three feet away, kept out of reach by a thin layer of grated black steel.

The van slowed suddenly and swerved to the left, tossing the occupants in the back to the other side. The driver straightened out the wheel and then drove down a long concrete driveway toward a white mansion.

The structure looked more like a huge compound. It towered over the other homes in the area and was easily twice the size in breadth and length. Palm trees lined both sides of the driveway, interspersed with monkey grass between.

When the van reached the end of the driveway and a six-car garage, he stopped the vehicle and got out. The guy in the passenger seat hopped out as well and hurried to open the side door. He leveled the weapon strapped to his shoulder, waving it menacingly at the three Americans. The driver stepped into view and ordered them to get out. His accent was thicker than Suit's and had a different sound to the letter "O."

"Speak of the devil," Sean said.

Suit appeared around the back of the van, stepping out of a white BMW sedan.

"Nice car," he added.

Suit didn't respond. He just motioned for the guards to take them into the building.

The Americans were ushered through the side door. Considering it was just an ancillary entryway, the opulence to the decor was incredible. Plaster lion heads popped out of the wall near the crown molding, jutting out every four feet or so. The tiled floor was made of white marble with the signature black ripples streaking through it.

Sean half expected to see a laundry room on the right with appliances made of pure gold. As he passed the door, he saw it was a closet for cleaning supplies.

The guards moved them quickly down the hall and up a flight of stairs next to a huge kitchen. When they reached the second floor, Sean thought they might stop there, but their journey upward continued until they reached the fourth level. They were then corralled through another door that led into a long corridor. Iron sconces lined the walls, casting artificial candlelight into the space to light the way.

The group passed two doors before turning right at the end of the hall. They walked into a room that was at least six hundred square feet—not little by any stretch.

There were three wooden chairs sitting next to each other in the middle of the floor. The simple seats all faced toward white double doors leading out onto a balcony that appeared to wrap around the entire level. A television hung from the wall between two sets of doors. A news anchor was rambling on about the U.S. economy and asking questions of a politician as to how he would make things better.

"Please, sit," Suit said, motioning to the three chairs.

The decorations in the room were sparse, to say the least. It was like the owner of the mansion had purposely kept the space just for such an occasion.

Emily and Sean did as told. Fitz hesitated.

"Mind if we watch ESPN instead? I mean, if you're going to keep us prisoner, the least you can do is—"

His sentence was cut off by Suit kicking him squarely in the back with the heel of his shoe.

Fitz grunted and collapsed to his knees. He grimaced while grabbing at the wounded area. "Jeez," he said between coughs. "Was just a legitimate question. Now I'm gonna be pissing blood for a week."

Suit motioned to two of his guards. The men pushed their weapons behind their backs and lifted the injured American to his feet, dragged him to the empty chair, and plopped him down.

Fitz winced again as his butt hit the seat, but he kept his balance.

"Not sure what all this is about," Sean said. "But we are American citizens. You're making a big mistake."

"Huge," Fitz grunted. His face had flushed red.

"So whatever it is you're planning, I'd suggest you let us go before we call the thunder down on this place."

A new voice entered the conversation. "And just what thunder are you planning on calling?" It was a smooth, even tone with just a hint of sinister spice.

All three Americans turned their heads to look in the direction the of the voice. In the far corner of the room, a figure with broad shoulders stood in the shadows. An orange tip from a cigar radiated for a moment and then dissipated. Smoke wafted out from near the figure's face.

A moment later the man stepped out. He wore a white suit with a black button-up shirt underneath, also unbuttoned at the top like his minion's.

Sean didn't know what to say in response to the question, which in and of itself was an achievement on the villain's part. It was a rare thing for Sean Wyatt to be speechless.

Emily spoke up after another lengthy silence. "Your friend here knows who we are," she motioned to Suit with a flick of her head. "That means you know who we work for and what we are capable of. If you kill us, they *will* come for you."

The man's roundish face appeared in the dim light coming from a single dome in the middle of the ceiling. His thin black eyebrows nearly came together over a thick, stubby nose. His brown eyes had dark bags under them and wrinkles stretching out from the corners.

"Of course we know who you are, Agent Starks. We know everything about you and your little operation. Although it was difficult to get information at first. My primary contact in Washington didn't seem to know anything about what you were doing. Fortunately, we had another source. How do you think we found your boat off the coast of Somalia?"

Emily had wondered about that. Only a few people knew they'd taken a yacht from Kenya to infiltrate Mogadishu. That meant Axis had a leak. Or there was another possibility.

She turned her head and faced Sean. "Looks like your friend has made some new acquaintances."

Sean clenched his eyebrows together. "What? Who? Tommy?" He shook his head as he scoffed at the insinuation. "He wouldn't."

Fitz interrupted their spat and asked their host, "Just exactly what are you planning here? Torturing us with nonstop CNN until we give you something you want? Because I gotta be honest, I'll break after five minutes. Maybe four."

"Always the sense of humor, Agent Fitzpatrick. No, we did not bring you here to torture you." He motioned to the television. "We want you to see events unfold that will change the course of history. From here, you will watch as our plan comes to fruition. You will see the reckoning take place, live."

"The reckoning?" Sean asked. "No offense; sounds kinda like a horror story based in New England."

The man in charge ignored him for the moment. "Ahmed?" he said to the guy in the gray suit. "Could you open the doors for our guests? It's a tad stuffy in here."

Sean sensed hints of Western culture in the man's verbiage. The way he worded things sounded like he'd possibly gone to school in America, maybe England.

Ahmed made quick work of the doors, and a cool morning breeze wafted in over the balcony. Cream-colored linen curtains fluttered in the gentle wind.

"That's better," the man in charge said. "I'm sorry. Where are my manners? I should have introduced myself."

"We know who you are," Emily said. "You're Omar Khalif. Billionaire. And you're supposed to be on our side."

He twisted his head to the right at an angle. "Side? Of course I'm on your side. I love America. This has nothing to do with you."

"Then why are you keeping us here?"

"Yeah," Sean piped in. "And what are you gonna do with all those missiles?"

"I already told you. The reckoning is upon us. Soon you will witness justice meted out upon the enemies of God's true people. And in a way, you'll have a front-row seat."

Fitz had semi-recovered from being kicked in the kidneys and sat up straight. "What do you mean...by all that?"

Khalif drew in a long breath through his nostrils and sighed with satisfaction. He stepped out onto the balcony and flicked the ash off his cigar before stepping back inside.

"I wasn't always a wealthy man," he began. "I was a poor boy, growing up on the streets of Cairo just a few miles from here. One day I met a man who took me in, taught me a righteous path, and saved me from a life of crime and poverty."

"Got a CliffsNotes version of this?" Sean asked.

Ahmed motioned to the guard nearest him. The man nodded and jammed the butt of his gun into Sean's upper back.

"Ah," Sean gasped and leaned over. He grimaced in pain and started rolling his shoulders to alleviate it. "That's gonna bruise."

"Talk to me when you're pissing blood on Monday," Fitz said.

"As I was saying," Khalif went on, "this man saved my life. In fact, he saved the lives of many young men like me who would have ended up on the streets. Then one day he and the entire academy where we lived was bombed and destroyed. All of my brothers died, as did my teacher."

Sean nodded as he straightened up. "Okay. That makes sense. You want revenge. I would too. But I'm pretty sure we didn't bomb your academy or whatever it was, although from the sound of it I'd be inclined to think you were running a terrorist training facility."

Khalif raised a finger in protest. "You would think that, Agent Wyatt. But that assumption couldn't be further from the truth. We were a peaceful group. We studied the scriptures and sought peaceful understanding of the universe and our world. You are correct, however, in your statement about the bombing. You three obviously didn't do it. And America didn't carry out the attack either."

Confused, Emily shook her head. "I don't understand. If you're not going to attack the United States with all that nerve gas, who are you going to..." She trailed off as the answer hit her square in the face.

The Americans' position was looking out to the northeast. Spatial intelligence was one of her assets, and she knew immediately why Khalif had put them where he had, facing that direction.

"You're going to attack Israel," she said bluntly.

Sean was a second behind her in putting the puzzle together. He twisted his head back and forth, first at Emily then at Khalif. "Israel bombed your little school?"

"Yes, Agents Starks and Wyatt. Israel was responsible for the attack. They were targeting a facility they believed was a radical Islamist installation. When the bombs hit, I alone survived. By Allah's blessing alone, I was not in the building. But I was close enough to see the fiery explosion incinerate everything, to see my brothers die in an instant. Now those responsible will pay."

"Ooooh," Sean said, elongating the word for effect. "Now I get it. So the Israelis killed your little group by accident, and now to make things right you're going to murder millions of innocent people who had nothing to do with it. Makes perfect sense."

Emily fired a warning glance at her partner as if to tell him not to push the guy's buttons.

"No one is innocent, Agent Wyatt. The Israelis took land that hadn't belonged to them for two millennia. I'm willing to overlook America's involvement in that little transaction. But now the time has come to remove them once again."

Sean's instincts were to stall, but he wasn't sure what good that would do. Even if he could manage some kind of superhero escape, kill the bad guys, and escape the mansion, he had no idea where the missiles were. And according to Khalif they were going to launch in six hours. High noon.

"I'm sorry," Sean said. "I guess I just have one more question. What's your end game with all this? I mean, are you trying to start a war, or what? You realize you will be hunted down, right? There's no way you get away with this." He said the words with conviction, partly to convince himself.

Khalif rolled his shoulders. "Perhaps. Though I suspect I *will* get away with it. After all, I am very wealthy. I have friends everywhere. Not that it matters. No one would suspect me. I am immune. Especially after I helped the Pakistani government locate a known terrorist within their borders. Now I have two countries in my debt.

"Of course, in the media I will denounce the horrific tragedy that has befallen Israel. I may even offer any assistance to locate the rogue terrorist group responsible. Ironically, it will be American missiles that deliver the deadly payload."

"Yeah, that much we already know." Fitz smarted off again, drawing Ahmed's ire. Lucky for the American, no more blows came his way.

Sean knew they'd stalled about as long as they could. He took a quick inventory of the room. Ahmed and Khalif plus six guards—two behind each prisoner. Eight on three plus six guns for the bad guys, probably seven—judging by the bulge sticking out of the side of Ahmed's jacket. Not good odds. One thing Sean had learned early on, however, was that inaction could get you killed just as easily as taking action.

The only question was what action to take. Whatever the answer, Sean needed it soon.

33

Cairo

"I'm afraid I'm going to have to leave you three here," Khalif said. "I have a very important diplomatic meeting in an hour, and I don't like to be late."

"So you're not going to oversee this whole thing?" Sean asked. "You kind of strike me as the micromanager type."

"No, Agent Wyatt. You see, I'm a planner. If you have a good plan, you don't have to supervise every little move. In this case, I will be meeting with high-ranking Egyptian officials. So even if—worst-case scenario—someone did try to connect me to the attacks, I have the perfect alibi."

"Sometimes things don't go according to plan."

Khalif shot him a wicked smile. "This one will."

A gun blast from the hallway shocked the room. The explosive sound seemed to come out of nowhere. Everyone—including the Americans—turned to see what had happened at the doorway. A thud on the floor signaled a body had dropped.

The sudden distraction was exactly what Sean had been waiting for. He spun out of his chair, lowered his shoulder like a linebacker, and plowed into the guard on the left. The shoulder dug into the man's abdomen. Sean pumped his legs hard until he felt the sudden stop of the man's back hitting the wall.

The jarring blow caused the guard to drop his weapon. Sean used the stunned moment to his advantage and in one move rose up, swinging his fist into the bottom of the opponent's jaw. Teeth broke, and the guard instantly lost consciousness. He slumped against the wall and slid to the floor. A few seconds later a fresh trickle of blood oozed from his lips.

Khalif watched the American's rapid attack in stunned awe. He wasn't silent long. "Kill him now," he ordered to the other guards.

More gunfire erupted from the other side of the doorway. Ahmed dove into the corner. A guard near Fitz was struck in the chest. Another near Emily took two rounds in the gut. The other three guards retreated to the balcony for cover between the doors.

In the chaos, Emily and Fitz dove to the floor, trying to stay clear of any stray shots.

The muzzle flashes popped loudly in quick succession as the shooter sprayed the room until the weapon clicked. For the first few seconds, the Americans could only see the pistol and the hands holding it.

When the remaining guards heard the attacker's weapon click, they stepped around the balcony doors and opened fire with their guns on full auto. The weapons filled the room with a repeating thunder. The doorframe and the wall around it shredded in seconds. Drywall exploded, wood splintered, and the light in the room flickered off as one of the rounds struck some wiring.

Emily and Fitz were still on the floor when the guards' magazines went dry. The two Americans glanced knowingly at each other. They bounced up and charged the two closest gunmen.

The guards hadn't expected that and were ill prepared.

Fitz went the brute-force route. Using his weight to his advantage, he replicated Sean's earlier tackle move and nailed his target in the chest. He drove the man back through the open door and out onto the balcony. The guard was smaller and lighter. For a panicked few seconds he swung his arms and kicked his legs. At the last moment, he tried desperately to slow his momentum by dragging his heels, but it wouldn't slow down the larger American's strength.

The guard's lower back hit the balcony railing. When Fitz felt his movement slow, he instantly pushed up and forklifted the guy up. The guard screamed as he toppled over the edge and tumbled head over heels to the ground below. His screams stopped suddenly as he hit the grass.

Emily jumped and twisted her body to the left. Her right foot whipped around at her target's head. His cheekbone cracked as the top of her foot struck. He let out a sort of yelp and stumbled backward. She landed on her toes, spun around, and kicked out with her left foot. The heel landed just below his ribcage, and the guard instantly doubled over with a grunt.

She saw the third guard nearest the wall out of the corner of her eye. He was panicking in an effort to reload his weapon.

"Fitz!" she yelled out.

Fitz turned around at the balcony just in time to see Emily snap-kick her opponent in the face. The guard flew back a few feet and into Fitz's arms. In a single fluid movement, the big American grabbed the guy under his armpits and used his momentum to hurl him over the railing. His scream was less pronounced than the previous guard's, probably due to Emily kicking him repeatedly.

She switched her attention to the last guard.

Inside the room, Ahmed dashed toward Sean. His initial attack was reckless and clumsy, a foolish charge that Sean dodged easily. Ahmed ran into the wall, shoulder first. The sound of the thud made the American wince.

"That had to hurt," he said.

He put up his hands, ready for a more well-conceived approach.

Ahmed's right eye twitched as he straightened up and turned to the side with his hands up and ready. He kept them moving in a fluid motion that instantly told Sean this guy had martial arts training.

Time to find out how much.

The American faked a roundhouse punch and went with a jab. Ahmed deflected and countered with his own. Sean blocked the counterpunch and swung his right elbow, stepping close to use his weight behind the blow.

The elbow never got there. He got too close to his opponent before he could finish the attack. Ahmed saw and reacted like lightning, ducking his head and driving his fist into Sean's gut.

Sean didn't have time to tense his abs, and the full force of Ahmed's fist sank deep beneath the skin. He grimaced and tried to hammer-fist his opponent's head, but Ahmed swung repeatedly at Sean's midsection.

Each strike sent a new round of pain through the American's body until Ahmed swung his left arm up to clear the way for a massive uppercut. All Sean could do was turn his head as much as possible to absorb the shot. It did little to ease the surge of fresh pain when Ahmed's knuckles hit between the jaw and cheek.

Sean spun away and hit the floor. Signals from nerves all over his body wrecked his thought process as he writhed on the tile. He noticed a couple of drops of blood on the floor near his face and wiped his lips with the back of his hand.

Ahmed wasted no time. He stepped toward Sean to finish him off.

Sean saw the approach and regained his senses enough to sweep his right leg at the attacker's shin. Ahmed saw the move and hopped over Sean's foot. The American didn't give up and scissored his other leg around, catching his opponent just as he landed.

Ahmed's feet tangled and he fell sideways, arms flailing in the air to keep his balance. He crashed to the floor and struck the hard tile with the side of his head.

The American struggled to his feet. Ahmed pressed his hand into the floor to push himself up, but he collapsed again—still dazed from the blow to his head. Sean wobbled for a moment, regaining his balance. The second he felt steady, Sean jumped on Ahmed's back. Sean's inertia caused him to roll Ahmed over onto his back. Sean took advantage and climbed on his chest, straddling Ahmed with both legs. At first he pummeled his victim's face with his knuckles, delivering one angry blow after another. With each successive punch Ahmed's head snapped one direction and then the other. When the muscles in Sean's arms started getting fatigued, he switched to hammer fists, dropping them down on Ahmed's bloody face until he felt the man's body go totally limp. Sean smacked the unconscious man's right cheek just to make sure. A cut over the right eye oozed blood down to his ear. Ahmed's face was already swelling and bruised in several spots.

Sean looked back through the balcony door as Emily flew at the lone remaining guard.

The man raised his weapon too slowly. Emily kicked it out of his hand. The gun smacked against the wall right behind him and clacked to the floor. He reacted fast and stepped at her. She jumped to kick him in the chest, but this guy wasn't as inept as the others. He spun around, grabbing her leg in midair. In a split second, he squeezed and twisted, flinging Emily to the ground.

She hit hard, but her side absorbed most of the blow. He raised his foot and brought it down to stomp on her head, but she rolled away and popped up.

Emily twitched her nose and shrugged the shoulder she'd landed on to work out the faint pain. She took a more conservative approach this time, stepping to the guard and lashing out with her right hand. He blocked the punch, but it was a decoy. In a flash, the base of her left hand crunched into the man's cheek and sent him back two steps.

Her hands swirled slowly in front of her face. The guard stared at her with furious curiosity. He'd likely never seen a woman with such training. The blow to the face only served to enrage the bull, and he lunged at her full force. Emily swung her right leg, but he knocked it down with his forearm. Her movement exposed her upper body for only a second, but it was all the guard needed. He fired a hard jab at her face and struck right next to the ear.

She gasped and staggered back.

Fitz watched what happened. As soon as Emily took the shot to the face, he stepped forward to end things. Or so he thought.

He reached out and wrapped his arm around the guy's neck. For a moment, the move worked. Fitz's big forearm squeezed the guard's throat and would have rendered him unconscious within half a minute had the man not shoved his thumbs back into Fitz's eyes.

The big American yelled as the guard applied greater and greater pressure until he released his grip. Fitz stumbled backward to the railing and dropped to the floor, rubbing his eyes with both fists.

The guard stalked toward him. He stopped and stood over Fitz for a second. Then he pulled a long knife out of a sheath on his belt and held it out as if to cut the American's throat.

"Didn't anyone ever tell you not to hit a lady?"

Emily's voice startled the guard, and he twisted around just in time to see the bottom of her foot flying at him. His eyes went wide for a brief second before the shoe struck at the base of his throat.

The force knocked him back against the railing and over the top. In his desperation, the guard's fingers managed to grab the outer ledge and hang on.

Emily reached a hand down to help Fitz up. He accepted the offer and kept blinking his eyes as he stood. He shook his head back and forth as if that would help.

"Thanks," he said.

"Right back at you."

They heard a grunt from the other side of the railing and saw the last guard holding onto the ledge for dear life. The two glanced at each other and then stepped over to the edge. His eyes were full of fear and rage all mingled together. He glared up at the Americans with fiery hatred. They looked at one another again and nodded. Then both of them reared back and punched the guard in the head. His fingers slipped off the ledge. He yelled much louder than the other two who'd fallen as he dropped through the air, flailing his arms until he struck the ground face first.

"All clear in there?" A familiar and unexpected voice came from back in the hallway.

Tommy stuck his head through the opening with his pistol extended, gripped with both hands.

Sean looked around. During the melee he'd lost track of Khalif. Now he saw why. The billionaire who'd thought himself invincible just moments before lay in the corner of the room with his hands over his chest.

He coughed hard several times. Spurt of blood came out with the air, splattering his white suit.

Sean didn't answer his friend. He instead ran over to the dying rich man in the corner and crouched down on one knee. Only one thought was going through Sean's mind.

"Omar," Sean said loudly. Khalif's eyes were staring at the ceiling. His breaths came in labored, gurgled gasps.

"Omar, tell me where the missiles are."

Khalif's teeth shone through his parted lips. "Nothing....can stop...it now. My...brothers...will...will be avenged..."

Emily, Fitz, and Tommy joined Sean next to Khalif. They stared down at him knowing that if he died, his secret of where the missiles were would die with him.

"Omar!" Sean nearly shouted as he smacked the man's face. "Don't you die on me."

Khalif started laughing. It was one of the creepiest, most sinister sounds any of the Americans had ever heard. The laughter ended when Khalif was struck with another round of coughs. Then his eyes fixed on a point in the ceiling and didn't move again. His chest ceased rising and falling.

Omar Khalif was dead.

34

Cairo

Sean looked down with disdain at the dead billionaire. Anger and frustration filled him. He fought off the temptation to kick the body repeatedly.

It wouldn't help to throw a tantrum. They had less than six hours to find the missiles and no clue how to do it.

"He must have been hit by a stray round or a ricochet," Fitz said as he stared at Khalif.

"I'm sorry, Sean," Tommy said. "I may have hit him."

Sean dismissed the apology. "You saved our lives. That's two I owe you." He clapped his hand on Tommy's shoulder. He turned to Emily. "Told you."

She blushed but said nothing.

"Told her what?" Tommy asked.

"Never mind that," Fitz interrupted. "How in the Sam Hill did you find us? I thought you stayed in Tanzania."

"I know my friend. He tends to find himself in trouble more often than not."

"Yeah but..."

Sean cut Fitz off. "He called me before I got on the plane to Nairobi. I told him I had a bad feeling about the way things had been playing out, like we were pawns on a chess board. I asked him to come to Kenya and follow us from a safe distance. That's what he did."

Emily appeared astounded. "Seriously?"

Tommy held out both hands. "What can I say? The man can beg." He faced Sean. "The second time you called me I knew there was trouble. So I hung back. And I did like you said. I identified the ping from the phone so that if the battery ran out, I could still triangulate it. Clever."

Fitz and Emily's mouths could have hit the floor.

"The rest was easy," Tommy went on. "Sean telegraphed pretty much every move these guys made. Obviously I lost contact on the flight. But once I got here, the signal was still good. Following you was easy."

When he was finished, Emily said, "I'm impressed. Maybe you *should* have been a government agent."

"Easy. I didn't say I liked this sort of thing. But when a friend is in trouble, I'm always gonna help."

Sean interrupted the conversation. "I don't mean to cut off his epic hero's tale, but we still have the small issue of a bunch of missiles with nerve gas that are going to be launched at Israel in the next five-plus hours. Might be good if we focus on that problem."

"Right," Fitz agreed. "But how do we do that?"

"Those tracking transmitters should still be working, right?"

Fitz nodded. "Yeah, they'll work for several days... Yes, the transmitters. They'll still be sending a signal."

"Good. And those work on a unique radio signal, correct?"

"Definitely."

"Then get on the phone with everyone you can think of: Air Force, Navy, any friendlies in the area with the capability to find those signals and give them the frequency. We should be able to lock in on the exact location of those warheads. As long as they're less than six hours away, we still have a shot."

Emily offered additional help. "I'll call Washington and let them know what's going on. They'll need to bring in the cavalry hot and heavy."

Sean realized that while they'd been focused on Khalif, he'd completely forgotten about Ahmed. Khalif's right-hand man had been knocked out, but it was doubtful he'd died. Sean turned around expecting to see him on the floor, but to his surprise, Ahmed was gone.

"Oh no."

"What?" Emily asked. Then she saw what he was staring at. The empty floor where Ahmed had been lying.

A surge of dread went through each stomach in the room.

"He's getting away," Emily stated the obvious.

Sean yanked the pistol out of Tommy's hand and took off toward the hallway. He didn't slow down as he yelled back. "Find those signals! I'll get Ahmed!"

He flew down the stairs two at a time, sliding his hand on a rail to keep his balance. He whipped around the corner of the first landing and pushed himself to go faster and nearly slipped on the edge of a step. He caught his fall and kept going, albeit more cautiously.

When Sean reached the ground floor, he turned down the hall they'd come through before and found the side door still open. A car engine revved outside. Tires squealed.

He burst through the door in time to see the BMW backing out toward the road. Sean looked at the van parked in the driveway.

No way I'll catch him in that thing.

Then he remembered the six garage doors. *There has to be something better in there.*

He darted back into the house and took the first hallway that looked like it would go to the garage. Luckily, he was right on the first guess. And there was a set of keys hanging from a well-organized key ring next to the door. No time to debate which one to steal. So he took the one with the Ducati badge on it.

Sean punched the garage door and snagged a helmet off a rung in the garage. He ran over to the 999 sport bike, jumped on, and put the key in the ignition. He revved the engine to life, shifted into gear, and the bike leaped out of the garage. Sean tore down the driveway and nearly slid the thing around the corner onto the street. He hadn't seen which direction the BMW went, but his gut told him Ahmed would go for the missiles to up the time frame for the attack. Based on where they'd been facing in the upstairs room, that would be northeast.

He twisted the throttle, zipping through the quiet early morning streets of the Garden District. There were hardly any people or cars out yet, which definitely helped in navigating the confusing roads.

Sean zoomed around a curve, leaning hard with his body. He'd not seen a trace of Ahmed's car and started to think perhaps his quarry had taken a side road. Coming out of the dramatic turn, the street straightened out. Less than a quarter of a mile ahead, Sean saw the tail lights of the BMW.

"Got you."

He twisted the throttle and felt the bike surge forward. Wind noise filled his ears. The cool, dry morning air coursed over him, raising the hair on his skin. He hadn't taken the time to secure the helmet, so it shook a little more than normal, but it would do. The only reason he grabbed the headgear in the first place was so he could see. Driving a motorcycle at speeds over 55 miles per hour made visibility difficult without some sort of eye protection.

The gap between the motorcycle and the sedan narrowed.

Sean reeled Ahmed to within forty feet. He didn't care if the car's driver could see him. This was going to end one way or another.

Sean raised the pistol he'd taken from Tommy and aimed at the back window.

Suddenly, the tail lights on the sedan brightened, and the car's nose dipped hard toward the pavement. Sean was preoccupied with getting off a shot, so his reaction to Ahmed's erratic move was slower.

He tapped the brakes with his hand and foot, then deftly swerved the bike around the car. He missed it by inches. Sean stuffed the gun back in his pocket and looked over his shoulder in time to see the white sedan disappear down a side street.

He shifted down, causing the engine to roar before he hit the brakes and did a sliding U-turn. He twisted the throttle. The rear tire slipped at first on the pavement before it took hold and launched the bike forward.

Sean whipped around the corner and down the street Ahmed had taken. It appeared to be a road leading out of the city. And the car was already out of sight.

He gunned the throttle again.

Shops and cafes blurred by as the bike neared 100 miles per hour. He caught a glimpse of the white sedan in the distance and leaned over the tank to get as aerodynamic as possible.

The mass collection of businesses and eateries ended abruptly, replaced by lower-income houses and rundown apartment buildings. Ahmed was still far ahead, but Sean was reeling him in again, although not as fast as before.

As he recalled, that model BMW had a top speed in the 150-mile per hour range. The Ducati 999 had been touted as capable of 170-ish.

He'd put that claim to the test. Sean hugged the fuel tank as the chase reached the outskirts of the city and roared into the desert.

The bright orange sun rippled over the dunes on the horizon to the east. Sean swerved around a dump truck in the right lane. The speedometer read 160. At that speed, steering the motorcycle wasn't an option. It was more like guiding a rocket. Movements had to be subtle. Anything sudden would mean a very quick and very messy death.

The BMW drew closer by a yard or two at a time.

Sean had never driven a motorcycle at this speed before. He'd topped out his Honda CBR at 156 once and figured that would be the pinnacle. Now he was doing 165.

The engine whined between his legs, and the wind pushed hard against his fingers. He didn't dare raise his head at this speed. It would be like getting your head grabbed and pulled back by a bodybuilder. And the sound was like standing in a wind tunnel. With no ear plugs.

A delivery truck was in the right lane ahead. Sean kept an eye on it until the second it whooshed by. Part of the danger of traveling so fast on a bike—or with any vehicle—is that other idiots on the road can do random things at the worst times, like swerve over for no reason.

The BMW was only sixty feet ahead. Sean would cover that gap in less than ten seconds. Wary of Ahmed's last trick, Sean eased up on the throttle. The bike's speed fell off, dropping to 140 and then 120. He made the move just in time.

The sedan slowed visibly, though the brake lights didn't come on. Ahmed was no fool. Hitting the brakes at that speed could have adverse effects, even in a car with top-of-the-line equipment.

Sean continued to let his speed drop in conjunction with the sedan until they were hovering over 100. He veered into the right lane and sped up. Ahmed saw the move and swerved into the same lane, blocking Sean's approach.

The American let off the gas again and fell back, merged left, and repeated the attack. This time, he saw Ahmed's window go down and knew what was coming next. A handgun poked out the opening and fired wildly. Sean retreated once more, falling back to within sixty feet. He felt the pistol tucked away in his pants, but using it would be tricky, especially at such high speeds.

He sped up again, approaching in the right lane. Predictably, Ahmed slowed down and cut him off. Sean leaned hard to the left, diving back to the other lane. Ahmed saw his move and corrected. The car's back end wiggled subtly for a moment. Within two seconds it fishtailed out of control.

Sean decelerated to keep a safe distance. Ahmed panicked, jerking the steering wheel back and forth. He overcorrected in his desperate attempt to keep the car on the road. The BMW twisted at an angle and sped across the right lane. It launched over a small ditch, slamming into mound of dirt and sand.

Sean tapped on the brakes and sat up on the bike. He pulled the bike over onto the side of the road and jumped off. He ripped off the helmet and tossed it on the ground as he ran to the wreckage.

Smoke and steam poured out of the crumpled hood. The smell of burned oil drifted through the air.

Sean took the pistol out of his belt and ran toward the vehicle with caution. He could see Ahmed's silhouette inside the car and assessed his condition on the approach.

No movement came from inside the sedan. Sean kept his weapon raised, the sights locked on the target.

As he rounded the trunk and crept around the passenger side, he saw why Ahmed wasn't moving. The impact had sent the driver's head through the windshield. His shoulders had stopped his momentum so only Ahmed's head stuck out. It was at a twisted, awkward angle. His lifeless eyes stared out toward the rising eastern sun.

Sean opened the passenger door. Alarms were dinging and beeping. As he suspected, Ahmed's body showed no signs of life. It hung limp on the dashboard and across the steering wheel.

The American agent lowered his weapon and sighed. He ran his hand through his hair and looked back down the road. The few cars and trucks on the road were slowing down to see what was happening or possibly if they needed to help.

Sean tucked the weapon in the back of his pants.

He turned his head and looked over his shoulder at the desert. "I need a vacation."

The American Navy had little trouble locking in on the location of the homing beacons. Once they had, it was all a matter of alerting the Egyptians to what was going on.

The Egyptian officials were shocked to learn what was about to happen from their own backyard. They immediately agreed to a joint-forces ground assault to take out the terrorists.

While an airstrike would have been more efficient, the Americans recommended against that due to the nature of the nerve gas contained in the warheads. Apache attack helicopters provided support for the ground forces during the attack.

Khalif's men put up little if any resistance.

The missiles were collected carefully and disarmed before being transported back to the nearest base.

With the world momentarily safe, Sean decided to return to Mbeya with his friend.

The two Americans stood behind the engineer who was staring at two computer screens. The images on the monitors were scans of the golden statue they'd found near the temple dig site.

"So the president called you to thank you personally?" Tommy asked.

Sean stared at the screens as he answered. "Yep. Kinda weird to think about it."

"I'll say. But that's pretty cool."

"Couldn't have done it without you, Schultzie. In fact, he probably should have called *you*."

"Who said he didn't?" Tommy looked over at his friend and winked.

Sean's tone turned sincere. "Listen. You saved my life. Twice. I'll never forget that. Thank you."

Tommy shrugged like it was no big deal. "That's what friends do for each other, right?"

"Yeah. Yeah it is." There was an appreciative tone in his voice.

The two of them never had been comfortable with things getting too sentimental. So Tommy changed the subject. "Did they ever find out how Khalif got those missiles and the nerve gas?"

"They're still working on who supplied the nerve gas. Khalif did a good job of covering his tracks. Not much of a paper trail to follow. The guy had accounts all over the world, and money was always moving from one place to another. Nearly impossible to trace. So that part will take some time."

"And the missiles?"

"Yeah, those came from the U.S. Turns out a senator named Harold Thorpe was dealing under the table with Khalif. Thorpe had his fingers in a lot of cookie jars. One of those jars is a weapons manufacturer. They're conducting a full investigation."

"Unreal," Tommy said, shaking his head. "They'll crucify Thorpe. I mean, treason? Jeez."

"Well, they would crucify him if he weren't already dead."

Tommy raised his eyebrows. "Dead? What, did he kill himself?"

"Reports said he died from a heart attack. If I had to guess, I'd say Khalif took him out. Thorpe was a loose end."

The engineer at the computer stopped scrolling and pointed at a line segmenting the statue's arm from the body.

He interrupted the Americans' conversation. "Okay, we have something."

They peered at the screen where the man's finger pointed.

"You see here," he said in a Scandinavian accent. "This arm is most definitely detachable. I think we have found the answer to how they were able to get the statue in there. There is a thin layer of gold over the joint to make it look like one piece." He tapped the screen to emphasize his point.

Tommy nodded. "Great. Now we just have to figure out how to cut that thing up without damaging the integrity of the piece."

"Yes," the engineer agreed. "But there is something else. I'm not sure what it is." He scrolled down a little farther and then to the left. In the center of the statue's torso was a round shape. It looked like some sort of disc.

Tommy leaned in and squinted his eyes. "That's inside the statue?"

The engineer nodded. "It appears so. Just below the neck, this part of the statue is hollow. Whatever that is, it seems no one was supposed to find it. That disc must have been extremely important to the people who left it there."

"I wonder what it could be," Tommy said.

It took two days for the crew to cut away the thin layers of gold separating the arms, legs, and head of the statue. The boat had been relatively easy to remove in that it was essentially sitting on the idol's hands.

The weight, however, made it extremely difficult to move. No one could come to a conclusion as to how the ancient people who put it there were able to do it. When the head was detached, Sean and Tommy climbed the scaffolding that had been constructed around the statue.

They reached the top and looked down inside the torso. Tommy shined a flashlight into the dark cavity. A small stone disc sat cradled in a golden cuff.

"It's not made of gold," Sean said.

Tommy shook his head. "No, you could tell from the scans that it was something else. I just wasn't sure what." He reached his hand down into the hole.

"Wait. You sure it's safe?"

Tommy snorted a laugh. "This isn't a movie, buddy. Poisoned darts aren't going to shoot out of the wall or something."

He grabbed the disc with his gloved fingers and gently lifted it out of the cradle. "Ah!" he shouted. His voice echoed throughout the chamber, startling Sean as well as some of the workers down below.

Then he grinned. "Got you."

"You're an idiot. Scared the crap out of me."

Tommy's eyes narrowed as he chuckled. "I know but you should have seen your face."

He pulled the disc out of the hole and put the light on it. "This is weird. I've never seen anything like this."

"What is it?"

Tommy frowned. "These hieroglyphs and the image."

"Looks like a mountain." Sean peered at the object and leaned close. "Is that some kind of a boat?"

"Maybe. The hieroglyphs on the other side are sort of vague. The gist of it means *home.*"

"Home? But where's home?"

Tommy's head turned back and forth slowly. "I have no idea. But look at this boat, if that's what it is. Why would a boat be sitting in the mountains unless..."

"Unless what?" Sean stared at him awaiting the answer.

"It can't be. That's impossible."

"What's impossible? Stop doing that."

Tommy looked over at his friend with wide eyes, like he'd seen a ghost.

"What?" Sean prodded.

"The Ark of Noah."

THANK YOU

First of all, I want to thank you for reading this story. I had a great time creating it, and I hope you enjoyed every minute.

There are millions of books you could have chosen to spend your time and money on, and you chose mine. So I appreciate that.

Thank you so much.

I'd appreciate it if you'd swing by your favorite online retailer and leave an honest review. Those reviews help other readers decide whether or not they should read a book or not. And they help authors, too. It only takes a few minutes for you to help.

Also, be sure to check out the author's notes on the next page if you want to know a little more about this story.

AUTHOR'S NOTES

I had a blast writing this story, and I hope you had just as much fun reading it.

If you're new to my Sean Wyatt series, you might be wondering why the story ended so abruptly with a cliffhanger.

That's because this story is a prequel to *The Secret of the Stones*, the first novel I published.

If you're interested in reading that story, you can get it for free by joining my VIP Reader list. Just visit ernestdempsey.net/vip-swag-page/, enter your email, and you'll get *The Secret of the Stones* and three other books totally FREE and on any ereader device.

As I mentioned in one of my other stories, I do not look to put Arabs or Muslims in a light that makes them all look like terrorists. Not all people from those groups are terrorists or hate America, or Israel. It only takes a short look at history to find that most terrorist attacks that have happened in America were done by Americans.

There are some radical Arabs and Islamists, however, who are terrorists. At the time of writing this book, those groups are more prevalent than others. Someday it might be a different ethnic and religious group. As an Irish-American, I'm well aware of the terror the Irish Republican Army spread through the United Kingdom for so long. So terror can come from anyone and anywhere. I would never want any group to think I'm singling them out and certainly don't want anyone to believe I think all people from a certain group are evil. They aren't. I'm proud to have several Arab/Muslim friends. They're good people and should be respected.

Okay, enough about that. Just wanted to clear the air.

The timeline for this story takes place a few years after the horrific events of September 11, 2001.

Going back in time to make sure the technology was correctly used in context was tricky, but I tried to put in my due diligence.

Cell phones were much different back then, and that alone was a challenge to remember while writing the tale.

As far as the locations are concerned, Tanzania is one of the most stable countries on the African continent. It is home to the vast Serengeti National Park and Mount Kilimanjaro, the largest mountain in all of Africa.

While the character of Baku Toli was fictional, there have been warlords who have committed the same atrocities I outlined in this story. The most notable was a man who operated in Uganda. His name is Joseph Kony, leader of what became known as the Lord's Resistance

Army. Between 1986 and 2009, over sixty-six thousand children were abducted for use as child soldiers or as sex slaves.

So you can see why I had to kill a character like that in this book.

Kony is purported to be in the Central African Republic but could be in one of the other nearby countries. He is on a number of international watch lists but to date has evaded capture.

The nerve gas and the missile type I describe in this story are entirely fictional, though I did a good deal of research regarding various types of missiles and nerve gasses.

The temple archaeological site in Tanzania was a figment of my imagination...sort of.

There is an identical site to it far to the north in Turkey. It is believed to be over ten thousand years old. I essentially modeled the temple in this story from that one.

Perhaps you could find a little mystery about that site.

While my wife disagrees with me on this point—since she loves BMWs—the Ducati 999 sport bike could reach a maximum speed of 170 mph, which gives it a faster top speed than most of the BMW lines of automobiles except for perhaps some from the M Series.

The conflict that seems to be going on perpetually in and around Israel is indeed tragic.

I have spoken to people on both sides—Palestinians and Israelis alike. It's sad for both sides. And the irony is that their origins are traced back to the same founding father, Abraham from the *Bible*.

While I do not engage in political expression in my books, I do believe it's important that I mention that Omar Khalif's statements—while misguided in many regards—are the thoughts behind many Palestinians or ancestors of those who were forcibly moved after the war.

It is my hope that someday these nations of brothers and sisters can come together in peace.

DEDICATION

For my Arden bean. You can't imagine how much you light up my life.

OTHER BOOKS BY ERNEST DEMPSEY

THE SECRET OF THE STONES
THE CLERIC'S VAULT
THE LAST CHAMBER
THE GRECIAN MANIFESTO
THE NORSE DIRECTIVE
GAME OF SHADOWS
THE JERUSALEM CREED
THE SAMURAI CIPHER
WAR OF THIEVES TRILOGY

COPYRIGHT

Made in the USA
Coppell, TX
03 June 2021